An Art Lover's
Guide to
Paris and Murder

Books by Dianne Freeman

A LADY'S GUIDE TO ETIQUETTE AND MURDER

A LADY'S GUIDE TO GOSSIP AND MURDER

A LADY'S GUIDE TO MISCHIEF AND MURDER

A FIANCÉE'S GUIDE TO FIRST WIVES AND MURDER

A BRIDE'S GUIDE TO MARRIAGE AND MURDER

A NEWLYWED'S GUIDE TO FORTUNE AND MURDER

AN ART LOVER'S GUIDE TO PARIS AND MURDER

Published by Kensington Publishing Corp.

An Art Lover's Guide to Paris and Murder

Dianne
Freeman

KENSINGTON
PUBLISHING CORP.

www.kensingtonbooks.com

KENSINGTON BOOKS are published by

Kensington Publishing Corp.
900 Third Avenue
New York, NY 10022

All Kensington titles, imprints, and distributed lines are available at special quantity discounts for bulk purchases for sales promotion, premiums, fund-raising, educational, or institutional use. Special book excerpts or customized printings can also be created to fit specific needs. For details, write or phone the office of the Kensington Special Sales Manager: Attn. Special Sales Department, Kensington Publishing Corp., 900 Third Avenue, New York, NY 10022. Phone: 1-800-221-2647.

Library of Congress Card Catalogue Number: 2024932263

The K with book logo Reg. U.S. Pat. & TM Off.

ISBN-13: 978-1-4967-4511-8
First Kensington Hardcover Edition: July 2024

ISBN-13: 978-1-4967-4513-2 (ebook)

10 9 8 7 6 5 4 3 2 1

Printed in the United States of America

An Art Lover's Guide to Paris and Murder

Chapter One

July 1900

"We should go to Paris."

George, my husband, glanced up from his work to remove his reading glasses and send a frown across the polished expanse of our partners desk. It was fitted sideways against the back wall of the office in our townhome in Belgravia. Our chairs sat on either side of the window, so we both enjoyed the view of the back garden as we attended to our morning routine, one that I feared was becoming a bit mundane.

From my side of the broad desk, I handled matters such as our schedule, pending invitations, correspondence, and weekly menus suggested by our chef.

Exhilarating work it was not.

On his side, George read the newspapers and dealt with his own correspondence, like the letter he'd just set aside when our butler, Jarvis, brought in the tea tray. I'd noticed the letter had come from Paris.

"Thank you, Jarvis," I said as he placed the heavy silver tray on the center of the desk, equidistant between us. "That's exactly what I need." The stocky butler, who looked more like a boxer, bowed and left us to it. I kept my gaze on the tray while I poured myself a cup.

George's chair creaked as he stretched his long frame up and backward, lacing his fingers behind his head. His lips turned upward at the corners, from a frown to something more like a smirk, as he watched me attempt to look guileless. "Paris, you say? Should we? Why now?"

I relaxed enough to allow my spine to touch the back of my chair and lifted my cup toward my lips. "To visit the World Exposition, of course, or Exposition Universelle, as the French call it."

"Are they doing that again? Isn't it like the Great Exhibition Prince Albert held in my father's day?"

"Exactly. In America we call them World's Fairs. I can't believe you haven't heard of this one. Everyone is talking about it." I took a sip of my tea. "They say Paris is now the City of Light quite literally, with buildings and streets illuminated at night. It must be breathtaking. People are traveling from every corner of the world to marvel at the display of art and industry collected in one place." I wagged my index finger at him. "You know you would enjoy it, and it would be educational for Rose." Rose was my eight-year-old daughter.

George watched me, smirk still in place, completely unmoved.

"As for why now," I continued, "I believe I've waited long enough for a wedding trip. We were married in February. It is now July, and here we are, still in London. Yes, we had good reasons for postponing our travel, but those reasons no longer exist, and it is well past time we go somewhere." After setting my cup on the desk, I crossed my arms and awaited his response.

George poured himself a cup of tea, gazing at me in assessment all the while. "Are you lying?"

It was my turn to smirk. "You tell me."

He eyed me while he stroked his beard—a recent addition to his handsome face that he had yet to become used to. I, on the other hand, took to it very quickly. Somehow, the dark whiskers along his jaw made his eyes even greener and his lips all the more inviting. Gazing at him, I became so distracted, I startled when he slapped his palm on the desk and took to his feet.

"All right, I'll admit I don't know." He leaned his hip against the desk, next to my chair. "Are you lying?"

I held up my index finger and thumb just a fraction apart. "A bit. Though my statements are true, they aren't the reason I want to go to Paris."

"That's the best way to spin a tale. Keep it as truthful as possible. I must say, you didn't give yourself away. I'm impressed."

My cheeks grew warm with his praise. "Thank you, darling. So I've passed the examination, have I?" George was something of an investigator. He'd worked for the Home Office for many years, even infiltrating criminal groups to uncover evidence of their illicit activity. He still accepted the occasional assignment from the government, but recently, we had been working on more personal investigations.

And yes, I did say *we*.

I've assisted in George's investigations and tackled one or two of my own, as well. Though I didn't have his expertise, I was learning. It was 1900, after all. Time for women to declare they could do more than decorate a man's arm or his table.

"You have most definitely passed," he said. "Not so much as a blush or twitch of those lovely blue eyes of yours." He cupped my chin with his palm and pressed a kiss against my lips. "Now," he said, propping a leg on the desk, "I'll take the truth, if you please. Why Paris? Why now?"

"Well, the part about our wedding trip is completely true.

First, my family caused a delay in our plans. Then you had to heal from your injuries. I had thought we'd go somewhere after you recovered, but then you took an assignment, and quite honestly, I fear we've fallen into a routine and are on the verge of becoming dull."

George's mouth formed a grimace as I spoke. "Perhaps a little less truth would be better." He held up his hands, as if measuring. "There must be a suitable place for me between perfect husband and dullard."

"Perhaps dull was too harsh," I said. "But I do believe it's time we share some excitement. If I can't run off with you to some romantic hideaway, at least we can go somewhere interesting, entertaining, and enjoyable, where we can take Rose. Thus, the Paris Exposition. I might even get a look at my new niece."

My sister, Lily, had married Leo Kendrick last October and had almost immediately moved to France for Leo's business. She'd given birth to a daughter early in May. Both sides of the family chose to ignore the timing. Leo's parents had met little Amelia Jane already. In fact, Patricia Kendrick, Leo's mother, had taken an apartment in Paris due to her work with Britain's Royal Commission for the exposition. Lily and Leo had left their home in Lille and moved in with Patricia when the baby was due so Lily would have the advantage of a Parisian doctor.

That was two months ago, however. Lily and her family had returned to their home, but even so, Lille was only a train ride away from Paris.

"I do miss my sister terribly," I continued. "It's very hard to hear how wonderful my niece is from Patricia Kendrick. She is a lovely woman, and yes, she's the child's grandmother, but she's still a third party. I'd like to see the baby for myself. In fact, Hetty might wish to come, too." Hetty was my aunt. It was she who had brought Lily to London from New York City over a year ago now. After Lily married, Hetty had stayed in London, then had taken over the lease on my house when I married George.

George tipped his head, which caused a lock of dark hair to fall across his forehead. He swept it back. "This sounds as though you weren't lying to me at all."

"I already admitted part of what I'd said was true."

"And the other part?"

"That letter you received from France." I wiggled a finger toward his side of the desk.

"How did you know it was from France?"

"It has French postage. I have the power of vision." I gave him a wink. "Quite the detective, aren't I?"

"Is this a roundabout way of asking who is writing to me from France?"

I lifted my cup to my lips, realized the tea had gone cool, and set it back down, conscious of George's regard. "All right. I suspect the letter involves an assignment. If it does, I'd like to be part of it." I arched a brow. "Does it?"

"Not exactly an assignment. More of a request."

I waited for more. George stared silently at his hands. "Isn't that how it all works?" I prompted. "First, you receive a request. Once you accept, it becomes an assignment. Does it involve going to Paris, and do you intend to accept?"

He released a heavy sigh. "It does, and I think I must."

His reaction and reply were not what I'd expected. George was always invigorated by a new case—excited and eager to get started. "This must be a disturbing case."

"It is . . . complicated. And confidential and potentially dangerous. The idea of making a holiday of it, with Rose and your aunt along . . ." He shook his head. "That is not possible."

"Fine. Then you and I shall go alone. Once we've completed this investigation, they can join us, and then we'll have our holiday."

"Frances, this is somewhat personal."

Warning bells sounded in my head. "Too personal for your wife?" All manner of horrors crossed my mind as I rose to my feet and took a step toward him, putting us nose to nose. "George Hazelton, if there is another Frenchwoman out there declaring herself to be your wife, so help me, I'll—"

"No!" George looked as though his life were passing before his eyes at the mention of events from last fall. He took me by the shoulders. "It's nothing like that. The letter is from my aunt Julia. It's of a confidential nature, and I simply don't know how much of it she'd be willing to let me divulge to you."

My racing pulse slowed. "Is she in some sort of trouble?" I'd met Julia Hazelton years ago, when I made my London debut and became friends with George's sister, Fiona. Lady Julia had chaperoned us once or twice when Fiona's mother wasn't available. We had always considered it a treat since she was only ten years older than us and far more indulgent than either of our mothers.

Lady Julia was the spinster aunt that all mothers warned their daughters they'd become if they didn't lower their standards and marry someone. From what I'd witnessed, hers didn't seem an unpleasant life. No worse than that of many of us who did marry, and far better than that of some.

I'd learned recently that Lady Julia had longed to travel and make her living painting, but for years the Earl of Hartfield, who was her brother and George's father, hadn't allowed it. Fiona thought her aunt Julia had been something of a prisoner in their home. George didn't see it quite so dramatically. Upon the old earl's death, George's brother had inherited the title and had set Lady Julia free, which is to say he'd given her a generous allowance and told her she should do with it as she wished.

My understanding was that she had been living a nomadic life ever since. She'd managed to attain the ripe old age of thirty-eight without ever having to follow society's rules. She was a veritable advertisement for the joy of spinsterhood. I was surprised she'd written to George. "Is she passing through Paris?"

"She has been living there for the past seven years."

"For seven years?" Not so nomadic, then. "Wouldn't that have been when she left the family home?"

George gave me a mirthless smile when he saw awareness dawn in my eyes. "This is my dilemma. The rest of the family thinks she is traveling the world, and she has made it clear to me that she wishes to perpetuate that ruse. She has contacted me twice over the years, and I've helped her with matters of business." He ran a hand down my arm. "I'd love to have you with me, my love, but there are elements of her life she wishes to keep private."

"But if the point of your trip is to help her with confidential business matters, I can stay at our hotel while you work with her. Or I could find something else to do. It is Paris, after all. She needn't even know I'm there if you fear that will distress her."

"That's not exactly what I'm worried about." He stepped around to his side of the desk and picked up Lady Julia's letter. When he opened it, something fell to the desk—a small fragment of paper. George swept it up and handed it to me. "I don't think sharing this with you will breach any confidentiality."

It was a newspaper clipping from July 11—two days ago. I unfolded it to reveal a death notice. "Paul Ducasse," I read. "The artist?"

George indicated that I should continue reading.

The newsprint was small and in French, so it took a moment to read. It was indeed Paul Ducasse, the artist, who had died— by accident, according to this. "It says he fell into the Seine and drowned on the evening of the tenth."

He held up the letter. "Aunt Julia thinks differently and would like me to investigate."

Ducasse must be of some importance to her if she wanted

George to investigate his death. It appeared that Lady Julia had a few secrets. One of them involved a man—a dead man.

"So, you must see why it would be better if you don't accompany me." The confident tone with which George began the statement faltered when he caught my eye.

I smiled. "Must I?"

"Surely you don't want to become involved in this, Frances."

I tipped my head.

"Egad, I've no choice, have I? You're going with me."

I rested my palm against his cheek. "I'll start packing now."

Chapter Two

By the following afternoon, George and I were crossing the English Channel. When necessary, I can be the model of efficiency. Our need to depart quickly had made obtaining hotel lodgings impossible. I had heard more than twenty million people had already visited the exposition since it opened in April, and at least that many more were expected before it closed. Which meant George and I might have found ourselves on the street if not for Patricia Kendrick, my sister's mother-in-law.

Patricia was deeply involved with the British exhibit at the exposition but was not currently occupying the apartment she leased in Paris. She'd returned to London last week for at least a month and suggested that George and I make use of her Paris apartment to visit the exposition, call on my sister, or investigate a suspicious death.

She didn't say that last part in so many words, but I was confident she wouldn't mind.

Modern woman that I was, I'd used our telephone to contact her the moment I knew we were bound for Paris. She could not have been more accommodating. She had sent the address and a set of keys with a footman within the hour and had promised to notify the housekeeper in Paris of our arrival. My aunt, Hetty, was happy to take charge of Rose for a week or so. And just as willing to bring her along to Paris later.

And voilà! Here we were a little over a day later, standing on the deck of the *Invictus* under a heavy sky. The cool sea air blew wisps of hair across my face. I lifted my hand to brush them aside, but George's fingers got there first and tucked the dark strands securely behind my ear.

He drew in a deep breath, clearly savoring the salty tang of the sea. "I knew it would be more enjoyable out here than in that tight cabin. Aren't you glad we came up on deck?"

"It's perfect," I replied, linking my arm with his and nestling into his side. We had come out on the covered deck almost an hour ago to watch our progress as we approached France. As we crept into the port of Calais, all sound was lost to the clamor of the coastal birds who screeched their objections at the steamer disturbing their pool. It was a shame we weren't traveling for pleasure, but with luck, that would come later—after Lady Julia's business.

I leaned against George's shoulder and watched the activity on the dock up ahead. There was no need to rush, as we had Bridget and Blakely, my maid and George's valet, along to take care that our bags were loaded onto the right train and that a suitable compartment was made ready for us.

"Lady Harleigh, what a surprise."

I glanced to our left to see none other than Alicia Stoke-Whitney standing on the other side of a support beam. As always, I couldn't help but draw a contrast between us. Alicia looked like a fairy princess—pocket size, with a pointed chin and bright cheeks and eyes. Even her hair was a vivacious red, which completely matched her personality. I, on the other hand, was a few scant inches shorter than George's six feet, with dark brown hair, blue eyes, and a pert nose. The only time my cheeks were bright was when I pinched them.

Alicia had left England months ago, after her husband died, intending to spend her mourning period on the Continent. Not that I thought she truly mourned her late husband, but that was beside the point. Mourning was a societal norm most widows followed. I had done so for my late husband, and he was a complete rotter. In fact, he'd been in Alicia's bed when he died. I'd quite forgotten about that, and the memory stung a bit, though I tried not to let it show. It was my late husband who'd broken our marriage vows, not Alicia. Since that time, she and I had become rather useful to one another.

Still, I did find it annoying that while the rest of us observed the formalities, she gadded about as she pleased. She'd clearly just come from England. And as clearly, she was in the company of a rather handsome man. He was of average height, but everything else about him was distinctive. Thick dark hair and mustache, piercing gray eyes, chiseled features, and broad shoulders. He looked to be in his early forties, which put him at the upper edges of Alicia's tastes. Her latest amours had been younger men.

George released a tsk that was audible only to me. Though I sympathized with his feelings, I was curious. "Hello, Alicia." I didn't bother correcting her use of my former title. I'd been Mrs. Hazelton since I married George. "I thought you'd forsaken England for the Continent."

She let out a tinkle of laughter and squeezed the gentleman's arm closer to her side. "I have certainly found much to love in France, but occasionally I must return to England for matters of business."

I wondered what business Mr. Dark and Handsome was helping her with. I shifted my gaze his way. Did Alicia intend to introduce him?

"Tell me, what brings you to France?" she asked. "Where are you staying?"

Hmm. Apparently, no introduction was forthcoming.

"The exposition, of course," I said. "You remember my brother-in-law, Mr. Kendrick? His mother is a member of the British commission. We are staying at her home in Paris."

"Such a small world," she said. "I, too, am a member of the commission. I took my late husband's place. I don't believe I've worked with Mrs. Kendrick, though the name sounds familiar."

The steam whistle sounded, vibrating from my feet up through my spine and reminding us it was time to disembark. "We should go to our cabin and gather our belongings," George said, taking my arm.

Alicia smiled. "And we must be off, as well. I'm sure we shall see each other again in Paris."

"Perhaps," I agreed before George nearly dragged me through the door. "I'm coming," I said once we were out of their hearing. "Heavens, I know you don't care for Alicia, but you needn't run in your attempt to get away."

George darted a glance behind us and slowed his pace. "I simply didn't want to be trapped into providing any further information. I'd really prefer that no one know we're here until after we've taken care of Aunt Julia's business."

We'd reached our cabin to find that Bridget and Blakely had already removed every sign of our previous occupation. "We have a private compartment on the train," I assured him. "She'll never find us."

George gave me a bewitching smile. "That sounds rather like an invitation."

"I thought you were avoiding invitations at the moment."

"Not from you, my love. Never from you." He pulled me into his arms, and goodness! We nearly missed our train.

* * *

We arrived in Paris about four hours later. Upon disembarking the train, we found Gare du Nord completely overrun with fellow travelers—some rushing across the platforms, heels ringing out on the metal grates, others waiting by stacks of baggage, each their own island within the flowing mass of people.

It was early evening, just after six. I suspected many of these people were returning home from their daily employment. The commuters scowled at the travelers who raised their voices to be heard over other voices, in every language imaginable. The noise echoed off the stone and metal structure and bombarded the ears like waves against the shore.

George gripped my hand so as not to lose track of me in the enormous building, and we stepped into the swirling mass. Bridget and Blakely had set out a good twenty minutes before us, so assuming we made it out of the station, they ought to have a cab waiting. I have never been so grateful for my height. I could see over most of the heads between us and the exit. When we finally made it out the doors, I expected to hear a *pop* like that of a cork released from its bottle.

"There's Bridget," George said. She stood on the back end of a hackney cab, or here in France, I suppose it would be a fiacre, waving her arms. Her fair Irish complexion was blotchy from the heat, and her blond curls had escaped her sedate bun.

"Blakely went on to the house with the luggage," she said as George and I climbed in. "And I got very lucky that this cabbie was willing to wait for you."

"Then hop in with us and enjoy the fruits of your labor," I told her. "Heavens, I had no idea it would be so crowded."

"You were the one who said the entire world was traveling to Paris," George said. "I should think you would have been prepared for this."

I bumped against the back of the seat as the cab took off. "I suppose I thought the world had already been and gone. I hope it's just the station, but I fear we will be up against crowds everywhere."

We had traveled along for thirty minutes or so when the carriage came to a standstill. I regarded the heavy traffic outside the window, wondering how long we'd be stuck here. We were south of the opera house and approaching the Louvre. I consulted my 1896 Baedeker guide. If it was correct, rue St. Honoré, and the Kendricks' apartment, ought to be close at hand—assuming the carriage would move at some point.

I heaved a sigh of impatience. "Why don't we walk? We've been traveling long enough today, and it's quite stifling in here."

"I'm game," George said. "Is the apartment nearby?"

A short consultation with our driver indicated it wasn't far at all.

"Shall we, then?" George said.

We left Bridget in the cab with our two small bags and payment for the driver. Then we picked our way around the multitude of carriages and even a few automobiles lined up on the broad boulevard. The sky was significantly brighter here than it had been on the coast, but without the breeze, the air felt sultry, and we were still dressed for the channel crossing. I considered myself lucky when we arrived at the apartment before I'd completely wilted.

That is to say we arrived at the entrance gate to the building. Suitable for a castle, the beautifully carved and ancient wood fit perfectly into an enormous arched opening in the stone wall. A knob was fitted into the side of the arch to ring the bell for the concierge. Before I could do so, Blakely opened one of the doors and stepped out. The valet was a head shorter than George, and the door he was manning was a good two Blakelys tall.

"Good to see you made it," George said as we followed the valet into the courtyard.

"I've been here just long enough to get your luggage brought in," he said. Neither the heat nor the exertion seemed to have had any effect on Blakely. His black suit and white shirt were just as crisp as when he left the house this morning. The pale skin that came along with his coppery brown hair was not even slightly flushed. I turned away with a sigh of envy and took notice of my surroundings.

"Why, it looks like a park in here," I said. A smallish park, anyway, enclosed on all sides with five-story buildings, the walls of which were covered with glossy green vines. The courtyard was paved with flagstones from the surrounding walls to a garden area in the center, filled with showy mophead hydrangeas and fuzzy ferns. Small palm trees in pots lined the two long walls of the rectangular space and framed matching stairways that climbed up the opposing walls to outdoor landings on the first floor. It was blessedly cool and shady here. A refreshing change from the street.

"We left Bridget and our bags in the cab a few blocks away," I told Blakely. "She should be along shortly."

"Very good, ma'am," he said. "Then, if you'll allow me to introduce the housekeeper, she can show you to your room, while I wait for Bridget."

"An excellent plan." We followed him up one of the stone stairways to the Kendricks' apartment, which took up the first and second floor on this side of the building. Blakely pushed open the door at the top of the stairs, and we preceded him inside.

I was familiar with the town houses of my little area of London and the brownstones in New York City, but I had never been inside a Paris apartment. If pushed, I'd admit I expected them to be small, if not actually cramped. I was completely unprepared for such luxury as met me in the foyer. The ceiling soared up to the second floor, where a softly glowing chandelier illuminated a railing around what must be a hallway above.

The foyer was paneled and painted a creamy white. It opened to a large salon and library on the right and a dining room on the left. A panel opposite the entry door slid open, and a woman emerged.

"Bonsoir, Monsieur and Madame Hazelton." She was dressed in a plain black dress with white cuffs, and a chatelaine hung from her belt. Her dark hair was upswept and arranged in a simple knot. She clasped her hands at her waist and crossed the foyer to stand before us.

"I am Madame Fontaine, the housekeeper here," she said in English with only the slightest accent. "I hope your journey was pleasant?"

We assured her that it was, then allowed her to lead us to our room, down a short hall and up a staircase to the second floor of the apartment. We walked along the railing I'd seen from the foyer, then entered a hallway.

"Madame Kendrick's chambers are to the left. All the guest rooms are down this way." Her skirts swished as she led us a few steps down the narrow hall to the first door.

"This will be your room." She pushed open the heavy door to a bright, airy room with glass doors on the opposite wall that opened to a balcony over the front of the building. "I hope this will be satisfactory?"

"This will do splendidly," I told her as George and I stepped inside.

"Excellent." Madame Fontaine stayed at the door. "Some messages arrived for you a short while ago. I've left them on the bureau, just there. And would you like coffee sent up or waiting for you in the salon?"

Coffee! Another reason it was so wonderful to be in Paris. "We'll go down for coffee, don't you think, George? That will give Bridget and Blakely a chance to unpack."

With a bob of her head, the housekeeper left, closing the door behind her. George and I both made for the closest of the two glass doors. There was a narrow table with two chairs just outside them. George stopped at the bureau to check our messages, while I parted the filmy curtains, pushed open the door, and stepped onto the balcony.

It was surrounded with ornamental wrought iron and stretched across all the windows on this floor. The street below was wide and bustling with cabs, carriages, pedestrians, and the occasional motorcar. It was noisy but pleasantly so. The air was beginning to cool, and I imagined myself out here in the morning with coffee and a croissant.

What more could one ask for?

I returned to the room to see George seated on the bed, reading our messages. "Can't those wait?" He continued reading. "I hear there's coffee downstairs," I added in a singsong voice.

"This will take but a moment," he said without looking up from the messages.

Since he was so engrossed, I took a seat on the sofa at the end of the bed to wait. "I assume one of those is from your aunt?"

"Yes. She's still in the country but expects to arrive in Paris tomorrow afternoon. She's asked us to dine with her tomorrow evening."

"In the country? I had assumed she lived right in Paris."

"She does have rooms here for when she's in town."

"But that isn't all the time?"

George let out a tsk. "Stop asking questions you know I won't answer."

I flapped a hand. "Fine. Let her be mysterious. As for dinner, it's something of a relief to put it off until tomorrow, don't you think? I don't know about you, but traveling since early this morning has left me exhausted."

George grinned and dangled the second message from his fingers. "That's a shame since we have also received an invitation. It's addressed to me and to Frances, Countess of Harleigh." He extracted a card from the envelope and reviewed it. "It's for this evening."

I frowned. "Who knows us well enough to send an invitation yet not be aware I'm Mrs. Hazelton?"

"The invitation is from a Monsieur Allard, and since no one else knows we're here, I'm guessing Mrs. Stoke-Whitney is behind this." He handed me the embossed card. "She probably assumes you've kept your title."

A name on the invitation made me sit up straight. "A reception in celebration of the life and work of Paul Ducasse," I read. "Well, I'm certainly not too tired for this."

Chapter Three

The reception was nearby, down the street and around a corner in a grand and artfully appointed gallery. A large selection of Ducasse paintings covered two of the walls. Lights hung from the ceiling above, illuminating the vibrant colors on the canvases. The center of the room was left for guests to mingle beneath the softer glow of two chandeliers.

George and I arrived about nine, which was an hour after the event began. We had assumed that guests would come and go throughout the evening, but the fashionably dressed crowd inside sipped champagne, nibbled canapés, chatted among themselves, and seemed content to spend the evening.

We showed our invitation to a man in formal dress at the door. He briefly perused it, then snapped his fingers at a nearby waiter, who offered his tray filled with glasses of champagne. George took two and handed one to me; then we wandered over to the first of the Ducasse paintings, a street scene. It depicted a broad boulevard lined with leafless trees and bustling with carriages and pedestrians wrapped in warm clothing. It might have been the street just outside, in a different season.

"This is more recent than the work I've seen from Ducasse," I said. "He was not using this pointillist technique in his paintings five or six years ago."

George threw me a sideways look, then took a step back and observed the painting, turning his head to the left, then to the right. "It looks blurry."

"Your eye is mixing the colors," I said, gesturing at the top of the painting. "See how he painted hundreds of tiny points in a multitude of colors so your eye can see a gray sky with just a weak light breaking through the clouds?"

"I wasn't aware you knew so much about art." George spoke with a note of admiration.

"Heavens, did I sound as though I knew what I was talking about?" I leaned toward him and lowered my voice. "I really don't. I wasn't even interested in learning about art until the first time I saw the Impressionists—Monet, Degas, Pissarro. They make me feel like I am looking at real life—real people. Not gods or characters from the Bible, or even some Lord Whoosis, painted as if he were in the midst of battle."

Laughter twinkled in George's eyes. "Even though he was probably reclining on a sofa during his sitting."

"Exactly. These paintings don't glorify their subjects or try to show their holiness or otherworldliness." I gestured to a painting of a woman—probably a working woman, based on her clothing—holding a cigarette between her fingers and staring into a cup of coffee. "This is modern. She is real," I said. "If we walked into any café, we might see someone just like her."

"Perhaps not any café." The male voice behind us, speaking slightly accented English, caused us both to turn around. "The woman is surely a prostitute," he continued, "so we are not likely to see one like her on *this* street."

It was the man who'd been with Alicia this afternoon. He looked more streamlined in evening clothes and carried himself with a confident sophistication. His mustache was now waxed into an upward curve that remained still when he spoke. Yes, he was every bit as striking as I remembered, and his matter-of-fact tone somehow saved me from blushing at the mention of prostitutes in mixed company.

"But you are correct," he continued. "Impressionism and Postimpressionism are meant to capture life, one moment at a time." He took a step back and executed a shallow bow. "I am Lucien Allard. You honor me with your presence this evening, monsieur and my lady."

The two men shook hands. "We almost met this afternoon aboard the *Invictus*, did we not?" George asked.

Monsieur Allard's lips tweaked upward. "Mrs. Stoke-Whitney did not wish to impose upon your time, but when she explained who you were, I felt I must send an invitation. I am delighted you accepted." He singled me out with his gaze. "Are you an admirer of Ducasse's work?"

"Based on this painting, I believe I could be," I replied. "But I haven't seen enough of it to be sure. And I must admit, I am no connoisseur."

"I assume you are a patron, Monsieur Allard," George said, "since you arranged this tribute. Perhaps you can walk us through this display and show us the finer points of his work."

Alicia Stoke-Whitney had stepped into view beside Allard. "There is no one who could do it better," she said. "If anyone knows Ducasse's particular style, it is Lucien."

Monsieur Allard smiled fondly at her, then turned back to me. "Paul Ducasse was my dearest friend. I managed all his exhibits and sales, freeing him to devote himself to his art."

He raised an arm to guide us along the long wall of Ducasse paintings. I let George move ahead with Allard and hung a step behind with Alicia. We listened attentively while Allard described technique and pointed out the nature of light, color, and expression. I simply knew I would have hung any of them on my walls with great pleasure. They were all of scenes the artist must have viewed every day and of people he knew—intimate, honest portraits that made me feel as if I knew them, too.

I tore my gaze from one canvas, only to see that I did indeed know the person depicted in the next painting. It was Lady Julia, but not as I'd ever seen her. No more than twenty-three or twenty-four years of age, she stood behind an easel, applying brush to canvas, wearing a paint-stained smock over her dress, with a paintbrush tucked behind one ear. Her dark brown hair fell from a loose chignon and formed frenzied waves around her face. The artist seemed to catch her as she glanced up from her work.

The look in her eyes was unmistakably one of love.

I couldn't help but stare. Unless someone had been standing behind Ducasse as he painted her, Lady Julia was obviously in love with the man.

"This is quite . . . something," George said. He did not seem as surprised as me.

Monsieur Allard gave George a narrow look. "This is an example of his earlier work. Not his best piece, by far." He shifted his regard from George to the painting and crossed his arms, nodding to himself. "It does show his promise, though, I must admit."

A woman stepped up next to Allard, oozing elegance, as so many Frenchwomen did. Her blond hair was drawn up with a minimum of twisting and fixed with a jet embellishment that matched the trim on the bodice of her gown. A wide waistband, almost like a cummerbund, separated it from the black silk skirt that swept the floor in a demi-train. She was as much a work of art as the paintings in this room.

Allard angled himself to include her in the conversation. "May I present Madame Ducasse?" he asked, then turned to her. "This is Lady Harleigh and her husband, Monsieur Hazelton, from England."

So, the artist had left a widow. "Please accept our condolences on your loss, madame," I said. "Such a tragic accident."

She gave me a wan smile as she turned from the painting to George. "Hazelton? I see the family resemblance. You are related, are you not?"

Monsieur Allard gasped. "Do you mean to say . . . ?" He let the words drift as he, too, looked from the painting to George and back. "I never knew that was Lady Julia," he said. "I never knew . . ."

My guess was that the man hadn't meant to repeat himself. If he had finished the second sentence, I suspect he would have said that he never knew Lady Julia was in love with Paul Ducasse.

"It was many years ago," Madame Ducasse said, and for a moment, I thought she had read my mind. Then I realized she was speaking to Allard's comment that he hadn't recognized Julia. "Perhaps she would like to have this one."

Allard's harrumph evoked a chuckle from her. "It is not one of his best works," she said. "You said so yourself."

"I can see why my aunt might be interested in purchasing the painting," George said, "but on the off chance she isn't, I certainly am."

Allard held up both hands, palms out, his expression pained, as if the conversation distressed him. "Nothing is for sale tonight, monsieur. The Ducasse estate is complicated, and things are not quite settled. This evening we are simply here to celebrate the man's life and work."

George held one of his calling cards between two fingers and extended it to Allard. "I assume at some point it will be for sale. Our stay in Paris is still indefinite. You know how to reach me here. But if the estate matters take longer to settle, you may contact me at the address on the card."

Allard tucked it into his waistcoat pocket and handed George one of his own cards. "When things are settled, I assure you I will."

He and Madame Ducasse excused themselves, leaving us with Alicia. She signaled to a waiter, who scurried over with a

tray of canapés. While she and George indulged themselves, I
noticed a woman strolling through the presentation. She didn't
look as though she belonged there. Or to be more accurate, she
looked as though she worked there. Her clothes, a hunter-
green suit and white cotton blouse, were neat and clean, but
certainly not evening wear. Her hat was a plain straw boater,
and beneath it, her caramel brown hair was styled in a simple
knot. And she was young—eighteen or nineteen. Not likely to
be purchasing expensive art in the near future.

Alicia reached up and placed a dainty gloved hand on my
shoulder. "I've added you and Hazelton to the invitation list
for the reception the British delegation is holding at the end of
the week." She inclined her head toward George, who was a
few steps away, trading in his empty glass for a fresh one.
"Hazelton says I shouldn't count on your attendance, since
your plans aren't currently fixed, but I do hope you'll come."

"We'll have a better idea of our availability in a day or two,"
I said. "What is the reception in honor of?"

"Who knows? One country or another holds a reception
every week. It was probably just our turn. Had I known these
committees spent so much of their time entertaining and celebrating, I'd have volunteered for this service long ago." Her
laugh tinkled over the low hum of conversation.

"How did you become involved in the exposition commission? I understand Arthur had been a delegate, but you've
never struck me as the type to sit on a committee."

She made a quick study of the room, as if preparing to im-
part a secret. George, who had been about to join us, rolled his
eyes and stepped away, feigning interest in one of the paintings.
Alicia leaned closer to me. "That is because the only committees I'd ever had an opportunity to join were filled with women,
and you know I don't get on with other women very well.
They just don't like me."

"Hmm," I said, with a shake of my head. Odd that she had

never realized the reason for that was her tendency to dally with other women's husbands.

"But the delegation to the exposition is almost entirely made up of men. I can't tell you how much fun it has been."

"I can imagine."

"The few women involved are the wives of businessmen, and they are far more congenial than the ladies of the upper class."

That reminded me of the young woman I'd noticed a moment ago. I scanned the room and saw her in the company of Monsieur Allard. He had her by the elbow and looked to be leading her, none too gently, to the front of the room.

"Do you know that woman?" I asked Alicia.

"I don't," she said with a note of interest. "But she's a pretty little thing, and the way Lucien is so eagerly escorting her out, I wonder if she is one of Paul Ducasse's little friends."

"What do you mean?" I asked, suspecting that I knew exactly what she meant.

"Ducasse was something of a libertine. I feel quite sorry for his wife."

"Do you, indeed?" Considering that married men, including my late husband, were some of Alicia's favorites, her statement took me by surprise.

"I know what you're thinking," she said.

"That Ducasse reminds me a great deal of my late husband?"

"Yes, that, too, but in addition, you think that I care nothing about the wife of a cheating husband."

That conclusion required no thought whatsoever. "Are you saying that you do care?"

She paused to consider. "I suppose not, but it is disheartening. When a man eschews discretion in his affairs, it's clear he no longer has any respect for his wife." She shook her head. "It's very sad."

I couldn't argue with that sentiment, but it seemed to me that a man who cheated had no respect for anyone, including his wife and his lovers, such as the woman Alicia had called Ducasse's little friend. If Alicia was correct, I wondered why the young woman showed up to his tribute.

George and I returned to the apartment after spending a little more than an hour at the gallery. I doubted we would have learned any more had we lingered. Other than Lucien Allard and Madame Ducasse, none of the attendees we met had had anything closer than a business relationship with Ducasse, and most had never met the man. The invitations seemed to have gone out to the elite of Paris society rather than to the man's friends. That struck me as odd, considering the purpose of the gathering. I said as much to George as we settled into the sofa at the end of our bed.

"Allard might have called it a tribute, but I'm quite sure he was giving potential collectors a chance to view what they may bid on as soon as he is given the approval to sell."

"Then why did he brush you off?" I asked, raising my eyebrows.

George bristled at that. "He took my card, didn't he? I suspect I'll hear from him as soon as he has an opening bid."

I bent forward and removed my shoes, wiggling my toes as I freed them. Since it had been such a long day, we had given Bridget and Blakely the evening to themselves. Whether they were out somewhere in the city or both sleeping by now, I couldn't call Bridget to help me undress.

I would have tucked my stockinged feet underneath me, but George captured them and pulled them onto his lap, a much better situation, in my opinion. "Who do you suppose has the authority to give him the approval to sell?" I asked.

"Now, that's interesting," he said. "I would have assumed the paintings all belonged to Madame Ducasse, but after our conversation with her and Allard, I have my doubts."

"Allard said the estate matters were complicated. That could mean anything, including that Ducasse didn't have a will. It doesn't mean Madame Ducasse won't inherit." I leaned back and pushed my feet against his hands. He quickly accommodated me with a massage.

"What about my feet?" he asked.

I crooked my finger. "Bring them up." Once we were both comfortable, I cast my thoughts back to the tribute. "I begin to understand why Lady Julia never married."

"You noticed it, too?"

"Oh, yes," I said. "Do you suppose your father wouldn't allow her to marry him? Or would matters have even gotten that far?"

"I don't know." George's head lolled back against the arm of the sofa. I shook his feet. "You can't fall asleep on me yet. I need answers."

"Years ago, I asked my mother why Aunt Julia never married. She told me only that Julia fell in love with a man she met in France. She had gained her majority, so she could have married him, but her parents thought him unsuitable and were against the match. She chose to honor their wishes. My father inherited the title a few years later. I don't know if he kept her from her love or if she never told him or if it was already too late. Ducasse did marry, after all."

"How very sad. Do you suppose she came to Paris hoping to pick up where they left off, only to find him married to someone else?"

"Dunno."

George was drifting off to sleep, and I wasn't far behind him. We had met two people closely involved in Paul Ducasse's life. Neither of them had denied that his death was accidental when I mentioned it. Perhaps Lady Julia was mistaken. I knew I should get up and get George up so we could go to bed, but I was so comfortable and so sleepy, I wanted nothing more than to close my eyes.

I'd think about murder tomorrow.

At some point during the night, we dragged ourselves from the sofa, changed our clothes, and climbed into bed. I woke what felt like two seconds later to a sunlit room and the sound of activity. Oddly, I was quite refreshed.

"How early is it?"

"A bit past eight, ma'am," Blakely replied.

I rolled over to see George slipping into a light gray morning coat, which Blakely held out for him. "Heavens, you are far ahead of me." I rolled to my other side and threw back the covers.

"I believe Bridget has a bath ready for you," George said as Blakely straightened the sleeves of his coat. "And breakfast awaits you in the dining room."

"Ah, life is good," I said. "A lie-in, a bath, and breakfast waiting."

Once Blakely had finished and left us alone, I took note of George's apparel. "Where are you going?"

"I am off in search of newspapers from the past few days to see if there is anything of Paul Ducasse's death other than the notice we read." He pressed a kiss against my temple. "With any luck, I'll return before you finish your breakfast."

"Wouldn't we have recent newspapers here?"

"The housekeeper says not. I thought the library might be of some help. I shan't be long."

George left on his quest, and I headed for the bath. An hour later, I was at the table on our balcony, enjoying my second cup of coffee and devouring the last bite of a buttery croissant. With a sigh, I slipped back through the doors into our room. I ought to send a letter to my sister, Lily, and let her know we were in Paris. With a new baby, she might not be able to come back to the city so soon. If not, perhaps George and I could visit her once we concluded Julia's business.

George still hadn't returned by the time I left the letter with the housekeeper to post, leaving me to wonder if he'd already begun his investigation without me. He had mentioned Lady Julia was a stickler for privacy. Not one to mope, I chose to make the best of the situation. After all, this was Paris, and there were the shops. I couldn't come to this lovely city and leave without paying at least one visit to the grand department-style store Le Printemps. Perhaps a new hat was in order.

Bridget was scowling at the wrinkles in the gown I'd fallen asleep in last night. "I don't know how you managed to do this, ma'am," she said.

"Leave that for now and join me," I said.

Within minutes we were headed for that magical building on boulevard Haussmann.

I made such a good job of it that we returned only in time to change for dinner. George, seated in the salon, drummed his fingers on the arm of his chair when I strolled into the room with the spoils of my outing. "It's not as bad as it looks," I said, stacking my purchases on the coffee table.

"Two hats?" George indicated the boxes.

"One is for you," I replied, working open the strings on the smaller box. I removed the lid and pulled out the most beautiful trilby. "Look! Is it not perfect?"

George took it from my hands and placed it on his head. "You tell me?"

I tipped the hat just a bit and took a step back for a better look. "Oh, yes! It suits you beautifully. You are even more handsome."

George laughed at my enthusiasm. "I don't believe I've ever seen you so excited over a few purchases."

I sank into the chair beside him and rested my chin in my palm. "You are right. This is very unlike me. It must be Paris. I haven't shopped here for ages, and everyone is so excited about this season's creations. It rather made me excited, as well." I tapped the unopened box on the table. "Wait until you see this hat. It is exquisite." I was smiling so hard, my face hurt, but I simply couldn't help myself. "It isn't even the shopping," I continued. "I just realized there is an energy over the city now—an air of excitement. Perhaps it's the exhibition or all the visitors." I waved a hand. "Je ne sais pas."

George pulled down the brim of his new hat and grinned at me. "Well, if the shopping wasn't necessary to put you in this lovely mood, I wish you'd realized it a few hours sooner."

"The shopping may have had something to do with it," I said with a shrug.

"Whatever it is, I approve. I don't recall the last time I've seen you this carefree and joyful. I almost hate to remind you that we are to meet my aunt for dinner in just above an hour."

"I'll be ready in less than thirty minutes."

I met George in the salon twenty minutes later and handed him my wrap, drinking in the vision of him before turning so he could place it on my shoulders. George, in evening clothes, was always a sight to behold.

The Kendricks had no carriage in Paris, but the footman had arranged a cab for us. It waited at the curb when we left through the courtyard gate. "Where are we meeting her?" I asked as George assisted me into the cab.

"Montmartre," he said, getting in beside me. "She asked to meet us at a restaurant called the Moulin de la Galette."

"Do you mean Renoir's Moulin de la Galette?"

George put an arm around me when the cab shifted to the right as it began moving. "It might be," he said. "I have no idea who owns it."

"No, no, no." I tapped his leg with each repetition of the word. "I mean Pierre-Auguste Renoir, the artist. I believe that café was the subject of one of his famous paintings. How exciting to see it in person."

"You do seem rather excited," he said with a grin.

"This is all very new to me. I've never been to that part of the city. Isn't it all artists and cabarets, music and dancing, drinking and devilment?"

"Sounds like an amusing place."

"Why doesn't Lady Julia want to meet us at her home?"

"She would have to answer that question."

"Fine. These questions are for you. Did you find the old newspapers you were looking for? Did you learn anything more about Paul Ducasse's death?"

"I did find them, and while I learned a bit about his death, nothing struck me as suspicious. It seems the police came to a reasonable conclusion when they ruled it a drowning. The man fell off his boat."

"He owns a boat? That rather tarnishes the image of a man starving for his art, doesn't it?"

"It was a houseboat. He lived there, and from my understanding, it was something of an old tub."

"Indeed?" The cab had turned into the evening breeze. Filled with the scent of flowers, it felt positively delicious on my face. Reluctantly, I turned away from the window and back to the thread of our conversation. "I have a difficult time imagining the sophisticated Madame Ducasse living on an old tub."

"They also own a more traditional residence in Paris," George said.

"By *traditional* you mean on land?"

"I do. From what I understand, Ducasse used the houseboat only occasionally and alone."

"I wonder about that. If Alicia is correct in her assessment of the man, he was not alone. That houseboat sounds more like a *nid d'amour*." I tsked.

"It may indeed be a love nest, but a neighbor saw him arrive alone the night he fell overboard."

That sounded off to me. "Perhaps he was the only person on his own boat, but weren't there other houseboats in the area?

The neighbor, for example. Did no one hear him? Isn't that suspicious?"

George took my hand. "Slow down. You are getting ahead of the story. There were other boats in the area, and someone might have heard a splash, but that may not be particularly unusual. Also, Ducasse struck his head against the boat when he fell. That likely rendered him unconscious and unable to shout for help. The officers of the Sûreté inspected the boat and found blood on the edge of the deck that would explain his head wound. They spoke to his wife and friends, all of whom, it seems, were doing something else at the time. The coroner gave the body only a perfunctory examination, but based on what I learned, it was correctly ruled an accident."

"Well, then," I said, squeezing his hand, "perhaps your investigation is over, and we can simply enjoy ourselves for the rest of our stay here. Wouldn't that be nice?"

"Nice, yes, but unlikely. I trust Aunt Julia's judgment. She wouldn't have asked me here unless she had some logical suspicion."

"Perhaps it isn't his death Lady Julia wants investigated but something else."

"I suppose we'll find out soon enough."

Montmartre was on a hill to the north of the city, but not far away. Once we zigged and zagged our way to the ninth arrondissement, we turned onto rue Laffitte, and about fifteen minutes later, we were on a street bustling with pedestrian activity. The cab slowed to a halt as men and women spilled from the pavement into the street.

"If the restaurant is nearby," George said to the driver, "you may drop us here. This street seems more suited to walking than driving."

The driver set us down. George paid the fare, and we made our way on foot. I linked my arm with his. The evening was warm, but a breeze cooled my face and stirred a curl that had slipped from my coiffure. As we passed others on the street, I noticed that we were among many elegantly dressed couples. I had assumed customers of cafés and dance halls would be of the middle class.

"I didn't expect to see such glamour on these streets," I said to George.

"I suspect many of the couples you see are tourists, curious to see how the bohemians live." He lowered his voice. "And the women may not be the wives of the gentlemen they are with. Either way, I suspect the upper-class ladies of Paris do not spend their evenings visiting the restaurants and cabarets of Montmartre."

"How fortunate for me I'm not a Parisian lady, then."

As we crossed the street, I noticed the asphaltum had worn thin, revealing the cobblestones beneath. My shoes slipped on the curved surface, and George tightened his grip on my arm. "The realities of middle-class life may not be as magical as you think," he said.

"Of course not," I replied. "But Montmartre has nothing to do with realities. It's all about possibilities and what could be, don't you think?"

"Possibilities," he mused. "I like that idea."

When we reached our destination, I was surprised to see a large wooden windmill surrounded by a walled garden, with a low building to the side. Fairy lights twinkled in the trees, casting a romantic glow on the couples dancing on the patio. Passing them, we followed several other people inside the restaurant.

The place was rustic and packed with a loud and cheerful crowd. I couldn't tell if the musicians were playing outside or in here. It was impossible to make out the tune. Strings of lights were draped from the ceiling. There were low tables with benches, tall tables for standing, and people surrounding them all. Everyone gave off an air of celebration.

As we delved farther into the dimly lit room, we came across a long table where at least a dozen people stood, talking and drinking.

A woman toward the middle of the group caught sight of us. "George!" She backed away from the table, only to step on the foot of a gentleman behind her, who let out a dramatic howl. "*Désolé, mon ami,*" she said, giving him a brilliant smile and a pat on his cheek, then turned to us and crooked her hand. "Come join us."

George cast me a look of confusion that I'm sure was matched by the one on my own face. This was obviously Lady Julia. But contrary to our expectations, she did not appear to be grieving a lost love.

Chapter Four

Lady Julia was nothing like the woman I remembered chaperoning Fiona and me ten years ago. Nor was she like the younger version of herself from the Ducasse painting. Yes, she was older now, her figure more rounded, and she had faint lines around her eyes, which indicated she smiled or laughed more than I recalled her doing in the past. But appearance was only part of the change in her. I'd always thought her reserved, introspective, certainly quiet. The Lady Julia across the table from us was anything but. Her expression, eyes, and voice sparkled with life and laughter. She looked happier than I'd ever seen her—like someone who fully enjoyed her independence.

George and I squeezed through the crowd surrounding the table. She did the same on the opposite side, and we all met at the end, where there was a little breathing space. After kissing us both on the cheeks, she ordered someone in the group to pour us each a glass of wine. When she spoke in French, her voice was lower than I recalled and velvety smooth.

"I hadn't expected this celebration," George said. "I was

under the impression you had some business to discuss with me—or at least something of a more solemn nature."

She tipped her head to the side as she studied him. "Celebration?" Her gaze traveled up the length of the table, then back to George. "I suppose someone here may be celebrating something, but I am not part of that. I arrived only a few minutes before you, so I was passing the time with a few friends."

There was some jostling behind her, and someone pushed a stemmed glass into her hand. "Ah, here we go, then." She handed the glass to me. "For you, Frances." When she turned around again, another two glasses waited for her on the table. She handed one to George and raised the other. "Since I was unable to attend your wedding, may I take this opportunity to congratulate you both and wish you many happy years together?"

George and I thanked her, and we all took a sip of what turned out to be a delightful champagne. Perhaps it was the bubbles that made Lady Julia so vivacious. Almost immediately a waiter wearing the customary long white apron, along with his white shirt, waistcoat, and short black jacket, arrived to lead us to our table.

Julia waved farewell to her friends, and we followed the waiter to our table. Though only a few steps away, this section was a shade quieter, though I would not have called it private. We seated ourselves at the small white cloth–covered table, barely a foot from those on either side of us.

"This is quite a lively place," I remarked.

"Isn't it wonderful?" She gave George a serious look. "I doubt these are the kind of people or surroundings you are used to, but many of my friends come here. They do not think about class, only about art."

George arched a brow. "Am I giving you a sense that I would prefer to be somewhere else? Or are you just assuming I'm a snob?"

Lady Julia released a peal of laughter. "This is why you are my favorite nephew. No one else in the family speaks so directly." She patted my hand. "You have quite a gem in George, do you know that?"

"Indeed, I do." I would have elaborated, but I cut myself off when she crossed her arms and looked me up and down.

"There was a time, before your first marriage, when I thought you two might make a match."

I smiled politely. "Did you?"

"Yes, but then I set the idea aside. You seemed a touch too meek to me."

George nearly choked on his champagne.

I stared at the woman. "Too meek?"

She reached for her glass. "I may have got that wrong, or perhaps it's just no longer the case," she said. "If so, I'm glad for it. It isn't good for George to always have his own way."

"Once in a while would be nice," George added.

The waiter came for our order, which left me a moment to decide if I was insulted or not. At the time I knew Lady Julia, I was rather meekly allowing my mother to make my decisions for me. She couldn't be faulted for believing I might have stayed that way. And I had to agree with her, it wouldn't be good for George to always have his own way.

The waiter left with our order and instructions to bring another bottle of champagne. I finished my glass and tried to recall what we'd been talking about before discussing the subject of George's gemlike qualities and my meekness. Oh, yes, this café. "I, for one, quite like this place. It feels like Paris to me. Since we arrived, I have noticed almost a current of electricity humming through the city. I feel it here, too. Is this the place in Monsieur Renoir's painting? I saw it at a museum a good ten years ago. I can't recall the name of the piece, but it stayed with me."

"It is called *Bal du moulin de la Galette*," she said, good humor twinkling in her eyes. "And you are correct. This is that place. But Renoir painted it from over there, by the dancers."

I glanced in the direction where she tipped her head. "You are right! I must go and view the painting again now that I have seen the original. But even from memory, I know he captured the essence of this place."

The three of us looked up when a shadow fell across the table. A large man with russet hair, eyebrows, and beard stood beside Lady Julia's chair. He removed his hat and looked at her with a solemn expression.

"Bonsoir, Edouard," she said. "You were not at the studio today."

"I did not know you would be there," he replied in a deep voice with a charming accent. After greeting him, Julia had slipped into English, and he had answered in kind.

Julia introduced Edouard Legrand to us as her friend and landlord. "You should join us," she said, then turned to George. "Do not give me that look. We are not discussing business tonight. Not on such a beautiful evening and when I am just reacquainting myself with your lovely bride. There will be time enough for business tomorrow."

George looked surprised but nodded his assent. "If that is your wish, Aunt. I'm willing to postpone our business until tomorrow."

I saw in Lady Julia's frown that she took his words in the same manner I had—as a warning. They *would* discuss business tomorrow. After all, that was why we had traveled all the way to Paris. Still, I was content to simply enjoy myself tonight.

Monsieur Legrand protested that he could not stay for dinner, but the waiter had just brought our champagne, and he was happy to sit long enough for one glass. While George poured, Legrand drew up a chair between Lady Julia and me. She caught his hand and said, "Frances was just telling me she likes Renoir."

He scoffed. "Everybody likes Renoir—now."

"Ah, but that's my point. Frances liked him ten years ago."

"Ten years ago, all the Impressionists were gaining popularity. Twenty years ago was when they were the outcasts. Tell me she appreciated them twenty years ago, and I'll be impressed."

Julia leaned forward and spread her hands open on the table. "As you should. Twenty years ago, Frances was a child. I doubt she had an opinion of Renoir or any artist. But when she saw your mentor's work, she felt he captured the essence of this place."

He regarded me with a hint of a smile on his lips. "That was precisely his intent," he said. "It is what we all hope to do—capture a moment in time."

George handed him a glass of champagne, and he went on to talk about his work. Apparently, the property Lady Julia leased from him was space in a studio that they both shared with other artists here in Montmartre. "None of us have gained public acclaim as of yet," he said. "Well, except for Paul." He looked at Julia until she met his eye. "If I have neglected to say so already, I am very sorry for your loss."

With a nod, she squeezed his hand, accepting his condolences. Interesting that he considered the artist's death as her loss.

When Julia picked up her wineglass again, I noticed Legrand gazing at his now empty hand, then at her as she spoke with George. Clearly, he admired her. I wondered if she'd rebuffed him or simply failed to notice his interest.

To distract him, I asked Monsieur Legrand about his work.

"I will be happy to show you when you come by the studio, but do not expect too much," he warned. "As I said, Paul was far ahead of the rest of us."

"Are there many of you sharing this space?"

"At the moment, there are four of us. Well, three now. I don't know if we'll fill Paul's spot. We have all become such good friends, it would be hard to find someone else to fit in."

"Friends," Lady Julia said, a note of scorn in her voice. "We are family, like brothers and sisters."

Legrand's gaze spoke of longing for a much closer relationship. If Julia didn't return his feelings, and given the way she blushed and turned away from him, it appeared she did not, I don't know how they managed to share a space day after day. He tore his attention from her and came to his feet. "That we are," he said in a monotone. "Now I must be off and leave you with your other family." He nodded to George and me and kissed Lady Julia's hand. "Come by the studio sometime," he said to me before walking away.

"He is right. You must come visit me at the studio. And do not believe Edouard. His work is wonderful. He just expects too much of himself." She sighed. "He is never happy."

He did look solemn, but was he generally unhappy or unhappy in love?

George eased back in his chair. "Tell me about this studio. Can you not paint at your home?"

Julia took a sip from her glass before replying. "It is not a case of one place being more conducive to painting. I paint in both." She turned to me. "I have a lovely studio in the country, but in Paris I have access to the masters." She let out a sigh. "I still do little more than emulate Renoir and Monet, but I am developing my own style. And it is enormously helpful to be around other artists who are still working toward their own styles, too. It makes one feel less alone."

She startled at the sound of a crash just behind us. Someone had turned headlong into a waiter. With no time to maneuver, his tray had flipped into the air and the glasses had hit the floor. This was followed by a stream of angry words shouted in French. It took only a second or two for someone to emerge from the kitchen to smooth things over and have the mess cleared.

I returned my attention to our table and was surprised to see

Lady Julia on her feet and leaning against the back of George's chair, her head down, drawing deep breaths, as if she was recovering from a fright.

George stood and took her arm to help her back to her seat.

She waved him off and settled in. "I'm fine," she said. "Perhaps a little jittery, that's all."

"Because of Ducasse's death?" George suggested.

"Not now," she said, glancing around. With all the noise of the diners around us, was she concerned about someone hearing George? She placed a hand on his arm. "This is not the time or place for that conversation. We shall discuss something less gloomy, if you please."

"I was surprised to learn you have a residence outside of Paris," I said. "Do you come to the city every day?"

"Chartres is only an hour or so from Paris by train, so I suppose I could, but when I come here, I stay for a few days at least. I have a small flat above the studio. It's not much more than a place to sleep, but when I need to be here, it is serviceable."

"It sounds as though everything you need is in Paris," George said. "Why not sell your country home and live here?"

She chuckled. "I could do that, but then how would I live?" She leaned toward him. "Believe it or not, people are not lining up to buy my paintings. Your brother provides a generous allowance, but even I can't stretch it to cover all my expenses. Housing in Paris is dear, and my place above the studio is far too small for . . . my needs. Besides, I am beginning to see an income from the perfumery."

"You own a perfumery?" I asked.

"That's right," George said. "You were just beginning that venture when I last saw you. How is business?"

"Toddling along," she said, then turned to me. "But you do not know the history. I bought the *maison* in Chartres almost as soon as I arrived here, so close to eight years ago. It came with land to farm, but since I know nothing about farming, I lease it to a neighbor. It also came with a barn. A friend of mine is an excellent gardener. She grows flowers and fragrant herbs, and she and I have turned the barn into a perfumery. We started several years ago."

"Several years ago?" George echoed.

"Yes, it took quite a bit of time to develop a scent that would be marketable to the public. Then one needs an eye-catching bottle, then the most important thing—someone who will sell it for me." She shrugged. "That all takes time. It's a very small operation, but we are turning a profit, I'm proud to say."

She did indeed look proud of herself, and rightfully so. When I met her ten years ago, George's aunt Julia had seemed nice and quiet. I had liked her well enough then, but I absolutely adored the woman she was today. Blue blood notwithstanding, she spoke about her business like my father or even Aunt Hetty. She was a free-spirited artist and an independent woman, and I couldn't help but admire her.

George clearly felt as I did. "You never fail to amaze me, Aunt Julia. Or impress me. You and Frances have that in common."

"What a lovely thing to say." Julia and I spoke nearly in unison, then laughed.

She placed a hand atop George's. "As I recall, you didn't always have such faith in my abilities—not when I first started this venture."

"You withheld important information," he said. "You never said you were starting a business when you purchased the farm and house. If you had wanted my advice on the matter, I think you ought to have provided all the facts."

The waiter brought our first course then, saving Julia from a reply. She did, however, request another bottle of wine. Once the waiter left and we started our entrées, I ventured a comment. "It seems George has a tendency to withhold information, as well. At least one of his siblings believes you are traveling the world." I hoped I wasn't overstepping my bounds, but this seemed almost cruel to her niece and nephews. "Fiona, for one, has no idea you are settled in Paris."

Julia gave me a sad smile. "I do miss them, but secrecy was necessary, at least up to now. That may change." She patted George on the hand. "We'll discuss that tomorrow, too. Along with my business."

George frowned. "We are here now. What is wrong with now?"

She set down her fork and lifted her glass. "I might have overreacted when I asked for your help. I need some time to decide." She lowered her voice. "Regarding Ducasse, that is. The funeral is tomorrow morning. I need at least until then to get everything settled in my mind."

"Could you be a little more cryptic, Aunt? I may have understood a word or two of what you've just said."

She chuckled. "I must be the mysterious woman a bit longer. Perhaps you will escort me to the funeral tomorrow? I will decide then whether or not I need your investigative assistance." As she spoke, she leaned in and whispered the last two words.

She certainly was being mysterious.

"You would not mind, would you," she asked me, "if I borrow my nephew for a few hours?"

I agreed that I had no objections.

"Excellent," she said. "Now we focus on pleasure and enjoyment. I want to ensure you are both properly welcomed to Paris—" She cut herself off when she caught sight of someone in the crowd. A woman of about my age stood a few feet away. She had a waiflike look to her, with light brown curls that floated around a pallid complexion and large dark eyes. She wore unrelieved black from head to toe and was looking at Julia as if wondering whether to approach.

"Martine!" Julia smiled at the younger woman. "I missed

you this afternoon," she said in French. "Would you like to join us?"

The compressed line of Martine's mouth ticked upward in response. "No," she said, her voice surprisingly high pitched. "I don't wish to interrupt. I wonder, though, have you heard anything of Paul's funeral?" Martine reached back and rubbed her neck, almost as if she were comforting herself.

"Tomorrow morning," Julia said. "Saint Sulpice."

"A large affair or small?"

"We will have to wait and see. I suspect Lucien will want something very public and showy. Gabrielle wants something private. It's difficult to say who will win that battle."

Martine narrowed her eyes. "Have you told her yet?"

Julia stiffened, and Martine shook her head. "I can see you have not. Poor Lissette. She will not thank you for keeping her in the dark."

I'd noticed Julia had modulated her voice when speaking to her acquaintance, using a calm, almost soothing tone. After Martine's last comment, a touch of ice crept into her voice. "Why is it that everyone else is so certain that they know better than I how to manage my life?"

The younger woman seemed about to protest, but Julia would not hear her. "This is not your affair, Martine. I will handle the matter as I see fit."

"You will not handle it at all." Martine regarded George and me with a frown. "Do not let me disturb your dinner," she said before heading back to the entrance of the restaurant and melting into the crowd.

"Too late," George muttered, turning to his aunt. "Who was that?"

Julia pushed her plate away and poured herself more champagne. "Someone from the studio."

He lifted a brow. "One of the family, eh? Must be the black sheep."

"Do not judge," she said before taking a sip from her glass. "Her path has not been easy. She was very close to Paul. His loss hurts her."

"The man did have a wife, you know," George said. "Perhaps he should not have been so close to a young woman like her." I could tell George was holding himself back, itching to ask just how close Julia and Paul were, and whether that was distant or recent past.

Julia let out a tsk. "You should meet Gabrielle."

"We did," George countered. "Just last night, in fact, at what was meant to be a tribute to Paul Ducasse."

Julia had been leaning her chin on the knuckles of her folded hand. She drew her head back in response to George's statement. "No!" she said in a hushed tone. "You must tell me about it. I assume Lucien was in attendance? How did you come to be there?"

George explained about meeting Monsieur Allard on the steamer when we crossed the channel and how that led to our invitation to the tribute.

Though Julia's eyes widened and she let out several huffs, she said nothing until the waiter arrived with the requested bottle of wine. "Unbelievable," she said as soon as he left. "No, what am I saying? It is quite believable from Lucien but wholly out of character for Gabrielle. I can't imagine how he talked her into that, but we can be sure Paul will have that very private funeral now. It's a shame I didn't know about this tribute when Martine asked about the arrangements."

With a shake of her head, she picked up her fork and returned to her meal, leaving George and me staring at each other and feeling a step behind. Julia's words were so matter of fact that I was no longer certain of my assumption that she was in love with Ducasse.

"My dear aunt," George began, "I was under the impression that you were rather distressed by Monsieur Ducasse's death and wanted me to dig into the particulars. Do you believe he met with foul play?"

Julia shushed him and peered around the room. "I told you we were not to discuss that business tonight."

George gazed at her through narrowed eyes. "Very well."

She lowered her fork and turned back to George. "Call on me at the studio tomorrow morning, and we shall go over my little problems before we go to the funeral. Afterward, we can meet Frances and proceed to the exposition. In the meantime, do not speak about foul play in relation to Paul Ducasse. Talk like that could get us all into trouble."

Chapter Five

After dinner, Lady Julia sent us on our way with no further mention of Paul Ducasse. It was somewhere around ten o'clock, and the narrow streets were crowded with revelers out for a night of dancing, eating, and drinking. Since George had to attend a funeral in the morning, we found a cab to take us home and caught a glimpse of the Eiffel Tower alight in the distance when we neared the apartment.

I pulled the bell for the concierge while George paid the cabdriver. Then we waited a few minutes before George reached for the bell again but stopped when a shout of "Who is there?" came from the concierge's loge. Even after we identified ourselves, it seemed to take forever for the older man to come out and open the gate. Then he grumbled about residents coming and going all night and disturbing his sleep.

"Cheeky fellow," George grumbled, but I saw him hand the man a few coins.

Once in the apartment and up in our room, I rang for Bridget, who came up with a tray of hot chocolate. She helped me change from my evening clothes to a night rail, then headed downstairs for her own bed.

George had slipped behind a screen to change his own clothing, and now he was fussing with the hot chocolate.

"Are you pouring whiskey in there?" I asked.

He turned to hand a cup to me. "Just a touch," he said. "It gives the chocolate a little bite."

We took our cups and settled onto the ends of the sofa, as we had the previous night, our legs tangled between us. I sipped the bitter chocolate brew. "Lady Julia is something of a puzzle," I said.

George let out a snort. "As you've seen for yourself, she is not exactly forthcoming with information. She always has kept her own counsel. Which is why," he said, directing a pointed look my way, "Fiona and my brothers don't know that she lives here. It was not my decision to keep them in ignorance."

"I came to that conclusion when she refused to discuss anything with you tonight and specifically requested that you leave me behind tomorrow. Do you think her reluctance to talk was because of my presence?"

""Perhaps," he said. "You were warned."

"Yes, yes, I know. She has every right to her privacy, and I wouldn't dream of infringing upon it, but I do hope she changes her mind about including her family in her life. I don't know about your brothers, but Fiona would love to see her aunt again."

"I'll talk to her about that in the morning."

The morning arrived all too soon. George had risen early and woke me just before he left for his meeting with Lady Julia.

"Any idea how long you'll be?" I asked, wiping the sleep from my eyes.

"Not really," he replied. "I hope to have our discussion about the investigation before leaving for the funeral. She may have a suspect in mind who will also be attending. That would give me a chance to observe and perhaps ask a few questions.

Since Aunt Julia wants to take us to the exposition, we can come here afterward to collect you."

"But that could be hours from now. I don't want to be stuck inside waiting for you when I could be out taking in the sights. Why don't we meet at the Fontaine des Mers instead? That will give me a chance for a stroll. And it's just outside the entrance to the exposition."

"You might have a long wait."

"I don't mind waiting. I just don't want to do it inside this apartment."

Eager to be off, he agreed. He crossed paths with Bridget as he left, and she entered the room with a tray with coffee and croissants. I took them out to the narrow table on our balcony. While visitors and Parisians alike bustled about on the street below, I closed my eyes and savored the brew—dark, rich, and invigorating. After just one cup, I was ready to bound from my chair and start my day.

It didn't take long for Bridget to get me dressed for a morning walk. A blue-and-gray-striped skirt in silk paired with a blue jacket and a white shirtwaist. It was an older ensemble, but it worked beautifully with my new hat, which dipped over one eye and sported both blue and gray plumes. I looked positively chic—perfect for Paris. I pulled on a pair of gray gloves and picked up a lacy parasol as I left.

It was a short walk to the rue de Rivoli, where I passed shops selling photographs, books, and assorted knickknacks as I made my way to the Tuileries Garden. The fountain where I was to meet George and his aunt was to the west of the garden, on la place de la Concorde—formerly the home of Madame Guillotine, now a public plaza. It was nearby, so I could take my time and stroll along the shady paths on my way.

The garden was spacious, with statuary, ponds and, of course, the horse chestnut trees that famously lined its Grande Allée. They provided welcome shade as I wandered down the

smaller paths, but also obstructed any view beyond a short distance. I suppose that is why I failed to see Lady Julia's friends
Edouard and Martine in conversation on a bench along one of
the narrow paths until I was about to walk past them. I wouldn't
have noticed them at all if Martine had not been shouting in
that high-pitched voice of hers. I didn't quite catch the words,
but the sound drew my attention as I walked by.

Edouard came to his feet, his hands fisted at his sides, as he
replied to her. His voice was too quiet for me to hear. I hesitated for just a moment, wondering if I ought to venture closer,
though I really had no reason to eavesdrop on them. Before I
could move on, an older woman stepped up beside me. "A
lovers' spat, I'm sure," she said in French. "We had best move
along."

Since she had barely slowed down to speak to me, I assumed
she was tactfully telling me *I* had better move along, and she
was right. Though it seemed as if Julia's newfound family were
at odds with one another, it was none of my concern. Frankly,
they reminded me very much of my own family.

I made it to the Fontaine des Mers before noon, surprised to
see George and his aunt were already watching for me—well,
Julia was involved in an animated conversation with two well-
dressed women, but George was watching. He raised a welcom-
ing hand when he saw me, but he looked out of sorts. Perhaps
their meeting had not gone well.

"Trouble?" I asked when I was close enough to be heard
over the splashing of the fountain.

"I have no idea," he said. "Now that we are in Paris, my aunt
is not so sure we should involve ourselves in Monsieur Ducasse's murder, after all."

"Interesting. She did sound as if she was having second
thoughts last night."

"Indeed, but now she's even conceded his death might possibly have been an accident." He glanced at Julia, who was still

chatting several feet away, then back at me. "We might have been lured here under false pretenses."

I huffed in outrage. "The nerve! How dare she take advantage of us?"

"Very amusing," George grumbled.

"How can you possibly complain about being in Paris, whatever the reason?" I lifted my hand toward the entrance to the exposition grounds. "It's even better if we haven't a murder to investigate, particularly in the midst of all this excitement."

"Yes, yes. I simply don't like being misled—if that is what she's doing. And I don't know if she is, which has me worried."

"I understand," I said. "But she might be unsure of her theory of his death and wary of presenting it to you. Or do you suppose the whole thing was a ruse to get you here? She has lost a friend and might simply want a loved one nearby. Her so-called family here in Paris might not have been sufficient. I could understand that."

"Either situation is possible, but I think the former more likely. Her solicitor was with us this morning. I appreciate her reticence to discuss a murder investigation while he was there, but the moment he left, we were off to the funeral. We stayed for the service and gave our condolences to the widow, and then she was urging me to come meet you here. I couldn't get her to tell me anything."

"As you said, she keeps her own counsel."

"Then why ask me to come in the first place?"

I assumed that was a rhetorical question. "Tell me, how did she and Madame Ducasse act toward each other?"

"With perfect cordiality."

We'd been watching the object of our conversation while we spoke. Perhaps feeling the weight of our regard, she turned and, catching sight of me, bid her companions farewell and joined us.

"Frances!" Julia took hold of my shoulders and kissed the air by my cheeks. "Now that you are here, we can be off." She placed herself between George and me, linked arms with us, and led us across the plaza.

The main entrance to the exposition had loomed over our shoulders all the while we'd been at the fountain. The enormous edifice had the shape of a turban, with a jeweled embellishment at the top. It was located at the end of la place de la Concorde. We merged with the crowd of visitors, offered our tickets, and made it through the gate with surprising speed.

Lady Julia confidently led us past two fabulous buildings and down a broad street toward the Seine. "The fairgrounds are extensive," she said, "but you can see all of it from the Eiffel Tower. We should go there first."

"Isn't that on the other side of the river?" I asked.

"Not to worry, my dear," Julia called over her shoulder as she bounded forward. "There are steamboats on the river that stop at several points throughout the exposition. There is a stop right by the tower and another right here at the new bridge. Do you see? The bridge itself is quite a work of art."

We scurried down the steps to the embankment and queued up for one of the steamboats that operated as a sort of omnibus on the river. "I have learned something quite amazing about you this morning," Julia said as we waited to board. "George tells me you and he have been investigating together and that you are every bit as good as he."

"Did he really say that?" I beamed at George. "I think that tells you more about him than about me."

She gave me a curious look.

"Plenty of women could do what I do," I said. "But it takes a man with character and more than the average amount of confidence to admit such a thing."

"Ah, yes. I have known for many years now that George is a most extraordinary man."

The extraordinary man heaved a sigh. "You ladies will have

me blushing in a moment." He helped us both to board, then hopped on himself just as the boat set off toward the Alexander III Bridge.

I settled into a seat next to Julia, with George on my other side.

He returned to our conversation. "I told Aunt Julia about our work together, hoping she'd take you into her confidence, since I have been shut out." He faced Julia, who scowled at him. "Is there anything you'd like to tell Frances about Ducasse? Or perhaps the break-in at your flat?"

Surely, I had misheard him. "Could you explain that last bit to me?"

George lowered his voice. "Someone broke into Aunt Julia's flat while she was out with us last night. They didn't take anything, or at least she won't admit to me that anything was missing, but the lock on the door had been broken. She had the locksmith in to replace it this morning."

"Have you any idea who might have done that?" I asked her. "Do you keep anything valuable there?"

"Do you think it had something to do with Paul Ducasse?" George added.

She held up her hands, palms out. "Yes."

That stopped us. George and I exchanged a glance before he continued. "Yes to what? We just asked you three different questions."

"Too many questions," she said. "I've changed my mind. I don't want to involve you in this." She crossed and uncrossed her hands abruptly, as if to put an end to this conversation. "Now, let us just enjoy the exposition. Look, we are moving, and you do not want to miss seeing the bridge."

Julia was correct; it was an impressive sight. The commanding winged horses of bronze and gilt that towered over each corner of the bridge were tempered by the elegant, sweeping lines of the structure and its ornamentation.

When we emerged on the other side, my gaze traveled over the vista along the river. "This is simply incredible!" Buildings of every shape and size lined the embankment ahead of us on either side of the Seine. I saw onion domes, church spires, and every sort of architectural form and structure one could imagine.

"That's the Street of Nations," Julia said. "Britain is represented somewhere in there, and look, there is the United States. Your countrymen, Frances."

The buildings boasted fabulously intricate façades. It was hard to believe they would all be demolished at the end of the exposition. But not before millions of people saw them. "I've been reading about the exposition for months," I said, "but nothing compares to seeing it for myself."

"It is amazing, isn't it?" Julia said.

While I was completely bowled over by the sights, George was not so easily put off. He leaned forward, and I caught the light in his eyes, which told me he'd had some sort of revelation.

"The break-in does have something to do with Ducasse, doesn't it?" he said.

I shrank back in my seat so he could speak to Julia around me.

"Someone knows you believe he was murdered." He observed her through narrowed eyes. "Or perhaps you've told other people how you feel about the matter. Whoever broke in might have intended to stop you from talking about Ducasse."

Julia drew back, as if she'd been slapped.

George took her reaction as his answer. "That's it. No wonder you don't want to tell us. You don't want to put our lives in danger."

The boat docked at the landing in the shadow of the Eiffel Tower. Our fellow travelers threw us curious glances as they scurried to the exit. We remained seated.

"You might wish to lower your voice when you speak of murder, George," I said.

"What if you'd been home last night?" he asked Julia, his

voice low and full of concern. "The intruder might have killed you. Allow Frances and me to take care of this. Let us take care of you." He glanced up at the exiting passengers streaming past us. "I'm not sure it's a good idea for you to be out admiring the sights if someone is threatening your life."

She waved off his concern. "Enough of this. You may be correct about my safety, but if I stop living and stay hidden away, then haven't they already succeeded?"

"I prefer to consider any hiding you do as temporary, so that you may live to, well, live another day."

"Do you really think anyone would attempt to harm her out in such a public place?" I patted George's arm when he scowled at me. "Not to mention that you and I are right beside her. How could she be in danger under these circumstances?" I turned to Julia, who was looking very self-righteous. "But if we are to investigate Paul Ducasse's death, we should do so quickly. Witnesses forget. Evidence becomes lost."

"And I still haven't decided if you are to investigate." She reached around me to poke her finger at George's chest. "Don't think you can tell me what to do. Those days are long over. Just give me time to decide how I want to manage this problem." She came to her feet and pulled me to mine. "Now, I have toured the fairgrounds a few times, so if you'll allow me, I shall be your guide."

George raised his gaze to the heavens. "By all means," he said, gesturing to the dock. "Can't let something like a little murder investigation stand in the way of art."

"And industry," Julia reminded him. "Besides, you can always investigate tomorrow."

We navigated the walkway to the embankment, only to be met with a mass of people. "We shall have to plan on multiple visits," George said. "It's already noon. I don't see us conquering more than this tower today. I caught a glimpse of the queue from the distance. We won't be ascending anytime soon."

We climbed the steps from the embankment to the street

level. "Come this way," Julia said, directing us around the imposing tower to the avenue de Suffren. We strolled down the street, then turned at the next corner and were startled by the sight of an enormous globe about three hundred yards away. Crowds were everywhere we looked. Fortunately, no one was in a hurry, so we simply flowed along with the foot traffic.

"That globe is impressive, don't you think?" George said.

It was—and right in our path, too, just across a footbridge.

"Shall we go closer?" Julia asked.

"I think the crowd is guiding us that way any—" I broke off when I heard a thunderous crash, followed by screams of horror.

About fifteen feet ahead of us, a hole opened up in the crowd—downward, as if the people had been sucked into the ground. It took a second or two for me to realize the footbridge had collapsed. Those ahead of us who had not fallen pushed back against us. Those behind us couldn't see what had happened, and continued to move forward. Caught between them, I felt as though I was being crushed. I lost sight of George and Julia as the crowd surged and ebbed like an image in a kaleidoscope.

I don't know how long it lasted. Though people around me screamed, I could barely draw a breath, nor could I move my arms. When the flow moved backward again, I was helpless against it. My feet no longer touched the pavement, and panic surged like an electric shock. I feared that if the people crushed against me should move, I'd fall to the ground and be trampled.

As that thought struck, the crowd gave way behind me. In the newly found space, I began to fall backward, flailing my arms, until a hand caught hold of mine. Then a strong arm circled my back and pulled me to my feet.

Dizziness overtook me as my lungs finally drew in some air. When I started to sink, the arm tightened, and a man's voice urged me on. "*Non, non. Allons!*" Staggering and leaning against him, I let him drag me away from the melee to a bench. Once there, he draped me over it like a newly laundered garment.

"If you are all right, madame," he said in French, "I will leave you here. There are others who need help."

"Yes, of course." I drew myself up to my elbows and looked around. "My husband and his aunt are still in there." I waved my hand toward the mass of people, though I could see the crowd was thinning. The police, blowing their whistles, ran into the area, and those who could helped those who had gone down with the debris of the footbridge. What had been a bright, shining Monday morning was now all rubble and dust.

I sent the man off with my thanks and pushed myself up from the bench, relieved that my legs remained steady. Remarkably, I still had my little reticule attached to my wrist with its strings, amazing considering the rest of me was in tatters. At least I was standing. At once I followed my rescuer's example and headed back to the rubble to see to the injured until actual medical personnel could take charge.

Perhaps thirty minutes later, the fire department had arrived, and along with the police, they were assisting the injured to ambulances. I had just helped a woman to a makeshift first aid area in a rubble-free section of lawn when I finally caught sight of George. Like me, he looked battered and gray with dust, but otherwise intact. He had never looked better to me. We stumbled into each other's arms, and for a moment, I thought all was well. If we were together, everything would be fine.

Then I recalled Julia and pulled away. He caught my face between his hands. "Are you injured?"

"No, I am fine." I was looking him over as I spoke. "You too?"

"Yes, but I lost track of my aunt."

"She was right next to me when it started." I glanced at the place where we'd all been walking such a short time ago. The police had cleared nearly everyone out. "Come with me." I indicated the busy first aid area. "If she hasn't already been taken to the hospital," I said, "she may be there."

We crossed the open expanse of pavement littered with debris: an odd assortment of clothing and hats, steel bars and chunks of concrete. As we came to the makeshift first aid area, there were perhaps a dozen people sitting or lying on the grass. I caught sight of purple tulle and clutched George's arm. "There she is. I can see her hat."

I could feel the relief flood through him as we rushed across the street. A uniformed policeman stepped in our path, putting up a hand to stop us. "Is there someone you know here?" he asked in French, indicating what I now saw were three people stretched out on the grass. My stomach knotted.

"My aunt is that woman there." George pointed to Julia. "Is she . . . ?"

The policeman placed a hand on his shoulder. "I am sorry, monsieur, madame. Your relative did not survive."

Chapter Six

George pushed past the officer and crouched down beside Julia's body.

"Please, let him have a moment," I said before the officer could go after him. "I can provide you with the particulars of her identity."

The officer, a bit younger than me, cast a sympathetic look at George, then pulled out a small notebook and asked me the expected questions. I gave him Julia's information, and since George was her next of kin, I also provided the address of the Kendricks' apartment, in case we were needed.

In exchange for my information, the officer told me where they were taking her and when we might be able to claim her remains—tomorrow was most likely. He also gave me the address and a telephone number to contact the coroner's office.

I went to George's side when more medical people came to take Julia's body away, and put my arm around him. Like a child disturbed from his slumber, he allowed me to guide him from the rubble of the collapsed footbridge, the dead and injured, and the survivors like us who were tattered, disheveled, and covered in dust.

Two blocks away, as we neared the river, Paris looked just as it had an hour ago. Excited tourists flooded the streets, pointing and chatting in multiple languages, eager to see the sights. They gave us wide berth, gaping at our appearance, as we crossed the Alexander III Bridge. I could have hailed a cab, since we were still quite a distance from the apartment, but I thought it might do George some good to walk.

By the time we reached the Tuileries Garden, he seemed somewhat recovered—that is, he was no longer lost somewhere inside his head. I suggested we sit on one of the benches scattered among the long rows of trees. Drenched in shade, it felt like a little bit of heaven, considering my dark blue jacket was hot to the touch. After a moment's silence, I took his hand in mine, only then noticing our gloves were tattered and filthy.

"I'm so sorry, darling. I can't believe she's gone. It all happened so quickly."

George tipped his head back and covered his face with his hands. "Far too quickly. While we were humoring her desire to forget that her life was in danger, she was killed."

"Strictly speaking, I was the one humoring her. You were trying to convince her to tell you what she knew. And I'm not sure it even matters if her life was in danger. No one murdered her. This was an accident. Tragic, but not something we could have prepared for."

George lowered his hands and leveled a look at me.

"Stop that. Are you saying you should have checked the integrity of the bridge before we went to the exposition?"

He scowled.

"Surely you aren't saying someone meddled with the structure as a method of murder? There was far too much havoc, and others died, too."

He turned tired eyes to me. Cement dust covered one side of his beard. I removed the remnants of my glove and attempted to brush the dust away with my fingers. He caught my hand in his and gently kissed the knuckles. "Are you trying to say there's nothing I could have done to protect her?" he asked.

"I believe I did say that, yes. It happens to be the truth, though I know it doesn't reduce your loss one whit."

"It doesn't. Gad, I haven't felt this heavyhearted since my mother died."

I pulled his head onto my shoulder and rested my hand on his hair.

Suddenly, he froze, then shot off the bench. "We have to get back to the apartment."

Startled, I jumped to my feet. "Why? What happened? What do you need there?"

He took my hand and rushed me down the path through the garden and toward our apartment building. "I must get to Aunt Julia's country house immediately." He threw the words over his shoulder.

"But why?" I scurried to keep up as he pulled me across the bustling rue de Rivoli without so much as a glance at the traffic. "Surely someone is taking care of things in her absence."

"Yes, I'm sure someone is, but blast it, I'm the guardian."

I dug in my heels once we reached the sidewalk. A couple crossing the street behind us had to do a quick side step to avoid a collision with us.

George seemed not to notice and simply tugged my arm. "We must go."

"You are making no sense, and I'm not entirely sure I shouldn't take you to a doctor. How could you be a guardian of her house, if that is what you are trying to say? I don't understand you."

He dropped my arm and placed his hands on his hips. "That's right. You don't know."

I drew in a breath, counted to five, and blew it out. All this secrecy surrounding Lady Julia was beginning to wear on me. "*Now*, what don't I know?"

George surveyed the broad avenue, where people flowed around us as if we were two muddy rocks in the middle of a stream, then took my hand again and indicated we should move on. "Let's return to the apartment, and I'll explain everything. I'd rather not discuss my aunt's personal business in public."

We walked the last few blocks in silence. Finally, we were admitted to the shaded courtyard by the very disapproving *madame la concierge*. I had no energy for excuses and simply suffered the scrutiny of the caretaker's wife as we climbed the curved staircase to the first floor. George unlocked the door, and we stepped into the cool foyer.

"Before we do anything," I said, heading for the stairs, "we must clean up."

George caught my arm and drew me to the salon. "Ring for Bridget and have her ready your bath. What I have to tell you oughtn't wait. And frankly, I could use a brandy."

George crossed the salon to a table behind the sofa, where a bottle of brandy and glasses waited. "I thought this might come in handy, but I didn't expect it would happen so soon."

I did as George had suggested, and when Bridget arrived, she took one look at the two of us, gasped in shock, or perhaps disgust, and left to arrange baths. Since that would take a little time, I pulled off my dirty jacket and took a seat on the sofa. George joined me and handed me a glass.

"You know the story of Aunt Julia as a young woman, I believe. Didn't Fiona tell you?"

I took a sip of the brandy and let it burn down my throat. "She did, but Fiona was mistaken about a few points. How long have you known Julia was in Paris?"

"Almost the whole time. She needed some legal advice when she purchased the country house. I did encourage her to tell the family she was here so they could visit or at least write, but she was vehemently against that idea."

"That sounds so sad to me." I shook my head. "What is it about her house that has you so concerned?"

He paused long enough for me to wonder if he had suffered some injury to his head. "It's not the house itself, but what's there."

"What is there?" I prompted.

He gave me a furtive glance.

"Cows? Chickens? Cheese? For heaven's sake, is this another secret?"

"She has a child."

I drew back sharply enough to bounce against the back of the sofa. "A child? Her own child?"

"A daughter. Ducasse is the father, though I'm sure you could have worked that out for yourself." He took a long drink of his brandy.

"A child. Is this the Lissette that her friend Martine mentioned?"

"I don't actually know her name, now that you mention it. I've never met her, but she is why Aunt Julia contacted me last year. That's when she told me she had a baby. She wanted to make sure Ducasse would never fight her for custody. He was agreeable at the time, but she was concerned for the future."

He put his glass on the table and rested his elbows on his knees before threading his fingers together. "If she hadn't needed my legal advice, I still would not know about the child."

"I suppose I can understand her desire for secrecy." In fact, this particular piece of information explained a lot. But there was one thing I didn't understand. I focused on George. "How old do you believe her child is?"

"More than a year. Less than two."

"I wondered why you called her a baby." I let out a tsk.

"You really ought to have asked to meet her when you were here, George."

"It was a delicate situation," he said. "I would have liked to meet her, but the whole idea of my aunt having a child out of wedlock in her late thirties, not to mention her demand that I keep that information to myself, well, it had me rather tiptoeing around the subject. I worked with a solicitor here in Paris. We drew up the documents, she signed, the solicitor took them off for Ducasse to sign, and I left." He pulled a face. "I could have been more of a loving nephew, couldn't I?"

I closed the distance between us on the sofa and leaned into his side. "She knew you loved her, George, and she clearly knew she could rely on you. It sounds as though she set the tone for your meeting, and that tone was secrecy. I know you, George. You would have respected her wishes. I just hope she didn't keep your family a secret from her daughter. I'd hate to think we are all strangers to her."

"She's just a baby, Frances. Everyone is a stranger."

"Oh, yes, that. I think you are mistaken there. It makes no sense that the child would be less than two years old."

George leaned back until he could look into my face. "You doubt me?"

"On this, I'm afraid I do. Upon meeting Lady Julia again, I could see that she was very independent. And though she may have been in love with Paul Ducasse at one time, I believe that time is well in the past. I can't see her having a love affair with a married man, particularly if she was no longer in love with him."

"But Ducasse is or was the father."

"That I do believe." I grinned at his confusion. I loved it when I managed to unravel a mystery before George did—not an admirable trait, I know. Shame on me. And not at all admirable when the poor man had just lost a beloved relative. Now was not the time to enjoy my success. "I am willing to wager that Lady Julia's daughter is significantly older than you estimate."

He studied me through narrowed eyes. "Indeed? How old do you suppose she is?"

"I'd say she's about fifteen years old."

Watching his face, I saw when his initial reaction to argue was supplanted by a willingness to at least entertain the possibility. "Aunt Julia would still have been living in England then," he said.

"Here's how I suspect it happened," I said. "Long ago, your aunt made a trip to Paris and fell in love with a penniless artist. Her father disapproved. Her mother was likely horrified. They refused their permission, and for whatever reason, perhaps financial, perhaps out of a sense of duty, Julia chose not to defy them—at least not outright. However, she refused to marry anyone else, as I'm certain she was encouraged to do. I also suspect that refusal was because she was pregnant with Paul Ducasse's child."

"An interesting story, but difficult to prove."

"That depends on how much proof you require. You may recall that while you were off working for the Home Office, I was stuck at Harleigh Manor, relying on friends, like your sister, for any spark of entertainment. I remember her writing to me when Julia left for her so-called world tour. That was eight years ago. Fiona mused that she'd always thought Julia would settle in France because she had traveled there once or twice a year for the previous seven years.

"Fiona then speculated that Julia had a lover, and maybe she did, but I believe Julia was visiting her child. I just did the math. Eight and seven equals fifteen." I lifted one shoulder. "She could be older, I suppose."

George stared at me in amazement. "Fiona wrote you a letter eight years ago—one of many, I'd imagine—and you recall the people, places, and dates she wrote about?"

"Did I mention my husband had left me in the country? During shooting season there were neighbors about, but otherwise, I was desperate for company. I read Fiona's letters until the paper wore thin."

He pulled me into his shoulder and kissed the top of my head. "Assuming you are correct, what do you suppose happened when she moved to France? Someone must have been caring for her child while Aunt Julia was still living in England."

"She probably hired a family to do so. Perhaps in the town where her house is located. Nonetheless, I suspect as soon as she could, she reclaimed her child and has since made a home for her. Ducasse was married, so she may not have told him he was the father. I wonder if he only learned of it before she called on you to help her with the custody issue."

"We'll find out soon enough. I'm sure you're correct and someone is caring for her child, whatever age she may be, but I still feel we need to go to her and break the news of her mother's death just as soon as we can."

"Of course. Do you know where her home is? Or how to get there?"

"It's mentioned in the paperwork we went over today, but her solicitor took it to his office. I believe he gave me his card."

"Why don't we just go to her studio?" I suggested. "There might be something in her garret about the property, or one of her artist friends may know. Heavens, we should make them aware of her passing, too."

"Yes, perhaps we should make a list, but Aunt Julia's child must be among the first things we attend to." He gave me a close look. "I haven't fully explained our situation. When Julia told me about her child, we also discussed who would care for her in the event of my aunt's death." He opened his hands. "She asked me, and I agreed to do it. I am the child's legal guardian. We are her guardians. I'm sorry I didn't tell you before now about my agreement, but I never imagined ... and with Julia's demand for secrecy ..."

Poor George looked to be at his wit's end. It occurred to me that he was like a man who had just become a father for the first time. I leaned my dusty head on his shoulder. "I do understand your predicament and concern. It is not cows or chickens. We now have a child—or really a young woman—in our care. It will be fine. We have room in our home and in our lives. We will do our best for her."

George pulled me into his arms. "Thank you for being so calm while I try to drag the pieces of my wits together." He let out a sigh. "I like your suggestion. Once we've had a chance to clean up, let's go to the studio and find out what we can about Julia's daughter and if she is indeed in the country. Then perhaps we can have a meal before we go to her. You might have Bridget and Blakely pack a bag for us, in case we spend the night there."

I gave him a quick kiss and regretfully left his arms. "I'll see to it now."

He downed the rest of his brandy. "I'll check with Madame Fontaine about the possibility of a meal."

I'd just reached the second-floor landing when a knock sounded at the door. I waited while George answered it.

"Monsieur Hazelton?" a male voice inquired.

I turned around and descended the stairs out of curiosity.

George verified his identity.

"Monsieur, I need you and Madame Hazelton to accompany me to la Sûreté, if you please."

"What is la Sûreté?" I asked, stepping up behind George.

"It's a branch of the police," George said, "involving criminal investigations." He returned his attention to the uniformed officer at the door. "Why are we needed?"

"It is in relation to a Madame Julia Hazelton. I believe she is your relative? The inspector has some questions for you."

"That's rather peculiar," George said. "We identified her at the scene of the accident. I can't imagine what questions your inspector could have."

The man tipped his head and looked at George in confusion. "It is not at all unusual, in the event of murder, to ask a great many questions, monsieur."

"Yes, I understand that, but her death was a tragic accident."

"No, monsieur. This was very definitely murder."

Chapter Seven

The officer allowed us enough time to change from our tattered clothing and clean ourselves up. After a quick bath, Bridget brushed the dust from my hair and put me into my most readily available outfit before attempting to arrange my hair into some sort of order. Sitting at the dressing table, I caught sight of George in the mirror as Blakely helped him into a clean suit coat. As soon as Bridget relaxed her grip on my hair, I turned around to see him walking toward me, with a grim expression. I took his hand and brought him to the dressing table before Bridget once again took control of my head.

"I'm so sorry to see you in pain, George. I know Lady Julia meant a great deal to you. Surely, the police can be put off until tomorrow."

"She did mean a lot to me," he said. "Before I really came to know Aunt Julia, I thought of all women as mothers and sisters, people to be taken care of."

Bridget let out a tsk, and I curled my lip in disgust. "Heavens, you were one of those creatures."

He chuckled. "I was. Then I saw Aunt Julia stand up to her

father and then my father. I learned that not only did women have their own minds and opinions, but they also had the ability to take care of themselves and, apparently, their children perfectly well unless the men in their lives denied them the wherewithal to do so."

"Then I am very grateful to her, since I am reaping the rewards of your expanded outlook on the role of women in the world."

"As far as speaking with the police, I'm eager to do so. I'm very curious about how they concluded she was murdered. Moreover, the sooner we speak to them, the sooner we can go about finding Julia's daughter."

Bridget had finished with my hair and fastened a hat to my head, which was when I remembered my new hat had been lost somewhere on the fairgrounds. No matter. So much more of value had been lost today.

We joined the officer, who had waited, as instructed, in the foyer for our return. The three of us walked together through the courtyard while *monsieur le concierge* and his wife watched from a window in their gate-side loge. I was certain the Kendricks would hear some exaggerated tale of our interactions with the Sûreté. I supposed they were no worse than any other nosy neighbors.

The cab had waited while George and I were cleaning up. We squeezed into the narrow interior along with the officer. He imparted no further information along the way. Upon reaching the building that housed the Sûreté, he turned us over to another uniformed officer, who showed us to a room with a battered wooden table and chairs and left us there.

To wait.

After twenty minutes, I broke the silence. "This doesn't feel right, George. You don't suppose they think we had something to do with that collapsed bridge, do you?"

He gave me a look of astonishment. "I'd love to hear how that could be our fault. No, I doubt they know how the bridge came to collapse yet. For some reason, they suspect murder, and I am her next of kin. I'm sure they have questions for us. You needn't worry they suspect us of that crime. There's certainly no reason for them to think we were involved in anything untoward."

"Then why have they left us here if not to stew in our own juices, so to speak?"

George raised his brows. "It's been only ten minutes. If that."

"It's been twenty minutes."

I would have explained why I thought that was too long, but just then the door opened and a man in a finely tailored suit entered, his hand outstretched to shake George's. "Daniel Cadieux," he said. "Inspector with la Sûreté. Thank you for meeting with me. I am given to understand you are English, though you speak French."

The inspector spoke English briskly and with only a slight accent. That was until he took my hand in both of his, leaned toward me, and said, "*Enchanté, madame,*" as only a Frenchman could.

The experience left me with just a few goose bumps and a silly grin.

"Ahem!"

The goose bumps fled when I caught George scowling at me. I placed my hand over his. Cadieux might be charming, but he wasn't George.

The inspector was slightly upward of thirty, clean shaven, with dark eyes and straight dark hair, which he combed back from his forehead. He was shorter than George, possibly shorter than me, and lean. But I must say, his suit fit him much better than Inspector Delaney's ever did. Did all the French have some innate sense of style? I had never seen any of Delaney's police colleagues back in London dress as well as Cadieux.

After greeting us, he set a coffee cup on the table and removed some papers from under his arm. "We can conduct this interview in English if you prefer," he said while he pulled up a wooden chair from against the wall. He seated himself at the table, opposite the two of us, prepared to grill us, I was sure, until one of us confessed to something heinous. Or perhaps he meant to torture us or simply lock us up.

"If this is official," George said, "English might be best."

Cadieux seemed not to be listening. With a look of dismay, he gestured to the table. "But you have no refreshment. Has no one brought you coffee?" Before we could reply, he came to his feet. "Obviously, they have not. Allow me to remedy that." He took a step toward the door and turned back. "Or do you prefer tea?"

"Coffee will be fine," George said.

With two swift steps, he was out the door. He left it open so we could see that he and, more importantly, the coffee were just around the corner. He returned with two steaming cups and set them before us. "Milk or sugar?" he asked, but both of us took long draughts from our cups as our reply. Satisfied, he retook his seat.

Perhaps I had been hasty in my judgment of the police. After all, this man had brought us coffee. And since French was not my primary language, I did appreciate the opportunity to converse with him in English.

"Monsieur and Madame Hazelton, let me first express my most sincere condolences at the loss of your loved one." He turned to George. "Lady Julia Hazelton was your aunt, correct?"

"Thank you," George replied. "Yes, she was."

"Were you close?"

George leaned against the back of his chair. "She was part of our household when I was young, so yes, I saw her as something of an older sister. Since she moved to Paris, we, by necessity, became less close, but she was still a beloved aunt."

"Now, that I find very interesting." Cadieux leaned over the table, tapping his index finger in the air as if he had a twitch. "What brought her to Paris?"

"What brings anyone to Paris?" George replied. "History. Art. It's a beautiful city."

"But a woman in her middle years making such a change to her life—and doing it alone." He shook his head. "No, something must have prompted her."

George's jaw tightened just a fraction. "Her reasons were personal."

"Of course. I'm afraid I will need to know many personal details about your aunt."

"Then it's true, you believe she was murdered." George narrowed his eyes. "Why?"

Cadieux took a slurp of coffee and sank back in his chair. He kept his eyes on George and gestured with his cup. "The first indication was the knife wound the medical examiner found in her back. Since it is highly irregular for people to stab themselves in the back, murder seemed a reasonable conclusion."

Indeed. After a moment of stunned silence, I spoke. "I don't understand how that could be possible. We were packed so tightly together I was lifted off my feet. I couldn't even move my arms."

"So, you were caught up in it, too?" Cadieux asked.

"Yes. Lady Julia was standing right next to me until . . ."

He nodded. "Until she wasn't."

"What I mean to say is that one would need a certain amount of space to stab someone, wouldn't they? There was no such space. Is it possible that she was pushed against something sharp? A part of the fencing or some such thing?"

He bobbed his head slowly, as if he was considering my suggestion, then turned to George. "What about you, Monsieur Hazelton? Did you get stuck in the crowd?"

"Momentarily, but I was able to work my way out."

"Of course, a large man like you would have no difficulty moving his arms, yes?"

Goodness, he wore the most innocent look I'd ever seen, but I didn't like his implication. I parted my lips to object, but George spoke first.

"You say your medical examiner found the wound. Is a medical examiner usually called in when someone dies in an accident? Did you suspect murder before the body was even examined?"

"Not at all. Nine people died as a result of that footbridge collapsing. That's in addition to other deaths that occurred yesterday and today. More than is usual, you understand, due to all the tourists here this summer. Do you know they expect upward of sixty million visitors to the exposition by the time all is said and done?"

He glanced from George to me and back, as if expecting an answer. When we failed to provide one, he set his cup on the table and continued. "The coroner's office was simply overwhelmed, so the medical examiner was called in." He tipped his head to the side as he studied George's expression. "And a good thing he was, yes? It's possible that the coroner might have missed the wound. Of course, that might be what the killer hoped would happen."

George looked doubtful. "Surely, your coroners are better trained than that."

"They are very well trained, but they are not generally doctors. Similar to your coroners in England, they pronounce death, identify the victim, investigate the scene, but they are not medical examiners. In my occupation, I find the procedures of police in other countries very interesting." He lifted a brow. "I also find it interesting that you seem to be familiar with our procedures."

Cadieux had a way of asking questions without actually asking questions. It seemed he was trying to goad George, and I could think of only one reason for that. "I am getting the very strong impression that you, Inspector, believe, or would like to believe, that my husband had something to do with his aunt's death. I can't imagine how that could be possible, and I'd like to hear your evidence. You must have some evidence, don't you? You wouldn't just assume a man is guilty of murder based on nothing, would you?"

George leaned back in his chair and crossed his arms, gazing over the table at Cadieux with some amusement. "You thought she would be the easy one, didn't you?"

The inspector shrugged, his expression giving nothing away.

"I can answer your question," George said. "The police dispersed the crowd at the exposition. It was the right thing to do at the time. They had to be able to get to those who were injured by the collapse of the bridge. The crowd was in the way, causing more problems. But later, when they found that one of the victims had been stabbed, they realized they had chased away all the potential witnesses. It would therefore be very convenient for Inspector Cadieux if one of us turned out to be the murderer." He fixed his gaze on the inspector. "Isn't that true, Cadieux?"

His lips quirked infinitesimally. "You were both there at the time. You are both acquainted with her. I would be remiss in my duty if I did not inquire."

I let out a huff. "It seemed to me Lady Julia knew nearly everyone she came across. She was speaking with some friends just before we entered the exposition grounds. I saw two of her artist friends in the Tuileries Garden just before the three of us met today. She had friends everywhere."

At Cadieux's urging, I gave him the names of Julia's artist friends. George told him where their studio was located.

"As for us," I said, "the answer is no. Neither of us killed her."

"Somebody did. Perhaps you will indulge me by answering my questions so I can find out who that was."

I waved a hand, indicating he should begin.

Cadieux dug through the papers he had brought until he found a writing tablet, then pulled a pen from a drawer in the table. "Why did your aunt move to Paris? What was this personal reason?"

"She has a child living in Chartres," George began. "She is also unmarried and didn't want the family to know about her daughter."

"Yet you are family, and you know."

"She needed my legal assistance to set parameters for the child's father. She wanted complete custody."

Cadieux nodded, scribbling on the tablet. "What is the child's name and age?"

George cast me a look. "I don't know." When Cadieux glanced up with a frown, George sighed. "She was very secretive about the child."

"I do not judge." Cadieux raised his hands, palms out.

"You bloody well are judging."

I placed a hand on George's arm to calm him.

"No, no," the inspector said. "You are British. You are more reserved than we French. Now, the legal assistance, is that why you are visiting her?"

"No, that business was a year ago. She asked me to visit her this time regarding a different matter."

Cadieux waited patiently, his pen poised above the paper.

"She wanted me to look into the death of a friend."

"Indeed?" Cadieux leaned against the back of the chair and studied George. "Why would she want to do this? And why you?"

"I have a little experience in investigations," George said. "She suspected he was murdered."

"Who is this friend?"

"Paul Ducasse."

Cadieux dropped his pen as his dark eyes flitted from George to me. I had no idea what George was willing to tell the man, so I remained silent.

"What made her think he was murdered?" Cadieux asked.

"She refused to tell me. Once we were here, she said she had changed her mind and didn't want me to involve myself. Someone broke into her loft last night, and I believe that frightened her into making that decision."

Cadieux flipped to another page in his tablet and had George tell him what he knew about the break-in. When he'd finished, the inspector reviewed his notes with a frown. "You say at first, she was emphatic that Ducasse was murdered, but when you spoke with her this morning, she said he wasn't."

"No. She never said he wasn't murdered, only that she didn't want to involve me or Frances."

"How well did she know Ducasse?"

George caught my eye, as if to ask, "Should I?"

I compressed my lips. The man would likely find out, anyway.

"I assume she knew him very well," George said. "He was the father of her daughter."

Cadieux drummed his fingers on the table. "The daughter she told you about, but whom you have never met." He looked across at us from hooded eyes. "Had she lived, are you certain tomorrow she would not have denied she had a daughter?"

"I do not believe my aunt was mad, if that is what you are suggesting."

The inspector gathered his papers. "I will go over the file for Ducasse's death. I will also speak with Lady Julia's artist friends. Perhaps they have met her phantom daughter. I will also do my best to determine who stabbed your aunt." He straightened his notes and considered the two of us. "And you? What will you be doing?"

"We will go out to my aunt's house in Chartres, where I believe we will find her very corporeal daughter and can tell her of her loss."

Cadieux came to his feet and held out a hand to George, who took it. "Best of luck to you, Monsieur Hazelton."

"The same to you, Inspector Cadieux."

I thought we all would need a great deal of luck. Particularly if Cadieux believed Lady Julia was simply a dotty middle-aged woman.

Cadieux had offered an escort back to our residence, but George had turned him down. Instead, we found ourselves on the pavement outside the police station on Île de la Cité—an island in the Seine at the center of Paris. The buildings of the court and the gothic spires of Sainte-Chapelle shrouded us in shadow.

"You may dislike Cadieux," I said to George. "But you might have accepted his offer of a carriage. I don't relish the idea of walking all the way back to the apartment."

"We're not going to the apartment," he said. "And I didn't want one of Cadieux's men reporting back to him about our destination."

I took his arm as we walked down the narrow street in the direction of the Seine. We were two of only a dozen or so people I could see in the area. That made sense, I supposed. This was a small island. Everyone was here for either police, court, or church business. "Where are we going, then?"

"The studio." George directed me toward a cab that had just dropped off its passengers. He helped me into the seat and told the driver to take us to Montmartre. With that, he joined me inside and closed the door.

When the driver turned the cab toward the Right Bank and the horse clip-clopped over the bridge, I thought it safe for a private conversation.

"You've just told Cadieux about the studio. Is it wise to go there now?"

"If we are to get there before him, now may be the only time."

I gazed out to the right as we passed a small park. The gothic Saint Jacques Tower rose above the trees that lined the perimeter. Even in the midst of this tragedy, it was hard to resist the charms of this city. I forced my attention back to the matter at hand. "Do you plan to speak with the artists?"

"Perhaps, but primarily, I want to go through her flat. I don't know if she witnessed Paul Ducasse's murder or if she simply knew something that made her suspicious, but on the off chance she has some tangible evidence, I want to find it before the police confiscate it."

"Do you believe they won't look into Paul Ducasse's death? Or do you not trust they will do a thorough job of it?"

He raised his brows. "I suppose because we're dealing with my aunt, I hesitate to trust them at all. Cadieux seems more than competent, but Ducasse's death was ruled an accident, and the investigation closed. Cadieux now has to convince a prosecutor to let him continue the investigation without any new evidence. Will he bother when he seems to think Aunt Julia is, well, something of a cracked pot?"

"But the evidence you are speaking of would be about Paul Ducasse's death. I thought you were more interested in learning who murdered your aunt."

"I suspect their deaths are linked. Perhaps Aunt Julia was murdered because of what she knew about Ducasse's death. I believe she backed away from investigating because she felt threatened by the break-in at her flat."

"That's a reasonable assumption. But what makes you think she'll have evidence that Ducasse was murdered?"

"Because my aunt was not mad."

My heart swelled with sympathy. "We shall prove that she wasn't."

We turned off a broad avenue and onto one of the narrow streets leading to Montmartre. The cab rumbled and rocked over the partially paved cobblestone street until the horse slowed his pace.

"I understand why Cadieux suggested it," George continued, "but I think the change in her story was due to fear, not madness."

"I do not doubt her sanity, George, but it is possible she was overreacting to the death of her friend."

"The fact that she was murdered tells me otherwise. It seems she was right to be fearful that the killer might come after her, but I wish she'd trusted me to keep her safe."

"We will do whatever we must to find her killer." I held out my hand, and he took it in his. "I know we need to find an address for her house in the country, but apart from that, I don't suppose you have any idea what it is we're looking for?"

"I haven't the foggiest."

George directed the driver down a narrow street, past the Moulin de la Galette, where we'd dined with Julia, and had him stop at the end of the block. We climbed out, and while George paid the driver, I admired the bright window boxes and awnings adorning the stone buildings, which had mellowed to an amber hue. The afternoon was growing warm again, and I wished Bridget had chosen a lighter color for me in my rush to get dressed.

George stepped away from the cab and joined me on the pavement.

"The building is down this block and around the corner," he said, taking my arm.

Calling the studio a building was generous. It looked more like a two-story stone ruin and did not improve as we walked past the façade. The trim around the windows had recently been painted a spring green by someone with a great deal of optimism. The thick wooden door stood open and looked as if it had been stuck in that position for generations.

"Are you certain it's safe to go inside?" I asked as we stepped across the deep threshold. Once we entered, I didn't care if it was safe or not. It was blessedly cool. George chuckled as I sighed with contentment.

The room was a large rectangle with thick plaster walls and high ceilings. At the moment it was filled with light from the windows across the top of the front wall. The only divider was a half wall across the back, yet it felt sectioned off into four work areas, one in each of the corners, leaving an open space in the center.

Each area held a worktable, with various tools scattered across the surface, a straight-backed wooden chair, and a taller stool. Shelves along the walls held jars filled with paintbrushes and every color of paint imaginable.

Two areas had painted canvases of various sizes stacked on the tables, leaning against walls, or displayed on easels, but one was notably devoid of any artwork. That must be the space Ducasse had used.

Several blocks of stone and a great deal of rubble and dust cluttered another area. Before I could investigate, George touched my arm.

"We can look around here later," he said. "It's more important for us to get into her flat before anyone shows up to work." He led me to a set of daunting stone stairs along the side wall.

"I thought artists liked working in the morning light," I mused. "You don't suppose they have heard about Lady Julia already, do you?"

"Since the police didn't even know about this place, who would have told them?" He gestured to the staircase. "Shall we?"

I tested the metal railing, was surprised to find it quite solid, and led the way up.

"Perhaps the other artists have already been here and left to find a meal," George said, slipping around me on the upper-floor landing and turning into a dark, narrow hallway.

"Half past three is an odd time for a meal. Besides, I saw them in the Tuileries Garden this morning, remember? Unless they are quite the early birds, they have not been here today." I peered down the hallway. "There can't be much of a flat up here."

"There isn't," George said. "You should prepare yourself for something of a hovel, albeit a neat and tidy one." He stopped at an ancient door with a shiny new lock.

"How do you intend to pick that lock in this light?"

He held up a key and sighed. "It's as if you think me a novice. The locksmith left her two keys when he replaced the lock this morning. Not sure what I was thinking, but I took one when she wasn't looking."

He unlocked the door and held it open for me. "Heavens," I said. "This room might aspire to be a hovel one day, but frankly, I think it too small for even that designation."

Behind the door was one simple room with low ceilings, a window, a bed in the far corner, and a table with a chair in the near one. A basin of water sat atop a cabinet affixed to the wall. An iron stove next to that. "It shouldn't take long to search," I said, attempting to sound positive, then changed my mind. "Why was she living here?"

"I asked her the same thing just this morning. She said she stayed here only when she needed to be in Paris, two or three nights a week. The rooms up here really aren't meant to be lived in, but the landlord, who I believe is Legrand, agreed to allow it for a short term, so she put a lock on the door and moved in."

He ran a finger around his shirt collar. "Rather stifling, don't you think? The timber siding up here doesn't keep out the heat as well as the stone walls downstairs. Why don't you look through the papers on the table, and I'll check the cabinets. The sooner we get out of here, the better."

The papers George referred to were in a tidy stack weighted

down by a clay bird painted in patches of green, blue, and pink. I took a seat and began reviewing them, while he rifled through the table near the bed. We were so focused that neither of us took note of any activity in the building until the floor squeaked just outside the open door. I peeked over my shoulder to see Martine in the doorway. With her wide stance and her hands on her hips, she looked very angry.

"What are you two doing here? Where is Julia?"

Chapter Eight

I came to my feet and introduced George and myself, speaking in French, as she had done. I reminded her we'd met her last evening with Lady Julia. "I'm afraid we have some bad news, Martine."

The woman sagged against the doorframe, a move that alarmed me since, despite her slight, seemingly fragile form, I still thought the wall might give way. After scooting around the table, I guided her to the lone chair. While I comforted her, George ran downstairs. He returned with a cup of water, only to have it waved away when he offered it to her.

If this was how she reacted to a warning of bad tidings, I wasn't prepared to deliver the actual news. We might need medical assistance. She looked flushed. I took a large envelope from the stack on the table and fanned her face. "Are you well?" I asked, bending over to look into her eyes.

She shook her head. "It's the heat. I don't tolerate it." She held out a hand to George. "Perhaps I will have that water." She took a few swallows, then looked up at me with the largest, roundest, darkest eyes I'd ever seen that didn't belong to a kitten. "Your bad news is about Julia, isn't it? Something has happened to her."

I hesitated to mention murder for fear of sending her into a swoon. "I'm afraid she's died," I said in the softest voice I could manage.

Tears pooled in her eyes. "She's been murdered, hasn't she?"

I took a moment to translate her words a second time. Such an odd statement. First, she sensed something had happened to Julia; then she guessed that something was murder. Either she was the gloomiest of doomsayers or she already knew about Julia.

"What makes you say that?" George asked. Clearly, our suspicions were running along the same lines.

"First, tell me if I am right."

"That's what the police have told us," he replied.

With a sigh, she rested her forearms on the table and leaned forward. "This is horrible!" A sob crept into her voice. "A tragedy that didn't have to happen. Why didn't I believe her?" She raised her head and, with a gasp, put her hands to her cheeks. "And our last words to each other were spoken in anger. Will she ever forgive me?"

Prospects for forgiveness were unlikely at this point, but the rest of Martine's words led me to reconsider my suspicions of her. What hadn't she believed? What had Julia told her?

I glanced at George, who looked so uncomfortable, I worried he might run. The British simply did not show their emotions in this manner, and he was at a loss for what to do.

"She would want you to help us," I said, my tone comforting, "by telling us what you know of the matter." I pulled a handkerchief from my bag and handed it to her. "It almost seems as though you expected this news of her murder. Why?"

Martine mopped her eyes and sniffled. "She told me Paul had been murdered, but she wouldn't give me the details or report it to the police. She planned to find out herself who killed him. I didn't believe her suspicions, but I still thought poking around in his life could be dangerous. I cautioned her to leave it alone." Martine assessed the two of us. "She told me she'd have help. Did she mean you? Are you some sort of investigators?"

"Something like that," George said, seemingly more comfortable with the calmer version of Martine. "That is why she asked me to come to Paris. But I fear you are right, someone wanted to keep her from investigating the death of Monsieur Ducasse."

Since Martine had the only chair, George squatted beside the table, putting him on eye level with the diminutive woman. "It would be helpful if you would tell me everything she said about Monsieur Ducasse's murder. Why did she think it was murder? Did she have any suspects in mind?"

Martine shook her head. "She told me nothing. She said it would put me in danger."

"Why did she mention it at all, then?" I asked.

Martine dropped her gaze to her hands, which lay in her lap. "Because I am a fool. I thought Paul had taken his own life. I blamed her and told her that." She stood abruptly. "Let us go outside. It's too warm in here, and I want a cigarette."

We agreed and followed her downstairs to the main room, where she stepped over to the area that held the blocks of stone and picked up a rucksack next to an unfinished sculpture. She was the sculptor? The job seemed at odds with her size, but perhaps she was stronger than she appeared.

Rooting around, she found a cigarette case in the sack and showed us out the back door, where the building shaded a small, quiet yard paved with the requisite cobblestones and lined with a row of column-shaped trees opposite the building. Across the alley, two horses poked their heads out of their stalls, sniffing in curiosity. Birds, hidden in the trees, twittered madly upon our arrival. Martine leaned against the building, struck a match, and lit her cigarette. George and I faced her, waiting.

"If you are not aware of Lissette," she began without preamble, "you must be made aware, since I suppose she will be given into your care."

"If Lissette is her daughter, then yes, we are aware of her," George said. "You are not breaking trust with my aunt by telling us about her."

"She is Paul's child, too. The poor dear is an orphan now. I'm not even sure if she knows her father has died. That was the problem. Julia and Paul had a past, but Julia did not want him to play a role in her present. Whether she was honoring his marriage or she no longer cared for him, I don't know. You British are good at hiding your emotions until no one can tell how you feel."

"Was Ducasse aware Lissette was his daughter?" I asked.

"Not until recently. Well, maybe about a year ago. It was when he joined us here at the studio. Julia brought Lissette to Paris with her one day, not knowing Paul had started working here."

George grimaced. "I'm sure that ended well."

Martine rolled her eyes and took a draw from the cigarette. She tipped her head back to exhale the smoke upward. "He was angry that Julia would keep such a secret from him. That she would keep his daughter from him for so long."

"How long was that?" I asked. "How old is Lissette?"

"She is fifteen, so a very long time."

At least that was one thing I got right.

"I thought it was cruel," Martine continued, "and I did not keep my opinion to myself, but I suppose Julia had her reasons. This is part of why I thought Paul had taken his own life. It was obvious he was in love with Julia and not his wife." She sighed.

"Julia would have nothing to do with him, which made him very unhappy, so though his death was called an accident, I thought perhaps he had done himself in."

"And you and Julia discussed all that?" It surprised me that the two women would have been so close. Martine seemed to have a penchant for tragedy, which I did not think would endear her to Julia.

"I told her of my suspicions. She did not agree with me. She had the idea he was murdered."

"But she never said why she believed that or who she suspected?" I asked.

Martine shook her head. "Did she never tell you?"

"Sadly, no," George said. "She told me this morning she'd changed her mind about asking me to investigate, and refused to say anything further. That's why we were in her room, to see if she had any sort of evidence. Did you know that someone broke the lock on her door last night?"

She looked surprised. "No. The last time I saw Julia was at the restaurant with you."

"Do you not have a room here, as well?" I asked.

She scoffed. "I have an apartment not far from here. I told Julia she could stay with me, but she is so independent. Those garrets are too decrepit to live in. They are more for storing supplies or napping at best. Paul slept in one of them from time to time, but Julia was the only one to put a lock on her door. I have no idea who would want to break in, but I can understand why that frightened her."

"Enough that she decided to drop the investigation," George said. "I think that was the point of the break-in in the first place."

"Ah." Martine drew on the cigarette a final time, then dropped it on the cobbles and crushed it under the toe of her boot. "In that case, it might be Paul's family. Or Gabrielle's. If Julia spoke to one of them, or if word got back to them that she was hiring a private investigator to prove Paul was murdered, they would not like that. They don't like to see their names in the newspapers unless it's about some society or charitable event."

That sounded much like the British aristocrats I knew. I eyed the woman. "Would they dislike it enough to murder her?"

She pursed her lips while her fingers worked at a loose thread on her sleeve. Finally, she released a sigh, and the thread. "I am thinking about who might have broken into Julia's loft. I wouldn't be surprised if one of the families asked someone to frighten her off, but I'm quite sure they would never hurt her." She frowned. "I don't think they would."

Was she trying to convince us or herself?

"You didn't happen to see anyone around here this morning, did you?" George asked. "Were you here then?"

"Oh, yes. I was here all morning," she said without so much as a blink or flicker of her eyes as she lied to us. "I was working in the studio. No one came in that way, but as you see, someone could have entered through the back."

She was right. There was a staircase at the end of the building that led to something of a balcony along the upper floor. I could see a door that would lead inside, very near to Julia's loft space. Still, why was Martine lying about her morning?

"That's strange," I began, then stopped myself when George squeezed my fingers.

"Isn't it?" he said. "I hadn't even noticed that upper door until now. Perhaps we should go back inside." He raised a brow at Martine. "If you're finished out here."

We filed back into the studio to find Edouard there, seated on a wooden chair, studying a partially completed painting. He looked rumpled. Streaks of paint stained his dark shirt as well as his arms, which were exposed by the turned-up sleeves. "I wondered where you were," he said to Martine as she crossed the room and took a seat near his easel. Edouard appeared surprised to see George and me but gave us a polite nod before turning back to Martine, who had begun to cry again.

"What is it?" he asked.

She managed only a few words before racking sobs overtook her. George gave Edouard the sad news while I comforted Martine. At first, I thought Edouard would succumb, as well, but after a few sniffs and several deep breaths, he recovered enough to ask for more details.

"You are sure of this?" he asked, pacing in a circle in front of us. "What exactly happened, and how do you know it wasn't an accident?"

"I cannot listen to this," Martine said. "Nor can I work." She swiped at the tears on her cheeks, picked up her rucksack, and headed for the door. "I am going home," she announced. If I thought the friends would comfort each other, I couldn't have been more wrong.

Edouard, whose dark eyes were focused on George while he listened to the details of Julia's murder, completely ignored Martine's departure. When George mentioned that Julia's loft had been broken into and that Martine had suggested it might be the work of the Ducasse family, he shook his head and made a disgusted noise.

"Martine is not reliable. She was in love with Paul and jealous of Julia. She sees romance where there is none and drama everywhere. Why would Paul's family want to hurt or even frighten Julia? She was of no importance to them."

"She was the mother of his only child," I said.

Edouard pushed his reddish-brown hair back from his lined forehead. "I do not suggest Julia was of no importance, but that the Ducasse family would have seen her that way. I doubt they knew Paul had a child, and even if they did, the child would have been important, not the mother." His lean face twisted into a scowl. "They would not have acknowledged her."

George leaned back against a table stacked with drawings and the tools of Edouard's craft. "It's possible Julia brought herself to their attention. She believed Paul Ducasse was murdered."

That brought on a look of shock. "Why did she think that?" He narrowed his eyes and watched George suspiciously. "Are you saying she told that story to his family?"

"We don't know. Julia was killed before she could tell me, but I suspect she told someone else and that person didn't want her to investigate." George lifted a brow. "It sounds like she didn't mention it to you?"

"No, she never did. I thought the police said it was an accident? Paul fell from his boat into the river and drowned."

"That's what they believed, but now they're taking another look."

Edouard rubbed the stubble along his chin. It held equal amounts of brown and gray. "That's almost as hard to imagine as someone murdering Julia. They were both well liked. Paul has nothing but friends."

He paused for a moment. George and I remained silent.

"There is one man, Beaufoy. He was an art jurist for the annual Salon des artistes français. He rejected Paul's work each year he sat on the panel. His was not the only vote, but he was very persuasive." Edouard sighed. "You must show at the annual salon, or you will never show your work anywhere important. We all had to deal with it, but Beaufoy almost seemed to have something against Paul that was unrelated to his work."

"Why do you think he might have killed Monsieur Ducasse?" I asked.

Edouard held up his hands defensively. "I don't. I still think it was an accident. But he is one person I know who is not Paul's friend. Particularly now. Paul gave an interview to

Le Figaro about a month ago, and he said some things about Beaufoy that were uncomplimentary and embarrassing if true."

"Were they true?" George asked.

"I doubt it, but I'm sure Beaufoy was angry all the same. Would he have murdered Paul over it? Frankly, I doubt that, too. But he is the only person I know who was not on good terms with Paul."

"Were you here this morning?" I asked. "Did you happen to see anyone come into the building?"

"No, I was on the other side of Paris this morning, buying supplies."

Well, now I knew they'd both been up to something nefarious this morning. Why lie about being together? George caught my eye and frowned, so I knew better than to ask. Oh, well, onward.

"We are trying to learn what we can about Julia's murder by piecing together the events of her life over the past few weeks," I said. "Had you noticed anything different about her? Before Paul Ducasse's death, that is."

"She and Paul were coming to some sort of agreement about Lissette." He stopped speaking and studied us. "You do know Lissette?"

"We know about her," George said.

Edouard picked up a thin paintbrush and twisted it between his fingers. "Julia didn't trust Paul. Me, I can't picture him voluntarily taking care of another person, but Julia feared he wanted to take Lissette away from her. She mentioned it more than once. That might have been why she was spending more time at her house in the country. I suppose she could paint there just as easily as coming here. My point is, once Paul learned he was Lissette's father, we did not see as much of Julia."

"Why do you think Paul wasn't interested in caring for his daughter? Was he an irresponsible sort?" George asked.

Edouard seemed surprised by the question. "I would never use the term *responsible* in describing Paul, but that isn't exactly what I meant. I would be surprised to learn that he cared about anyone more than himself. I wouldn't trust him to care for a pet."

"What about a wife?" George asked.

"As a single man, what do I know of marriage? You must ask Madame Ducasse about that."

George asked where we could find Beaufoy. Edouard gave him an address and was about to return to his painting when George held up a hand. "What about Ducasse's houseboat? Do you know what became of it?"

"Nothing, as far as I know. It should be where it always is, on the Seine, near the pont de Sully."

George thanked him, and we went back upstairs to Julia's loft. Once we were on the upper floor, we huddled together near Julia's table.

"They both lied about how they spent their morning," I said in a hushed voice.

"Yes, I noticed that. We can mention it to the police, but I didn't think it wise to confront either of them with the fact that you'd seen them together. You've done your previous investigations among people you are familiar with and in a place where you are known. That's not the case here. For all we know, one of them may have killed Julia or Paul, or both. Better to let the police handle that."

"I'm pleased you're willing to let the police do their work, but what is your opinion? Did you notice that Martine never asked how Julia was murdered?"

"And she jumped very quickly to the conclusion that it was murder," he added. "I know Julia gave her cause to worry—"

"Or did she?" His brows rose, and I continued. "Martine seems like an odd confidant for Julia. Both artists were her friends, but she never mentioned her suspicions about Ducasse's death to Edouard."

"And he mentioned that Martine was in love with Paul." We exchanged a look. "As I said, tread cautiously. Let the police question them."

That was fine with me. "Here's a question for you. It sounds as though Julia called on you to draw up those custody documents as soon as Paul found out about Lissette."

"I thought you had a question."

"I do. Why did she only recently become concerned about Paul taking Lissette away from her?"

"Good question, but I've no answer. Perhaps he came into some money and thought he could support her better. Perhaps he wanted to take up with Julia again and was using their daughter as leverage. Perhaps, legal documentation aside, Julia would never get over the worry of losing her daughter to Ducasse."

That would be hard to get over. "I can't think of anything else. Shall we finish searching the room?"

George returned to the cabinets he'd been searching. I perused the room. "I can't believe she felt comfortable sleeping here, even for just a night or two a week," I said.

"Space in Paris is at a premium right now with all the tourists visiting the exposition, and apparently, she preferred it to staying with Martine."

I blew out a breath. "I can understand that. Julia was very reserved. Martine might ask questions she didn't want to answer."

George sorted through some correspondence he'd found in a drawer. "That's likely to be a recurring scenario. I have a feeling the only one who knew Julia's business was Ducasse, and he's dead."

I had a feeling the only person who knew Julia's business was Julia. How sad to go through life with no one to confide in. Or at least believing you had no one to confide in. I wondered if her daughter had a deeper understanding of Julia. Perhaps the woman was a different person outside of Paris. Perhaps she had friends in the country. I picked up the stack of papers I'd left on the table when Martine interrupted us earlier. "I'm very eager to get to Lady Julia's house tomorrow."

"To meet Lissette?" George asked.

"That, too, though I dread telling her the news. No, I just wonder if Julia has left more of an imprint on her home than she has here. I'd call this sterile if it weren't so shabby."

"Regardless, I think that's a good word." He crossed the room to flip through some canvases. "There seems to be an absence of humanity here. It's a cold place."

"I understand Paris is a squeeze at the moment, but she's lived here for eight years. Surely, she could have found something in that time. Your brother provides her with a good allowance, and she said something about running a perfumery at her house in the country. That may produce a respectable income, too."

"Perhaps she is saving money for her daughter." George looked around the room. "Perhaps there's more here than meets the eye. Aunt Julia has always known what she was doing."

I turned over the last of the pages on Julia's table and gave him a smile. "Perhaps you are using the word *perhaps* a great deal today."

"At this point, speculation seems to be all we can do." He held out a hand to me. "Why don't we move on, then? It's getting late, and I'd like to catch this Beaufoy chap."

We left the loft and locked the door after us. Descending the stairs, we found Edouard staring at a canvas. He never looked up when we said our farewells and left the studio. "Should I assume after we interview Monsieur Beaufoy, we'll be taking a walk along the Seine?" I asked. "Somewhere near the pont de Sully?"

George had stepped out to the street to hail an approaching cab. He gave me a grin. "You know me so well, my love."

Chapter Nine

❧

The address Edouard had given George for Monsieur Beaufoy was for his home, a neat building on rue de l'Éperon in the sixth arrondissement. Beaufoy's apartment was on the first floor, attained by a broad staircase. It was half past six o'clock, so we feared he might be dining, but to our surprise, not only was he available, but he also answered his own door.

Beaufoy was a small man, portly, and probably in his fifties or early sixties. George introduced me and himself in French while we stood on the man's doorstep. He explained his relationship to Lady Julia, but it wasn't until he told Beaufoy she was dead that the man let out a gasp and invited us inside.

He led us to a salon just off the foyer. The wood-paneled walls were covered with art. I recognized none of the work, but then, this man would know all the up-and-coming artists I had yet to see.

I tore my gaze away and took a seat next to George on a Baroque-style settee, then returned my attention to Monsieur Beaufoy, who sat opposite us. "I am so sorry to hear about Lady Julia," he said. "Please accept my condolences on your loss. It must have been sudden?"

"Very," George said. "She was murdered."

Beaufoy's dark eyes widened fractionally. "Murdered? When? By whom?"

George told the man what we knew. In the midst of the story, Beaufoy strode across the room to pour three glasses of brandy. Upon returning, he placed two on the table before us and settled himself across from us.

"As for who is the culprit," George was saying, "we've yet to learn that."

"The way it happened in a crowd, are the police certain it was no accident? I didn't know her well, but I can think of no one who wished the lady ill."

"What of Paul Ducasse?" I asked.

Beaufoy looked at me as if I'd lost my mind. "Paul? He would never have harmed a hair on her head."

"That's good to know," I said, "but I meant, do you know anyone who would want to harm him?"

"Are you saying he was murdered, too?" He leaned into the back of his chair, as if trying to put some distance between us.

"My aunt seemed to think so," George said. "She asked me to come here to investigate, but once I arrived, she was reluctant to provide me with details. Now she is dead. It's possible her murder had nothing to do with Ducasse, but it feels very coincidental."

"I see." Beaufoy's brow furrowed as he stared off into the distance. "Quite honestly, I can't think of anyone who disliked Ducasse enough to murder him, either. His wife perhaps."

"Indeed?" George asked.

The man turned his attention back to us. "That was a joke. In poor taste, I suppose. Though they were no love match, Ducasse was just now beginning to support her in the style she had always expected. To the best of my knowledge, she had no reason to kill him. Besides, I thought Paul's death was an accident. That's what the papers said." He paused. "I suppose his family may have put that about to avoid a scandal."

"I don't know if the family attempted to influence the investigation one way or the other, but the police are taking a second look." George leaned forward toward Beaufoy. "The thing is, if he was murdered, he must have had an enemy or adversary or, at the very least, managed to anger someone. How was your relationship with Ducasse?"

"Me? Aha! That is why you have come here. You must have heard about Ducasse's interview for *Le Figaro*. Well, let me tell you, what he said is nothing I haven't heard before. I sat on the jurist panel. I had a say in whose work was shown and whose wasn't. I received no love letters when I approved them, but I got plenty of poison-pen letters when I didn't. Then they all wanted me dead." He circled a finger in the air. "Not the other way around." He shrugged. "Besides, those days are in my past."

It sounded to me as if Beaufoy missed his power. "From what I understand, you frequently disapproved of Ducasse's paintings."

"Early in his career, yes, I did. Paul and I have known each other for ages. I saw his potential and have tried to help him." He placed his glass on the table; then after sitting back, he rested his elbows on the arms of the chair and steepled his fingers in front of him, glancing from me to George. "Let me tell you about Monsieur Ducasse. It may help your investigation to know what he was like."

I was very eager to hear this.

Beaufoy continued. "The Ducasse family are well-to-do. They have been so for generations. They are also very influential. If they want their child to attend a certain school, they simply have to say the word into the right ear, and he is in. His grades are not good? So sad, but that can be fixed, too. Paul Ducasse has never had to exert himself for anything. All was simply handed to him, so of course, he appreciates nothing." Beaufoy stopped himself and held up a finger. "No, he knows the value of nothing. And that is how he floated through his life for the first thirty years or so."

"Is that when he met Lady Julia?" I asked.

Beaufoy paused and grew reflective. "It was about that time, yes. I wish I could say she changed him, but that is not the case. He charmed her. She fell in love. But she cared about her family and went home to get their blessing. Had she received it, I do believe Paul would have married her. Instead, her family refused their permission. Perhaps they saw Paul as he really was—a man who could not care for anyone as much as himself."

Interesting. That was precisely what Edouard had told us.

"Not long after Lady Julia returned to England, Paul's family grew weary of the irresponsible life he was living. They expected him to enter the family business, marry well, and start a family. Paul was doing none of this. He didn't particularly want to settle down, but marriage was the least arduous of the responsibilities they wanted him to take on, and he thought if he accomplished that, it might appease his family and he could continue to pursue art as a career."

"It's a very unreliable career," I observed.

"The worst! But he was the spoiled child of a wealthy family. They were delighted that he finally gave in and proposed to Gabrielle. She was their choice for him. Paul wasn't exactly business minded. Perhaps they had second thoughts about bringing him into the business, after all. Whatever the reason, he continued painting and living off his allowance until only a few years ago, when he began to see success. Then the family who thought he was simply wasting his time decided that art was indeed worthwhile."

"That's all very interesting," George said, "but what has it to do with Ducasse insulting you in an interview with *Le Figaro*?"

"He cannot insult me unless I choose to be offended, and for me to take offense, I'd have to have some respect for the man.

I'll openly say I don't. I simply couldn't be angry enough at Ducasse to kill him. He isn't worth it."

As much as I appreciated Beaufoy's openness as to Paul Ducasse's background, I could see why the artist had chosen to insult Beaufoy in the newspaper. The man took judging to new levels. I couldn't decide if they were high or low, but he clearly relished delivering such judgment. Some people ought not to have power.

Beaufoy took to his feet and again crossed the room. This time stopping to rummage through a drawer in the desk and returning with a leather-bound book. His diary, I noted when he placed it on the table. It was open to a page that showed a calendar for the month of July.

"If you know which day Ducasse was murdered, let us see if I have an alibi. I've had a rather busy month, with the exposition going on."

The newspaper had said Paul Ducasse died on the tenth. While George leaned forward to look at Beaufoy's busy schedule, I checked it for this morning to see if he had been nearby when Julia was stabbed. Indeed, he hadn't been far away. In bold letters the word *conference* was printed in the little square on the calendar, followed by the words *Grand Palais*.

Once they determined that Beaufoy had been away from Paris at an exhibit on the tenth, I decided to inquire about today. "What time was your lecture this morning?"

"This morning?" He sat back and gazed at me, wearing a rather amused expression. "Are you thinking I murdered Lady Julia, too?" He tittered. "I must come across as quite the brute. My lecture ran from ten until noon. I arrived about fifteen minutes before it began and have about three hundred witnesses who can state that I was indeed there the whole time.

"Lady Julia was a lovely woman," he continued. "A good artist, too. Not a great one, mind you, strictly amateur, but I often told her there is nothing better than to do something only for the love of it. I hope you catch whoever killed her, but I have no idea who that might be."

We left shortly after that exchange. Back on the street, clouds had settled in, and the air was cooler. I took George's arm, and we ambled down the narrow street toward the river. There were still people out and about, in carriages, motorcars, and on foot, but in this neighborhood, there was nothing like the crowds around the exposition grounds. Possibly because everyone was dining. The cafés and restaurants we passed were full to bursting. Even the tables outside, along the sidewalks, were filled with cheerful patrons, chatting, laughing, and eating.

It all made me very hungry. Part of me was eager to go home and enjoy a delicious meal, but on the other hand, with both the heat and the crowds having dissipated, it was delightful to simply walk. We'd both had our fill of crowds today.

"Shall we cross Monsieur Beaufoy off our list?" I asked George.

"Not just yet. He seemed to have a petty grudge against Ducasse, don't you think?"

"Pettiness might make him stand in the way of Ducasse's success, but would it lead to murder?"

"Not likely. His alibis should be easy to check. If the police don't do it, I shall. Any thoughts on who ought to be on the list?"

"Julia's artist friends lied as to their whereabouts. That's not a good sign. And Edouard seemed rather annoyed with Martine. Said it wasn't worth our time listening to anything she had to say."

"Yes, I don't trust either of them myself." He glanced down at me. "Anyone else?"

I scoffed. "Such as?"

"You're right. We haven't spoken to anyone else. And tomorrow we must go to Aunt Julia's daughter."

"And I'm getting the impression you are planning another stop this evening, before we return home."

He gave me a look of pure innocence. "I can't imagine to what you refer. Oh. Are you suggesting we investigate Ducasse's boat? What an excellent idea."

"Don't try to suggest I put that idea into your devious mind. Now that I think about it, it seems unwise. How are we to board the boat without being seen?"

"We'll never know unless we investigate. This might be our only chance," he said. "If the police reopen the Ducasse case, they will be all over that boat, and we'll never get a look at it."

"You won't see much of it in this light, anyway."

"That's just the clouds playing tricks on you." He pulled out his pocket watch. "It's not yet eight o'clock. We've more than an hour of daylight to get up to no good."

We had stopped walking at the corner of rue Seguier and the quai along the Seine River. If we turned left toward pont Neuf, we'd be headed back to our apartment. To our right was Ducasse's boat and possible trouble.

"Look," I said, gesturing directly in front of us at the island in the middle of the Seine. "While you talk about committing a crime, the Sûreté is right there. I could throw a stone and hit their building."

George gave me a stern look. "I wouldn't do that if I were you. You might get arrested." He ignored my scowl and linked my arm with his, then led us to the right. "Honestly, Frances, such behavior is quite shocking."

"My behavior? I'm beginning to wonder if I got it wrong at the wedding. Tell me, dearest, is your middle name really Trouble? Or perhaps Danger?"

He frowned. "Now that you mention it, my mother was always calling out to me, 'George, be careful.'"

"I concur with your mother. Be careful."

"That's my middle name." He had the nerve to grin at me, the devil.

It was pointless to argue. Besides, I knew very well that George was quite stealthy in these situations. And it seemed we were finding ourselves in these situations frequently.

George casually strolled down the steps to the embankment. I did my best to emulate his air of nonchalance. There were few people down here to notice. Two boys scurried off as we walked past them. A young couple leaned against the wall of the Tournelle Bridge, but they had eyes only for each other. Once we passed under that bridge, we saw a scattering of houseboats moored alongside the embankment.

"Do you have any idea which is his?" I asked.

"Legrand mentioned the pont de Sully, which is the next bridge ahead. One of the reasons no one heard Ducasse fall in the water was that his boat was the last in the line. I'm hoping that's still the case."

I examined the boats as we passed. These were nothing like the yachts some of my wealthy acquaintances owned. Some barely looked seaworthy, or rather river-worthy. I was sure I'd be far too nervous ever to sleep on one of them. Yet they floated. It appeared they had been doing so for a long time. Some even had potted plants on their decks, along with small tables and chairs—things that made them look "homey."

At the end of the line of boats, we slowed our pace. This could be Ducasse's houseboat. It looked uninhabited. It also looked wide open, long, and flat, except for an odd little hut directly in the center. The word *exposed* came to mind. "How does one live on this? It's all"—I waved my hand at the old wooden vessel—"deck. Is that the correct term?"

"I suspect the living quarters are below. I'll go aboard and find out." George spoke in a low voice next to my ear. "You wait here."

I stopped him with a hand on his arm. "Are you quite serious? A lone woman standing out on the embankment in the evening? Next to Ducasse's supposed love nest, I might add. I couldn't be more conspicuous if I held a sign reading TWENTY-FIVE FRANCS."

George winced. "That's a little pricy for this neighborhood, but I see your point. I do need a lookout, though. You'd better do that from the deck."

That was hardly an improvement, but I agreed. A short plank allowed us to cross from land to boat easily. Surely if anyone were aboard, they would have pulled it in. I felt a bit more secure.

I followed George to the far side of the boat. "Here it is," he said. "This is where Ducasse must have gone over. The police report indicated they found blood on the edge, where the man might have struck his head as he fell overboard."

I saw a rather large dark spot on the light wood. "There is a sharpish edge there," I noted. "The police might be correct."

"They might at that," he said. He stepped away and opened a door to the hut, which turned out to be sheltering a stairway to the cabin below. He descended a few steps, thought better of it, and came back up.

"It's dark as a dungeon down there," he said. "I'll do a circuit of the deck, and we may as well leave."

"Or you could take that lamp." I pointed to an oil lamp hanging from a nail on the side of the hut.

George's grin grew as he turned my way. "Now you're getting into the spirit of things." He nearly skipped back to the lamp and snatched it from the nail. A tray built into the base of the lamp held a few matches. Once lit, it cast a yellow glow, which moved down the stairs with George. I turned to survey the upper deck and locked my gaze with that of a middle-aged woman glaring at me from the next boat.

"Heavens!" My hand rose to my chest automatically, perhaps to keep my heart from pounding itself right through my ribs. I took a breath to calm down. The woman never looked away, nor did she change her expression, which was far from friendly. Her hair was bound in a kerchief. Her face was round and florid, like that of someone who did her share of drinking. Or perhaps she'd been in the sun too long. Who was I to judge?

"He will never marry you," she said in French with a little bob of her head.

The woman thought I was one of Ducasse's lady friends. Well, that was to be expected. Odd that she hadn't heard of his death. If the police had questioned anyone, one would think the person in the boat next door would have been at the top of the list.

"Do you live here?" I asked.

"Don't worry. I see nothing." The way she shook her head made me think she actually saw quite a bit. Unfortunately, she turned her back on me and walked away, crossing over her own plank to the embankment.

"Wait," I called. "Did you hear any sort of ruckus here one night last week?"

She threw me a look of contempt. "I hear nothing!"

She heard nothing. Fine. I wandered back across the deck as George came up from below. "Did you find anything interesting?"

His expression was glum. "Nothing to indicate he was murdered. Just bare necessities down there." He took in our surroundings. "Who were you speaking to?"

"The neighbor came out and spotted me. I couldn't very well hide from her."

"Did she have anything to say?"

I sighed. "Only that Ducasse would never marry me."

George bit his lip, then covered his mouth with his fist, clearly trying to stifle his chortles.

"Go ahead and laugh," I said.

He did. Leaning against the hut, he took a moment to wind down. "She's not wrong," he said, swiping at his eyes.

I caught his arm and took the oil lamp "I'll hold on to this while you recover from your fit of hilarity, lest you set us aflame."

When I lowered the lamp to my side, it illuminated something odd on the floor—or deck, I suppose. It was a stain of some sort, with dark and light patches, and swirl marks, as if someone had tried to clean it.

George stepped next to me as I peered down at the deck. "What is it?"

"I couldn't say for certain, but my guess would be blood." I gestured to the polished wood, where light smudges of reddish brown were barely visible in the lamplight. "Someone attempted to clean it."

George took the lamp from me, then stooped over for a better look. "I believe you're correct. This is blood, and the way it's smeared along the planks, it looks like the victim, presumably Ducasse, was dragged across the deck toward the river." He stood and gave me a beaming smile. "Fine observation, my love. Have I told you lately how absolutely wonderful you are?"

"Even if Ducasse will never marry me?"

He caught me up in a hug. "Even if he could, I would never let you go. This is the evidence, Frances. Ducasse might have drowned, but this shows he was at least badly injured before going into the water. At worst, he was already dead."

Chapter Ten

The officers of the Sûreté were less than pleased to hear our accusations of foul play. When George and I left Ducasse's boat, we knew we couldn't leave it until the morning to tell the police what we'd found, but we hoped Cadieux would still be on duty.

Sadly, he was not, and no one else had heard of reopening the Ducasse case. It took several recitations of our story and our insistence that Inspector Cadieux would want this information before one officer agreed to write a report. They had no intention of inspecting the alleged crime scene now that it was dark, and when George suggested sending someone to guard it overnight, they showed us to the door. Feeling we had done the best we could to preserve the scene, we decided it was time to go home. Hopefully, it wouldn't rain tonight and wash away our evidence.

We finally reached the apartment at half past nine. The sun was casting the last of its reds and pinks into the night sky. *Monsieur le concierge* grumbled and gave us his usual suspicious glare but opened the gate for us. It was clear the man was once tall and sturdy, but age had crept up on him, bowing his back and narrowing his shoulders.

"You have a caller," he muttered. "I hope he will not be late."

With a thank-you, we passed through the courtyard and climbed the stairs. It had been a long day, and it seemed it was not over yet. Bridget greeted us at the door, and after a glance to see that my clothing was still in one piece, she tipped her head toward a gentleman waiting in the salon.

"That's Mr. Hubert, ma'am," she said, pronouncing the name "Ooh-bear." "He says he's Lady Julia's solicitor and asked if he could wait for you both. I thought it was for you to decide, though if you ask me, it's awfully brash for him to call on you and Mr. Hazelton with Lady Julia just dying this morning." She leaned closer to me. "The poor woman's barely cold."

George handed her his hat and peered into the room. "It's all right, Bridget. I believe we should speak with him."

I handed Bridget my hat and gloves. "We'll go right in. Do we have any coffee?"

"I'll have some sent in, ma'am."

I stopped her before she could leave. "What about food? I'm famished."

She nodded. "I'm sure the housekeeper will find something."

"Then we definitely won't keep Monsieur Hubert long," I said.

Hubert came to his feet when we entered the room. He was middle-aged, with a round face and spectacles perched on the end of a short nose. George greeted him in French, so I continued in that language when I asked him to take a seat.

Hubert chose one of two wing chairs facing the tea table. George and I sat across from him on the sofa. "I assume this is about Lissette," George said.

"In part," he said. "I hope you will forgive the liberty I take in calling on you so soon after your aunt has passed, but her daughter must be told the tragic news. I thought if you were not planning to go to her soon, I could take it upon myself to do so."

"We had intended to go to her today but were detained by the police, so our travel was necessarily delayed," George said. "We will leave tomorrow morning."

"Is anyone with her now?" I asked. "Is there someone who cared for her when Lady Julia came to the city?"

"There is a young woman who lives with them, but I doubt word has reached them yet about Lady Julia's death."

At least she was not alone. "Have you met Lissette?" I asked.

Hubert made a few weak attempts to smile, instead merely compressing his lips. "Ah, yes. Mademoiselle Lissette is a very interesting young lady. Very interesting. I'm sure you'll find her so."

That was daunting. When a man used the word *interesting* to describe a woman of any age, interesting was rarely what he meant. She was either eccentric or difficult, a word that in itself could cover anything from willful to murderous. I'd been described as difficult before, now that I thought about it. Perhaps Lissette and I would be kindred spirits.

"Do you know what Lady Julia's wishes were regarding her daughter?" I asked. "Did she leave any specific instructions as to her education or, well, anything?"

Monsieur Hubert bobbed his head and released a sigh. "She most certainly did, madame. Lady Julia was very thorough and seldom left anything to chance, thus everything is spelled out in her will." Reaching down, he lifted a briefcase up to his lap, sprang the latch, and removed a paperboard cylinder.

"My reason for contacting you tonight was twofold. Mademoiselle Lissette was my primary concern, but Lady Julia gave this to me late last week, before she returned to Chartres. She asked me to keep it with her will and turn it over to you at the appropriate time."

George took the tube from him, and after opening one end, he pulled out a rolled canvas. Had Julia bequeathed George a painting? He pulled at the string and unrolled the canvas on the tea table.

The three of us simply stared at it for a moment.

"What is this?" George waved his hand over the strangest painting I'd ever seen.

"It's just—black," Hubert said, as if we couldn't see that for ourselves. Indeed, it was nothing more than a thick layer of black paint that covered most of the canvas.

"Did she give you an explanation about this?" George asked while I shook the tube, hoping a note would fall out.

Hubert looked befuddled. "Everything she told me I've relayed to you."

While George absorbed this information, Bridget arrived with the coffee. I moved the canvas so she could place the tray on the table. Then I poured each of us a cup. Once we'd enjoyed our first few sips, George asked about Julia's home.

Hubert's glasses had steamed up from the coffee. He took them off and cleaned them with a handkerchief. "It's more of a farm," he said. "Not at all large, but she has a tenant who works it and pays a reasonable rent. Should the family choose to sell the property, he might be interested in purchasing it."

"That sounds like a great deal of work for you, Monsieur Hubert," I said.

George heaved a sigh. "I'm afraid we will be the ones taking on that work. I told you I was Lissette's guardian, but I might have neglected to mention that I'll be responsible for Aunt Julia's property until Lissette comes of age."

Hubert wanted to save the actual reading of Lady Julia's will for a later date, when her daughter could be there, and left as soon as he'd finished his coffee. After rolling up the painting, we practically ran to the dining room, where a dinner of crusty bread, cheese, and wine waited on the table for us.

"This is dinner?" George frowned at the offering Madame Fontaine had managed to put together. "I'm really quite hungry."

"At this hour, you should be thankful to have anything. The housekeeper rises very early. She has every right to seek her bed. It's after ten."

With a grumble, he sat down and tore a hunk off the baguette while I poured us each a glass of wine.

"Think of it as a picnic," I suggested. "Dinner was fish with a cream sauce. Madame Fontaine could keep that warm only for so long." I decided not to tell him how delicious Bridget had found the meal. I tore off my own portion of bread and added some cheese. Personally, I liked the intimacy of a private meal with George and no servants.

"Did you bring any black clothing?" I asked. "I'm certain Bridget packed something for me. One never travels without a black gown."

"We will not be donning mourning clothes," George said. "That was one of my aunt's wishes—no mourning."

"Are you certain? We haven't seen the actual will yet."

"She told me that part outright. No mourning."

"Did she also have a 'no relatives at the funeral' clause somewhere in her will? That's what will happen, you know, if we don't notify them soon about her passing."

George had just taken a hearty bite of bread and cheese, so there was a moment before he could speak. "We shall have to send telegrams. Fiona is the only one of my siblings with a telephone."

I imagined the convoluted conversation with Fiona, over the static of the London telephone lines, as we tried to explain what we were doing in France and why George knew their aunt lived here. "Telegrams will do just fine." The conversation would still necessarily take place, but it would be later and in person. At the moment, that felt more manageable.

"What do you suppose is the meaning of that painting?" I asked.

"I haven't the foggiest," he said. "Initially, I thought she'd documented her suspicions, but clearly, it's nothing of the sort."

"You don't believe it's some clue?"

"My aunt was not one for puzzles."

"Perhaps one of the artists at her studio would understand the meaning of it," I suggested.

"Do you really think there's some meaning there?"

"Your aunt was not mad, George. She didn't paint a study in black to be delivered to you in the event of her death."

His gaze softened. "You are right. It might be worth a try, but I don't want to put off going to Lissette any longer. The painting must wait."

He put down his wine and took hold of my hand. "Here is what I propose. Tomorrow morning we send the telegrams to my family, then contact Inspector Cadieux. I'd like to know if he has officially opened a case on Ducasse. Then we take the train to Aunt Julia's house and see what's facing us there."

I squeezed his hand. "Whatever it is, we'll get through it together."

It was no surprise that George was up and dressed at what felt like first light the following morning. "Are you going to the Sûreté at this hour?" I muttered, barely lifting my head from the pillow.

"I'll get to the Sûreté, but I plan to stop by Ducasse's boat first."

"Won't the police consider that as interference in their case?"

"Whatever they consider it, I can't get back to sleep, so I'm going to check on it." Even with my eyes closed, I felt him looming over the bed. "Tossed and turned all night," he said. "Not that you noticed."

"My powers of observation are far less acute when I'm sleeping."

"You should work on that."

"Mm-hmm."

He moved away from the bed. "Besides, I don't feel a great deal of confidence that those officers posted a guard at the houseboat last night or that they're interested in Ducasse's case or that there even is one yet."

I forced my eyes open to see George standing at the foot of the bed, his head tipped upward while Blakely tied his tie. Heavens, he'd dragged poor Blakely out of bed, too.

"It takes an absurdly long time to get the process rolling over here," George continued.

"Cadieux said that wouldn't stop him from investigating."

"But does he even know about the evidence we found on the boat?"

I closed my eyes and snuggled into the comforter. "Give them a little time, George. It's only been a few hours."

"It's been ten hours since we reported it. And that is almost twelve, and that's half a day. It's not as early as you think, my love. It's almost half seven."

"Really? I feel as though I've just lain down." I pulled the coverlet around me and swung my legs over the side of the bed, but I still couldn't raise my head from the pillow. This might take some time.

"You needn't get up," George said, moving closer. "When I return, we'll take the train to Chartres. There's nothing else to be done here."

"No, I'll get up." I raised myself to a seated position. "We need to send the telegrams to your family. I'll see to that while you're gone. Just be careful."

"Echoes of my mother," he said, then gave me a kiss that was anything but motherly. It went a long way toward brightening my morning. "I shan't be long."

Blakely held open the door. "I'll send Bridget to you," he said as he followed George out.

"Ask her to bring coffee," I called after him, then came to

my feet and stumbled to the dressing room George and I shared. I found my lap desk on a shelf next to our shoes and brought it back to the bed. After climbing up, I placed it across my lap, lifted the hinged writing surface to find paper and pens below, and got to work. By the time Bridget arrived with my coffee, I had the text for three telegrams—one for George's eldest brother, Brandon, another for the second eldest,Colin, and the last for Fiona—ready to deliver the tragic news.

Bridget left the coffee and set off with the notes to find someone to take them to the telegraph office. Then she returned to help me get ready for the day. Once I was dressed and she was doing my hair, I gave her the news that she and Blakely would be free for the next day or two. George and I had decided to travel by ourselves to Julia's house. We didn't expect to be gone longer than two days and had no idea what sort of accommodations we'd find.

"I can't say precisely how long we'll be, but once we're off, you and Blakely should consider yourselves free to explore the exposition or Paris or whatever takes your fancy."

Bridget's eyes lit up. "I don't know if I'm ready to visit the exposition again, what with bridges collapsing and all, but I'm that eager to explore this city properly. Thank you, ma'am."

I felt a sudden dizziness with the memory of being swept off my feet by the crowd. When it passed, I was left with the sadness of loss—for George and Fiona, and for Julia's daughter.

"I can't imagine how Lissette will take the news." I'd already told Bridget that George was the guardian of Lady Julia's daughter.

"It won't be easy for her, I'm sure. I don't see much of my mum, but it's comforting to know she's around."

I felt the same. Though I'd endured a heavy dose of my mother, and her incessant criticism, from last autumn to the beginning of this year, now that she was traveling with my father, I rather missed her.

There must be something wrong with me.

"All the same, she couldn't do better than to have you and Mr. Hazelton as guardians."

"That's kind of you to say, Bridget. We'll certainly do our best."

Our conversation was cut short by a knock at the door. Bridget opened it to the housekeeper, who took one step inside the room. "Madame," she said, "there is a man at the gate who wishes to speak with you. He has a message from Monsieur Hazelton, and he will not give it up to anyone but you."

I was out of my seat in an instant, imagining every possible horror. What could have happened?

Both women followed me to the front door, but Madame Fontaine stayed with me all the way to the courtyard gate, where the concierge's wife waited with . . . a cabdriver?

"I am Madame Hazelton. Do you have a message for me?" I was well aware of the two women pressing in to hear what the man had to say, but right now I couldn't be bothered to send them away.

The man touched his fingers to the soft felt hat that slouched over his brow and bowed his head. "Yes, madame. I'm afraid officers of la Sûreté have arrested your husband. He asks that you come as soon as possible."

Chapter Eleven

❧

Was it odd that news of George's arrest filled me with relief? Perhaps, but at least he had not been hurt or murdered or any of the other fates I had imagined. The police, we could deal with, though it was a bit of a problem.

"Did they take him to the building on Île de la Cité?" I asked. Was there even another option?

"I would think so, madame. We were near there. He had me take him to a boat moored by the pont de Sully."

"Yes, I know where he was. Thank you so much for coming here to tell me."

"The monsieur, he asked that I do so, specifically."

I reached into my pocket and pulled out a few francs for the man. "Did he say anything else? Is there something more I should know?"

The man shook his head. "He was not happy, but neither did he appear concerned."

That was good to know. It was likely George had been arrested because he'd been caught on Ducasse's boat, something Inspector Cadieux would be able to clear up. I could think of no other way to contact the inspector than to go myself to the Sûreté. "I will need to gather my things," I told the man. "Can you wait another few minutes and take me there?"

He nodded. "Your husband has hired me for the day."

"Excellent." When I turned back to the courtyard, the two women sprang back and tried to appear as if they hadn't been listening at my shoulder. *Madame la concierge* gave Madame Fontaine a knowing look before returning to her rooms above the gate. The housekeeper walked with me back to the apartment.

"Is Monsieur Hazelton in much trouble, madame? A friend of mine has a nephew who is with the Sûreté. Perhaps he can help?"

"That is very kind of you, madame, but I'm sure it's just a misunderstanding. We shall sort it out quickly." I ignored her doubtful expression and forged onward up the stairs. "By the way, Monsieur Hazelton and I leave this afternoon for the home of his aunt in Chartres and will not likely return until tomorrow at the soonest."

That was assuming the police let him go.

When we reached the foyer, Madame Fontaine headed toward the kitchen and left me to get along on my own, which I did with all due haste. Bridget was still in my room, so I had her fetch a hat and gloves, along with a good supply of francs for my bag, just in case. I was back downstairs in the foyer in less than five minutes.

While I debated whether to go straight to the Sûreté or attempt to call on Monsieur Hubert first in case we needed legal assistance, someone rang the doorbell.

I pulled open the door to see Cadieux on the other side, crisp and fresh in a gray linen suit, his lips turned up in a smile, casually leaning against a stone pillar at the top of the stairs.

He straightened. "Bonjour, Lady Harleigh. I did not expect to see you."

"No? Then whom are you calling for? Mr. Hazelton is already at your police station. Surely, you aren't here for my maid or his valet?"

His gaze was full of amusement. "I only meant I was surprised to see you answer your own door."

"Well, as you see, I am quite capable." I stepped back to allow him entry. "I am likewise surprised to see you here. Is this about my husband?"

"I had hoped to speak with him. Did you say he was at the Sûreté? Was he looking for me?"

"Looking for you?" I stepped back and placed my hands on my hips. He truly seemed not to know that George had been picked up by his own men. I guided him into the salon and explained that George and I had found more blood on the deck of Ducasse's boat the previous evening.

He took a step back and gave me an assessing look. "You *found* it, did you? What a fortunate accident." His air of goodwill had disappeared. "Tell me, why were you even on Ducasse's boat?"

In hindsight, perhaps I shouldn't have said anything. "Looking for evidence?"

He sighed.

"We took our information to the Sûreté immediately, filed a report, and suggested they post a guard at the boat. I don't think we did anything wrong."

"Except trespass on private property."

"Well, yes, that, but with you seeming to doubt Lady Julia's sanity, we didn't think you'd reopen the case without more evidence."

He frowned. "When did I doubt her sanity?"

"You questioned her change of mind about having my husband investigate Ducasse's death."

"Ah, well, I was taking your word that your aunt believed

Ducasse was murdered. I had to determine if she was prone to exaggeration."

That was a slightly kinder way to say it. "And have you made that determination?"

"In fact, I have heard from the prosecutor this morning that he would approve further investigation."

"That's excellent news, but it doesn't explain why my husband was arrested."

That clearly took him by surprise. "Are you telling me officers came here and arrested Monsieur Hazelton?"

"Well, no. He wasn't here."

Cadieux released another sigh. "Not here? Perhaps he was snooping around the Ducasse houseboat this morning?"

I admitted that he was.

"You did say you requested that we post a guard at the boat, did you not? Guards tend not to appreciate people poking around the thing they are guarding."

"Yes, I suppose that's the explanation."

"It must be. They wouldn't have known about the will. That was my purpose in calling on you today."

I indicated that Cadieux should take a seat and joined him across the tea table. "Are you referring to Lady Julia's will?"

"Indeed. We received a copy of it late yesterday."

"How does her will signify?"

"I will be happy to tell you all about it, but first, why don't we join your husband? He should be part of this conversation, too."

"He did want to speak with you."

Cadieux chuckled. "He was, perhaps, a bit too eager."

"Or your colleagues were."

"You say they found him at Ducasse's boat." He lifted his hands in a helpless gesture. "It's suspicious. I know you are not our adversaries. Now, let us go explain that to my officers."

"Yes, let us go." I came to my feet. "Did you walk here?"

"I did, but I saw a cab waiting at your gate."

"Yes, he's waiting for me. Allow me to give my maid some instructions." I slipped up the stairs to find both Bridget and Blakely listening in the hallway. They followed me into the bedroom.

"I'll be happy to accompany you, ma'am," Blakely said. "I'm not sure that man is to be trusted."

"It's just a short ride to the police station, Blakely. I'll be fine."

"But the other officers arrested Mr. Hazelton. How do you know this bloke doesn't mean to do the same to you?"

"Thank you for your concern, Blakely, but I'm going to trust that Inspector Cadieux doesn't believe Mr. Hazelton and I had anything to do with his aunt's murder. We weren't even in France when Monsieur Ducasse was murdered. We shall return before you know it."

I then instructed them to pack a small bag for George and me. We'd pick it up this afternoon, assuming we could finally proceed to Lady Julia's then. I waited a moment while Bridget found a hatpin that was suitably long and lethal and replaced it for the one that was currently securing my hat to my hair. Now that I was armed, I was ready to go.

When I entered the salon, Cadieux came to his feet and accompanied me to the foyer with the smooth stride of a cat. He made me a slight bow when he opened the door, which would have seemed courtly if not for the mischievous glint in his eye. Was he simply being gracious or poking fun at me?

I swept through the doorway and down the stairs without checking to see that he followed. When we arrived at the cab, his hand reached around me to open the small door, then took my elbow to help me to my seat. Cadieux had such an easy manner about him that all his movements seemed natural and casual. Perhaps the mischief was simply part of his makeup, too.

He asked the driver to take us to the Sûreté, sat down beside me, then closed the door just as we took off. I told him we'd notified family in England, and asked when he thought we might be able to have a funeral service for Lady Julia. He consented to contact the medical examiner and let me know. With that out of the way, I asked him what was in the will that had prompted him to call on George.

He raised his brows. "Have you not seen it?"

"No. We've spoken with Monsieur Hubert. He's given us the salient points, but he wanted to reserve reading the will until Mademoiselle Hazelton was available."

Cadieux frowned while he took in the information. "Was one of those salient points that your husband will now have access to a great fortune?"

I let out a tsk. "He is Mademoiselle Hazelton's guardian. He will likely be charged with overseeing her fortune until she is of age. We have no reason to believe it will be particularly large. Nevertheless, George will not be spending it on himself. He has a difficult enough time spending a gift of money my father has given us." My mouth drooped open as an idea came to me. "Is that it? You think my husband is so eager to get his hands on his aunt's fortune that he murdered her?"

Cadieux spread his hands. "How was I to know your husband had an aversion to money?"

"He doesn't. I never said that."

"I'm glad to hear it. I do not trust a man who rejects all worldly goods."

"That would definitely be overstating the fact."

"I am coming to know that Lady Julia was quite secretive, and I suspected Monsieur Hazelton might not be aware of the details of her will. Regardless, I thought it worth a conversation."

"I understand, but you will find George could not possibly have murdered his own aunt."

"Well said, madame."

The cab drew up next to the broad façade of the police station that overlooked the Seine. Cadieux assisted me from the cab, then led me through the large double doors. "I hope one day to have a wife who will fight for me like that," he said. "Though I suspect Hazelton is holding his own with my officers."

I repressed a snort of laughter. It had been an hour since George sent his message to me. "I wouldn't be surprised if they were all playing cards and having a jolly time by now."

Cadieux grinned. "Shall we find out?"

We ascended the central staircase that turned left every eight or nine steps and made me rather dizzy to look up. Fortunately, we soon stepped off into a hallway with doors along one side, with windows beside them. Cadieux peered into the windows and found George and the officers in the second room. They were not playing cards, but I hadn't been too far off track. The room simply reeked of bonhomie, and George looked as relaxed as if he were in the cardroom of one of his clubs. He clearly needed no rescue.

He came to his feet when we stepped through the doorway. "Frances!" His smile faded. "And Cadieux. Is something amiss?"

"Only that I think these gentlemen have taken enough of your time, monsieur." Tipping his head to the door, Cadieux drew the two officers out to the hall. "If you will excuse us for a moment?"

"You seemed to be getting along just fine," I observed, sidling up next to George.

"Don't be fooled. Without you and Cadieux, I'd be facing another hour or more of grilling."

Cadieux returned alone, appearing a bit disgruntled. "It seems it was not a guard we have to thank for your arrest, Monsieur Hazelton, but the woman from the next houseboat. She alerted a patrolling officer."

"Huh. Don't know why she objected to me. I was perfectly pleasant when I greeted her."

I couldn't believe it. "Is that the same woman who *hears nothing* and *says nothing*?"

"Clearly, she has regained the use of her senses." Cadieux turned to George. "You are free to go, but I hope you and your lovely wife will do me the honor of taking coffee with me. There is a quiet place around the corner where we can discuss the case in a more pleasant environment."

We agreed and followed Cadieux back down the stairs and out an exit. We walked down the street to a café that had seating outdoors under large colorful umbrellas. A waiter swept us to a table, where George held my chair and Cadieux ordered coffee for three.

"The inspector stopped by this morning to ask if you murdered Julia for her money," I said to George.

"Didn't think she had any to speak of," he said.

"We will be looking into that, as well as your finances."

"Understandable," George said.

Cadieux folded his hands on the table. "Now, as a gesture of goodwill, allow me to share our findings on the death of Monsieur Ducasse."

George's gaze sharpened with interest. "You reviewed the police file?"

"And I asked the medical examiner to review it, as well. He found it very interesting." He paused while the waiter placed steaming hot cups of coffee before us.

"One thing you must understand," Cadieux continued once the waiter had left, "is our coroners and medical examiners have had much more work since the exposition began back in April."

George nodded. "I can imagine that they are very likely overworked."

"The coroner who examined the scene when Ducasse's body

was found looked at the laceration on the man's head and concluded he fell into the water, striking his head on the boat on
his way down. He was possibly unconscious when he went
into the river and unable to save himself. The coroner called the
cause of death drowning."

"What part of that did your medical examiner find interesting?" I asked.

"He thinks Ducasse was dead before he ever hit the water."

George looked up from his coffee. "Why is that?"

Cadieux grinned. "Because the man is an excellent doctor."

"I'm more apt to think him a medium," George said. "Ducasse
was buried yesterday, after all."

"We interviewed the funeral director." Cadieux took a sip of
coffee. "There was no water in Ducasse's lungs."

"Well, that rather rules out drowning," George said.

"And if Ducasse was already dead, he certainly didn't throw
himself into the river," I added.

"I had a feeling the two of you would catch on quickly,"
Cadieux said. "I understand you found more blood on the deck
of Ducasse's boat. We will look into that, as well. I have come
to believe this was no accident. We are opening an investigation
into Monsieur Ducasse's murder. Since you say your aunt suspected as much, I think there's a chance their deaths are
linked." He leaned against the back of his chair and regarded
the two of us. "What can you tell me about their relationship?"

"Not as much as we'd like, I'm afraid," I said.

George sighed. "I wish she had been a little more forthcoming
about her life. But all I really know is that they have a daughter
together. She is about fifteen, which means she was born before
my aunt moved to France."

"So fifteen years ago they were lovers. Do you know when
Ducasse married? Did they continue their relationship after his
marriage and up to the present day?"

"He wasn't aware of their child until recently, so I suspect they did not," I said. "We hope to learn something from her daughter. Julia and Ducasse worked together with other artists in their studio. I got the impression the four of them were friends, so they may be able to tell you something."

"However, I don't think it was their relationship that got my aunt killed," George said. "I think it was something she knew or saw. She called me here to investigate his murder, but her confidence faltered once I arrived. Then someone broke into her garret above the studio where they all work. After that, she wanted to drop the matter entirely." He shrugged. "I think that frightened her. Find out who broke in and you may find her killer."

Chapter Twelve

Finally, more than a full day after Lady Julia's murder, we were in a coupe carriage on the train bound for Chartres, on our way to tell Julia's daughter about her mother's death. The poor child. She was now an orphan, having lost both parents in the space of a week. We weren't even sure she knew about her father's death.

George found and squeezed my hand. "Are you as nervous as I am?"

"Terrified. But I'm also relieved to hear that you are not as calm as you appear. She's suffered a horrible loss, and her life is about to change tremendously. She's lived in France all her life—in the country. And I assume we will take her back to London with us?"

"Perhaps not immediately, but yes, that is our home."

"She will feel that her life is up in the air. I hope we can make a sort of soft landing place for her."

"How do you think Rose will feel about another young person living with us?"

"I think Rose will be delighted to have someone other than her male cousins for companionship."

George leaned over and gave me a kiss. "You have made me feel much better. Part of my anxiety was that you might be angry that I dragged you into this. I should have remembered what a kind heart you have."

"There is definitely space in it for Lissette."

The trip southwest to Chartres took little more than an hour. We allowed ourselves a moment to gaze at the majestic cathedral, then George found someone with a carriage to take us past that wonder, through the town, and down a country road along the river. We gave vague replies to the man's inquiries as to Julia's whereabouts. Neither of us wanted to reveal the truth until we'd spoken to her daughter.

And now was the time. Our driver had set us and our bag down outside the gate of a lovely home. Much larger than I'd anticipated, it was a two-story cottage-style house made of stone and brick, surrounded by a low wall of the same stone alongside the road. All the windows were framed with shutters of periwinkle blue, some open, some closed.

A second structure stood off to the left of the house, directly on the riverbank. It was also two stories, but of wood construction. I suspected it was used as a barn. A gravel path ran from the gate to the space between the buildings. It was intersected by a narrower one from the barn to a door at the side of the house. Otherwise, the broad area between the two structures was ablaze with colorful flowers and shrubs. The Eure River ran, or rather strolled lazily, beside the property, just behind the barn.

The water lapped against the steep banks, and the bees worked among the flowers. The sun was high and bright, yet it was much cooler here than in the city. "It looks like a Monet painting," I said, more to myself than to George. Then I realized he'd been waiting for me. I straightened my clothes. "Am I presentable?"

He grinned. "Always, my love." He drew a deep breath and picked up our bag. "Shall we?"

We stepped up to the door and applied the knocker. After a few moments, it was answered by a woman somewhere between eighteen and twenty, with light brown hair worn in a loose plait that draped over her shoulder. She was too old to be Lissette, but though her skirt and shirtwaist were somewhat workaday, they weren't the dress of a servant.

"How may I help you?" she asked.

George introduced us. "I'm afraid we are here with tragic news for Mademoiselle Hazelton."

She took a step back and opened the door wider, allowing us inside a small, closed-off entry hall with an arched doorway leading to the rest of the house. "I wish you'd been here just a bit earlier," she said, leaning closer to us. "One of Lady Julia's friends is with Lissette now. I think it would have been better if a relative had broken the news to her."

George dropped our bag near the door. "Who is it?" he asked.

"Gabrielle Ducasse. I'm just glad there's family here now. If that woman had tried to take Lissette back to Paris with her, she'd have had a fight from me." She tossed the plait off her shoulder. "Let me take you to the salon."

The news that Gabrielle Ducasse was here was a bit disturbing, but there was something about this young woman that bothered me, too. She seemed familiar, though I couldn't place her. I touched her arm as she would have turned away. "It sounds as though you are a good friend to Lissette. Will you not tell us who you are?"

"Of course," she said. "I am Christine Granger. Please call me Christine. Madame Hazelton employed me as Mademoiselle Lissette's governess." She gestured for us to follow her to the salon, then turned to speak over her shoulder. "And occasional housekeeper. And sometimes I make perfume."

This was an unusual household, to say the least. With Julia here only part time, I imagined she was very grateful to Christine for filling in where needed. She led us down a short hallway, then opened a door to a good-sized salon and preceded us inside. "Lissette," she said. "You have more callers."

Gabrielle's expression of surprise said our appearance was unexpected. She came to her feet and drew the thin, lanky young woman beside her to hers. Lissette had the Hazelton height and seemed uncomfortable with it. Wearing the plain dress of a schoolgirl, she stood rather stooped next to Gabrielle and brushed aside a cluster of dark, wispy curls. She blotted her eyes with a handkerchief while Christine introduced us as Lissette's cousins from London.

George stepped forward and gently took Lissette's hand in his. "Your mother was one of my favorite people. I am so sorry, my dear cousin, that you will not know her as long as I have. I see Madame Ducasse has already given you the sad tidings."

Gabrielle's cheeks reddened. "I apologize if I've overstepped. I heard only this morning that this poor girl has lost not only her father but her mother, as well." She placed a gloved hand on Lissette's shoulder as George released the girl's hand. "I knew at once I had to come and offer her comfort." She glanced from George to me and gave us a tentative smile. "It is good to know she is not alone in the world."

Christine cleared her throat. "I'm sure you would like some refreshment after your journey." With a glance to Lissette, she left the room to see to it.

We all took our seats, slightly less comfortable without Christine's presence.

"We are late in coming," George said. "But we were working with the police regarding your mother's murder, so I hope you can forgive us."

"Murder?"

It struck me, in a rather darkly humorous way, as appropriate that the first word George's ward uttered to us was *murder*. Even if it was posed as a question, which meant she hadn't known. George and I exchanged a look.

"Didn't Madame Ducasse tell you that?" he asked her.

Gabrielle put a protective arm around Lissette's shoulders and pulled her closer. "I wasn't aware. There was nothing of it in the newspaper."

Lissette turned toward Gabrielle while putting some space between them. "You said she died in an accident. A bridge collapsed." She turned to George. "You say she was murdered. What exactly happened?" There was a plaintive tone to her voice that reminded me of the bleating of a lamb.

"Everything happened at the same time," George replied. "Initially, we all thought your mother's death was an accident, including the police. Madame Ducasse was not lying to you. Frances and I were with her at the time, but perhaps we should save those details until we can discuss them in private."

Her narrowed gaze traveled between George and me. "If you were there at the time, why did you not try to save her?"

Christine had returned to the room, balancing a tray of coffee and the accompanying accessories. She placed it on the table and turned to her charge. "That is unfair, Lissette. You are not in possession of all the facts, and your tone of voice was disrespectful. Your mother and I taught you better manners than that."

"I beg your pardon, madame and monsieur," Lissette said, glaring at me, despite the words.

I resisted the urge to offer some excuse. Lissette had just received the worst news possible. All she needed at the moment was comfort.

"How do you take your coffee, Madame Hazelton?"

I gave Christine my preference, and she handed me a cup of black coffee and moved on to Gabrielle, who seemed quite comfortable in Julia's home. "Do you visit here often, Madame Ducasse?" I asked.

She took a sip of her coffee and placed the cup on the table. "No, but then I have learned only recently that Lissette is my stepdaughter."

Uh-oh. That statement sounded just the tiniest bit possessive. I wondered what she meant by *recently*. Before or after Ducasse's death?

Gabrielle ran a hand down Lissette's unbound hair. She sighed. "There are just the two of us now."

That started more sniffles from Lissette, followed by a few tears. George and I shared a look over our cups. What exactly was the woman suggesting?

"Though no one can replace her parents, Lissette has family, including several cousins she has yet to meet," I said. As Lissette looked at me with curiosity, I added, "I'm sure they will all love you."

"I don't know if you are familiar with your mother's wishes, Lissette," George said, "but she has asked me to be your guardian until you are of age. And I hope we can be a family to you much longer than that."

"Julia has made you her guardian?" Gabrielle stammered, then seemed to regain her composure. "Lissette is Paul's daughter, too. I hope you will allow me to help if there is anything I can do. You live in England. If it does not suit you to remain in France while the estate is settled, I assure you, Lissette will always be welcome in my home."

Heavens! This might be the most unusual circumstance I had ever encountered. Her husband had a child with another woman. Yes, it was before their marriage, but by all reports, he had remained in love with Julia. Yet Gabrielle, his widow, wanted to mother that child. Perhaps she was desperately trying to hold on to some piece of her late husband. Such intentions were understandable, but not necessarily the best thing for Lissette.

"Madame Ducasse," I said as kindly as possible. "Her mother put her faith in Monsieur Hazelton, and we are more than willing to welcome her to the family. Still, you can be sure that we have no plans to make Lissette a stranger to her country or her friends."

George placed a hand over mine. "Lissette, please believe your happiness is important to us."

Christine caught my eye and gave me an encouraging nod from behind her cup.

"Furthermore," George continued, "since we will be staying here with you, at least for tonight, I don't think it's necessary for you to stay, as well, Madame Ducasse."

Gabrielle pulled a handkerchief from her bag and dabbed at her eyes. "Yes, I suppose you must get to know your family, *ma chère*," she said, taking Lissette's hand. "But do not forget, I will be here if you need me."

Lissette nodded. "*Merci, madame.*"

Gabrielle stood and nodded at us. "That goes for you, as well. I want nothing but happiness for my dear stepdaughter."

Well, now I felt positively cruel for asking her to leave. "Madame—"

"Our neighbor will take you to the station, madame." Everyone in the room was surprised to hear Christine speak up. She came to her feet and drew herself up just a bit taller than the widow. "You would not wish to miss the last train back to Paris."

Gabrielle agreed. We said rather stiff farewells and waited silently while Gabrielle followed Christine out of the room. That was when I realized where I had seen Christine Granger before. She'd been at the reception in honor of Paul Ducasse. She was the young woman Lucien Allard had escorted from the room. The one Alicia had referred to as *one of Ducasse's little friends.*

Chapter Thirteen

～

Once Christine had escorted Madame Ducasse from the room, Lissette took to her feet and turned, with some ferocity, on us. The sun shone through the window to her back, making her tousled hair appear to be crackling with electricity. "You did not have to send her away," she said. "I'm not a child to be told who I will and will not associate with. Certainly not by you, of all people."

Before George or I could utter a word, she stormed off to her room. At least I assumed that was where she went. We heard her running up the stairs, and a few seconds later, a distant door slammed. I'd heard that sequence of sounds a time or two when I'd failed to give in to some desire of my daughter, Rose.

George turned to me. "How do you think that went?"

It took a moment to realize he was serious. "Let me see. We've just separated stepmother and daughter. For good or ill, I don't know. They may have been a comfort to one another, but since Lissette will be living with us, I think it's for the best. However, Lissette seems to resent our intrusion, might possibly blame us for not saving her mother, and has run off. I'm sure she'll speak to us someday. Overall, I think it went quite well."

He frowned. "I think you're teasing me, but I suppose this guardianship involves learning as one goes."

"It will. But you are a quick study. The hardest part will be for Lissette to trust us. Once she does, things will go more smoothly." I gave him a confident smile. "Now, before Christine returns," I added in a lowered voice, "tell me, did you recognize her?"

George looked confused. "I did not. Have we met before?"

"Not exactly. She was at the tribute to Ducasse. I asked Alicia about her, and she suggested Christine was—and I quote—one of Ducasse's little friends."

George reacted with raised eyebrows.

"Granted, Alicia could be wrong about that, but I later saw Monsieur Allard escorting her, none too gently, out of the room. It would seem that he didn't think she belonged there."

"I suggest we ask her," he replied just as footsteps sounded in the hall.

Christine Granger stepped into view and leaned against the door of the salon. "It may be difficult to see at the moment, but Lissette really is a lovely girl."

"Come join us," I called to her. "Perhaps you can tell us the best way to befriend her."

"I believe she's a bit frightened of the situation she's in right now—not knowing what's to become of her." Christine sat across from us and poured herself a cup of coffee.

"That's completely understandable," I said. "Her mother was the only family she's known, and now she's gone."

"That depends on who you count as family," she said sharply. "I suspect she includes me. Perhaps even one or two of our neighbors. Sometimes family is who you come to depend upon."

"How long have you been with Lissette?" George asked.

"All her life. My mother raised her."

"Heavens," I said, "you must have been very young at the time."

"Yes, madame. I don't remember all the details of that time, but back when Julia was still living in England, she asked my mother to foster Lissette. I can't recall how they met each other, but my mother was struggling to raise me by herself."

She looked down at her hands for a moment, then directed her gaze at us. "My mother was also unmarried. Her family would not help her after my father abandoned her in Paris. You can imagine that she eagerly took the opportunity Julia offered.

"Julia swore she'd be back someday to take custody of her daughter," Christine continued. "In the meantime, she bought this place and paid my mother to run it and take care of Lissette. She did so for seven years. Julia would visit once or twice a year, whenever she could get away, I suppose. Then, just before Julia returned for good, my mother died."

I must have made some sound of distress, because she turned to me and nodded. "At that time, I was only thirteen. My mother had been ill for a while, but I wasn't prepared for her death. Both Lissette and I were devastated. The neighbors helped as much as they could, and I wrote to Julia. I don't know how long it was before she came home—maybe a few weeks—but in that time, while we were healing from our loss, Lissette and I became more like sisters. I've been the longest constant in her life. Then Julia."

"She's suffered too much loss in her short life," I said to George. "We must take those constants, as Christine calls them, into consideration before we ask her to go anywhere."

His brow furrowed. "I understand, but you and I cannot stay here."

"I'm sure we'll all work something out, but staying here is not impossible if it becomes necessary."

"I'm willing to help in any way I can," Christine said. "Julia was good to me after my mother died. She gave me a home and employment as Lissette's governess. Then when we started the perfumery, she let me take charge."

"My aunt spoke of it as a going concern," George said. "I'm curious to learn how it's managed, along with her farmland."

"I'd be happy to go over the perfumery business with you. Lissette's had a hand in it, too, but I don't know much about Julia's agreement with Denis. He's the neighbor who farms the land here." She chuckled. "Now, the chickens, those belonged to Julia. Lissette and I can tell you all about caring for them."

George leaned forward. "There is something I'd like to have you tell us, if you don't mind, Mademoiselle Granger."

"Please call me Christine," she said quickly. "We have never been formal around here. Even Madame Hazelton was simply Julia."

"Very well, then, Christine. What brought you to Paul Ducasse's tribute three nights ago?"

She blushed and dropped her gaze. "Goodness, you noticed me."

"It seems odd that even though Julia wasn't there, you were," I added. "Do you visit Paris frequently?"

"No, not very often at all. Julia sent me there about the business. Monsieur Allard was supposed to have arranged a meeting with someone from Worth, the fashion designer."

"I'm quite familiar with the House of Worth," I said. "What sort of business would you have had with them?"

"Perfume, of course. They don't have a scent of their own. We hoped to convince them to carry ours."

"Julia must have trusted you a great deal to give you such an important assignment," George said.

"She treated me like a partner." Christine looked down at her folded hands. When she returned her gaze to us, it held a glint of steel. "Unfortunately, Monsieur Allard did not live up to his word. No one was available to meet me when I arrived at the appointed time. They had no idea what I was talking about. Afterward, I couldn't find Monsieur Allard at his home. I'd heard about the tribute and went there to confront him. He was not pleased to see me."

I was coming to like this spirited young woman, but I still didn't believe her story. I didn't think George did, either. Julia had clearly preferred to control every aspect of her life, business, and family. I couldn't see her turning over such an important negotiation to Christine, whether she considered her a partner or not.

Still, since this was George's family, I thought it up to him to pursue the matter, or not.

"Sounds as though Allard wasted your time," he said. "What reason did he give when you asked him about it?"

"He told me I must be mistaken, that I had either the date or time wrong. He was angry I came to the tribute and barely took the time to speak to me at all before scooting me out the door."

"I'm sure that was a disappointment," he said. "Rather than returning home victorious, you had to tell Julia the meeting never took place."

"Or did you stay and try again?" I asked.

"Erm, no. That is, I spent the night in Paris and returned the following morning. Julia needed to go to Paris that day, and we would not leave Lissette home alone. We agreed to try again later."

"That's the spirit," George said, getting to his feet. "Of course, we'll have to see how Aunt Julia has left everything before making any plans." He stepped over to the window and peered out. "It looks like the neighbor farmer is here. I'll go out and have a chat with him. I don't suppose he's heard the bad news yet."

"We've only just found out ourselves," Christine said.

George turned away from the window. "He should be told, and perhaps he can enlighten me as to his business arrangements with Julia. If you ladies will excuse me?"

When he left, I poured another cup of coffee for myself and Christine, who was intent on watching her fingers as she laced and unlaced them.

"I wonder if you will let me ask a favor of you, Madame Hazelton."

"You may ask, of course," I said cautiously. "And if we are to be informal here, you may call me Frances."

She gave me a polite smile. "You mentioned that you are free to stay in France for a time, but it's clear you are not certain what the future holds for the two of you and Lissette. Is that true?"

"Yes, it is. Even if we stay here, it will not likely be for long. I have a daughter waiting at home." I smiled at the thought of Rose.

"Julia trusted me to care for Lissette," Christine said. "You could just leave things as they are."

"I don't believe that's what Julia intended. Lissette has family in England. They would always have loved her, and it's a shame that she was ever kept apart from them. I'm grateful she has you, but she shouldn't be isolated from her relations."

Christine nodded slowly. "Then you will take Lissette to England?"

"I don't know when, but yes, I'm certain we will at some point."

"That's what I thought. I wonder if you'll allow me to accompany you and help Lissette settle in?"

"Is that the favor you mentioned?" I asked.

"It is. I doubt that I'd stay with you for long, but I'd hate for her to lose another person from her life anytime soon."

"I think that would be a splendid idea, Christine. In fact, from my perspective, you would be the one doing us a favor."

"Good," she said. "It's always best if there is benefit to both sides of an agreement."

Lissette refused to leave her room while I was in the house. In her grief, she needed someone to blame. It appeared I was that someone. George returned and wanted to discuss the matter with her, but to be honest, the day was fine and far cooler than it had been in the city, and the idea of a solitary walk struck me as a very good one indeed.

"I don't like you leaving because Lissette is being stubborn," George said.

I donned a wide-brimmed hat I'd borrowed from Christine. "She's not stubborn. She's grieving and frightened. Try to have a talk with her yourself while I'm gone. You've both suffered a loss. Perhaps you can help put her at ease."

Stepping outside, I thought I'd forgo Julia's property for the moment and walk back toward the town where the train had dropped us. It was early evening, and I still had at least two hours of daylight. Julia's farm sat at a bend in the road. One direction led to hills and trees and likely more farmhouses. The other direction followed the river. That seemed the safest bet to avoid becoming lost, so when I left the yard, I rounded the barn and followed the country road and the river. It was remarkable how many houses, like Julia's barn, backed up to the Eure. It was quite hypnotic watching the gentle ripples break the surface, reflect the sun, then recede with a quiet splash against the bank.

I'd walked only a few hundred yards before someone called out to me from a nearby house.

"Are you lost?" asked a woman wearing a straw hat like mine.

I moved up the drive to the other side of the railed porch where she sat. Under the brim of her hat, she had brown eyes, broad cheeks, and a friendly expression. Her hands were busy shelling peas.

"I've just come from Julia Hazelton's home," I told her after introducing myself as Frances Hazelton. "So, I haven't had a chance to become lost yet, but given time, I'm sure that's a possibility."

She laughed and told me she was Suzanne Dupont. "Is Julia back already? I thought she expected to be in Paris for the week."

There was no point in lying; there would be something about it in the paper soon if there wasn't already. I moved closer to the porch and rested my hands on the railing. Leaning closer, I explained that Julia had died, mentioned the collapse of the footbridge, and left it at that. Considering her stricken face, I knew that news was bad enough. I didn't have to include the detail that she'd been murdered.

"How is poor Lissette taking it? I'm sure this has shaken her down to the ground."

I agreed that she was indeed distraught. "My husband is Julia's nephew and Lissette's guardian. We came here to give her the news and comfort her as best we can."

With a frown, she let her gaze travel from me to the farm and back, as if to say, "And yet she is there and you are here."

I sighed. "I'm afraid she's not very happy with me at the moment. I was with her mother when she died, and I . . . didn't . . ."

She winced, then gave me a sympathetic look, her hands still working on the peas. "You poor dear. I'm sure she will see things differently in time."

"That is my hope, but for now I thought it best to make myself scarce and take a walk."

"Then I won't hold you up any longer," she said with a

smile. "If you see my boys along the way, tell them to come home. I have work for them."

Suzanne's husband emerged from the house, and she told him the sad news about Julia. He asked me to deliver their condolences and let them know if there was anything they could do to help. "We will send a hearty stew up for your dinner tonight. Christine must have her hands full already."

I thanked them and walked on—past more houses nestled on the riverbank, framed by weeping trees and gardens of bright flowers. I wished Rose could have been there to enjoy it with me.

Just as I was about to turn back, a low rumble and a high-pitched creak announced a cart coming in my direction before I ever saw it. I moved off the dirt road to stand among the grass and wildflowers until the cart rumbled into view. Pulled by one sturdy horse, it held bags of grain and pottery containers, which were likely full of milk. My knowledge of farm goods might have been lacking, but I was able to identify two boys in the cart, along with the other goods, and guessed they belonged to Suzanne.

The driver slowed to a stop as he reached me. The boys were both under ten years of age and having a delightful time trying to keep their balance as they stumbled to the front of the cart. The driver admonished them to sit back down, then turned to me. "Good evening, madame. Are you lost?"

"You are the second person to ask me that," I said. "It must be an unusual sight for someone to be strolling down this road, but it is good to know the residents here are all kind enough to direct me, if I need it."

He laughed. "Most of us are working all day and haven't time or the energy for an evening stroll." He jerked his thumb over his shoulder and raised his voice. "Except for the likes of those two. They seem to have nothing to do all day."

This brought out chuckles from the boys.

"Well, if their mother is Suzanne Dupont, I've just spoken to her, and she has plenty for them to do."

"I'd better get you boys home, then. Madame, it feels like rain may be coming through soon. May I offer you a ride? I assume you are one of the people staying at Madame Hazelton's home."

I glanced at the sky, which seemed a little darker but not threatening. All the same it would take me almost an hour to walk back, and in that time, the rain could become more than a threat. I thanked him and took both his offer and the hand he reached out to help me climb up next to him.

Once I was settled, we were off, moving at a pace that, while not exactly quick, was faster than I could walk. The boys tumbled farther away in the cart.

"Are you a neighbor to Julia Hazelton?" I asked, bracing myself to break the sad news yet again.

"My family lives next to the Duponts. I have known Julia since she moved here. I'm Denis Vernier. She leases her farmland to me."

"I'm Frances Hazelton. I believe my husband spoke to you about Julia earlier today."

"He did, but I still don't understand," he said. "Was she killed by the crowd itself? How did that happen?"

"The police are still investigating, so I can't tell you much, but they found evidence that Julia had been stabbed."

He drew in his breath in a gasp. Apparently, George hadn't told him everything.

"It's shocking," I said. "I did not mention that part to Madame Dupont."

"But Lissette knows? How is she managing?"

"She does know, and she's managing as well as can be expected, I suppose."

He leaned closer to me and lowered his voice. "When did it happen?"

"Yesterday, late in the morning. Why?"

He sighed. "She knew," he said, turning his gaze back to the road ahead. "I was at Julia's place yesterday. Lissette was home alone. She ran out to the field where I was working and begged me to come in for lunch. She said she felt unwell and didn't want to be alone. She couldn't express what was wrong, but by the time lunch was over, she felt better, so I left. I think she had a premonition."

"She must have been terrified." We had pulled up outside the Dupont house to let the boys down. I saw Denis's cottage right next door and decided I'd walk back from here. I thanked him for the ride and set off. I reached the farmyard all too quickly. I wasn't ready to go back in just yet, and I was certain Lissette wasn't ready for me to return.

The barn looked rather interesting. I wandered inside through the open door and found a lightbulb and chain hanging overhead. Goodness, it was electrified. I pulled the chain, and the bulb cast a yellow glow over the immediate area. Even in the darker corners, I could see that this was not a barn for animals. There were shelves along the walls with bags, boxes, and crates of, well, something. Set up on a long table in the center of the ground floor was something that looked like a chemistry experiment. If I didn't know Julia had a perfume business, I'd have sworn someone was distilling spirits in here. The small bottles at the end of the table were too much to resist. I pulled the cork on one of them and took a sniff.

It was underwhelming. But then I'd been told before that one should always smell a perfume on the skin. I resisted the idea. I didn't want anyone to know I'd been snooping, and the scent would follow me for many hours.

While I resisted the perfume, a staircase right in front of me tempted me sorely. I was no expert on barns, but the one or two I had seen in my youth had had open lofts overhead. This one was enclosed. The staircase was a surprise, too. I would have expected something more ladderlike. Curious, I ventured up. The stairs ended at a short landing and a closed, but not locked, door with a hand-lettered sign that proclaimed I AM WORKING!

I suspected this was Julia's studio and the sign was to make the casual visitor, daughter or not, determine if they truly needed to disturb her before knocking. After pulling open the door and stepping into the room, I jumped when I walked into another chain dangling in the dark. Once my heart settled, I pulled the chain, illuminating the art studio.

But no natural light for an artist? I eyed the far wall, covered with paintings. I moved to the closest one and removed it to find latched wooden shutters. The latch moved easily, and voilà, one side of the shutter swung outward. I pushed the other side and looked out.

The river was directly below. Past the opposite bank lay a meadow, distant trees, and a glimpse of the horizon. Closer by, birds chirped and scratched at the dirt, while bees raided the flowers for pollen. It was the very image of serenity. She must have loved it here.

Turning away from the window, I took in the room. Now that there was daylight in the space, I could see that Julia had everything she might need available here. A table against the far wall held jars full of brushes, tubes of paint, palettes, and even a few small canvases. There was a comfortable chair by the table, and a stool next to the window, where I assumed she would set up the easel, which now stood in the corner, along with quite a few canvases leaning against the wall.

I flipped through them, saw that most were indeed of the view through the window, but some depicted other scenes, as they contained a number of cows. I chuckled to myself, wondering who would buy a painting of cows, but then remembered the jurist's opinion of Julia's work. She painted for the love of it, and these must be the things she loved. A little farther into the stack, I found even more evidence to prove that point—portraits of Lissette.

Julia must have thought she was in danger to have George made guardian of her daughter. Why didn't she go to the police with her concerns? Or at least trust George and me? We simply had to find her killer now.

Chapter Fourteen

❦

I stumbled down the stairs to the kitchen the following morning, hoping to find a cup of coffee. Since Bridget had always brought my first cup to my room for the past ten or eleven years, I'd forgotten how difficult it could be to move around without that hot, steamy brew. In this case, I simply followed my nose and found Christine and Lissette deep in conversation over their own cups at the kitchen table.

Christine jumped to her feet when she saw me, but not before I'd heard her utter the words "Don't you forget" to Lissette. Judging by the closed expressions on both their faces, I was unlikely to learn just what she was not to forget.

"Good morning, Frances. Would you like some coffee?" Without bothering to wait for an answer, Christine filled a heavy mug and set it on the table where she'd been sitting.

"There's no need for you to move on my account," I said, thinking I'd take my coffee outside.

"Nonsense." She waved me to the table with the towel she'd been using to wipe her hands. "It's time we started breakfast, anyway. The bread's just out of the oven. Come help me, Lissette."

Lissette came slowly to her feet, watching me seat myself from the corner of her eye. "I don't suppose you know how to cook," she said in that soft voice that made me want to protect her, despite the fact she was clearly trying to goad me.

"No, I'm afraid not." I tipped the mug and drank deeply of its elixir.

"Well, if you don't cook, you should go and collect the eggs. Surely you don't wish to be a layabout."

Had I just thought I wanted to protect her? Regardless of her attitude, I was delighted to have done something to make Lissette speak to me, look at me, or do anything to acknowledge my presence other than walking—no, stomping—out of the room. She'd done exactly that when I returned from my walk last evening. Then refused to dine with us. George said she'd been disagreeable with him when they spoke, but at least they spoke. He didn't care for her manner toward me at all and intended to take her to task for it.

I asked that he wait until the morning, and now, look, she was indeed speaking to me—for the moment, anyway. "I never had cause or the opportunity to learn," I said. "And I'm afraid I know even less about chickens."

"She is teasing you," Christine said. "We already have the eggs. Enjoy your coffee."

I did enjoy it but felt slightly guilty about allowing them to do all the work. "I suspect I could slice that bread as well as anyone else." I pointed to the loaf resting on a metal rack near the open window.

Christine chuckled as she broke eggs into a pan. "Go ahead, then. It should be cooled by now."

Lissette added vegetables to a pan where chunks of ham already sizzled, and muttered something that I had to assume was less than complimentary.

"Come now, it's not as if I've never sliced bread before," I said, sawing through the loaf and wondering when I *had* last done this myself.

"Of course you have," Christine said. "When you are done, you can put it in the frame and toast it over the stove."

It was as if she was speaking Greek. "Well, now you've completely lost me."

The comment set them both to giggling. Splendid. My pretended ineptitude had broken down another barrier with Lissette. All right, there was no pretending involved. I had no idea what a toast frame might be or look like. "Why would anyone want to toast this lovely bread, anyway?"

Slice after slice joined the first one on the plate, soft inside and slightly steamy. The aroma had me licking my lips. I couldn't wait to melt some butter on it and pop it into my mouth.

I turned around with the plate full of bread in my hands just as George stepped into the room and pulled a chair out from the table. He stopped in his tracks when he saw me. "Are you cooking?" he asked with an expression of real concern.

"Yes, dear. I slipped out of bed a few hours ago to bake this bread and make everything else you see here." I waved a hand toward the stove. "Learned just this morning."

Christine chuckled, Lissette snorted, and I felt like that was a minor victory. "Not to worry, George. I'm not ready to sack our chef just yet."

"You have a chef?" Christine brought a plate of perfectly fried eggs to the table, and Lissette was right behind her with the ham and vegetables. "I hope you don't mind the informality, but we generally serve breakfast in here."

I set the plate of bread next to the steaming eggs and took a seat. "As long as we have butter for that bread, I am happy to eat any way you wish."

"You are in the country, Frances." Christine pulled a cloth off a bowl filled with scoops of butter. "Of course we have butter here."

Cool air, butter, and coffee. The country was looking better all the time.

Once we were all seated, we served ourselves from the plates at the center. George leveled his gaze at Lissette before speaking. "I mentioned to you yesterday that I was investigating your mother's murder," he began.

Lissette gave him a wary look. "Yes?"

"I think it might help to learn a little about her relationship with Paul Ducasse," he said. "If it isn't too painful to speak of them, could you enlighten us?"

She gazed at George in surprise, looking a great deal like a startled fawn. "You think that might help you find her killer— or his?"

"It might help us find both, but in all honesty, it might be of no help at all. We can't know until you tell us."

"All right. Where should I start?"

George looked at me, and I made a go-ahead motion. Lissette seemed more willing to talk with him. "How long have you known Paul Ducasse was your father?" he asked.

"Me? As long as I can remember. *Maman* didn't want him to know, but she didn't mind my knowing." She glanced across the table at her governess. "Did you always know, Christine?"

"Not until Julia came to France to live, when she warned me to watch out for Monsieur Ducasse. I'm not sure what she wanted me to watch out for, but I know she didn't trust him. She worried that if he knew Lissette was his daughter, he'd want to acknowledge her."

That surprised me. "He would?"

Christine chuckled. "It is different in England, I think. In France, or at least in Paris, it isn't unusual for people of the upper class to have love affairs. The big scandal for them would be to marry someone not of their class."

"It isn't uncommon in England, either, but most men

would balk at acknowledging a child born outside of wedlock as their own."

She nodded knowingly. "If Ducasse had acknowledged Lissette, Julia would have been pushed to the background. She would have been seen as his mistress, even though their liaison was prior to his marriage. She was still British, and that bothered her."

"That may be true, but I think more importantly, she didn't want her British relations to find out about me," Lissette put in. "She was worried she would lose their respect."

George shook his head. "Her concern might have been warranted for the family members of her generation—my father and mother, but she should have realized that all her nieces and nephews would have embraced you and her. I'm sorry she didn't trust us."

"I'm curious as to how she managed to keep all of this from her family," I added. "How did she manage to hide her pregnancy from them, and where did she give birth?"

"My understanding is that her sister-in-law helped her," Christine said.

George frowned until he realized who Aunt Julia's sister-in-law was. Then he stared at Christine in shock. "My mother? I never would have believed that she could organize such a clandestine operation."

"Apparently, you come by it honestly," I said.

He chuckled and returned his attention to the others. "Do you know how they worked everything out?"

"Not all the details," Christine said. "Your mother arranged a cover story—the two of them were going to visit one of her relatives in France."

"I didn't know she had any relatives in France." George looked confused.

"Maybe she did, maybe she didn't, but the point is that Julia's father believed the story." Christine took a sip of her coffee. I noted Lissette was hanging on every word. Christine cleared her throat and continued. "Julia's parents thought the trip would do her good. They'd rejected her French suitor. She hadn't had a letter from him, and though they didn't know it, she was carrying his child. She was crushed, and her father was concerned about her lack of spirits, so off the two women went, with his blessing.

"They traveled to Paris first," she continued, "to find Ducasse. Both ladies thought the best thing would be for the couple to marry. I'm sure you can imagine Julia's surprise when she learned Paul was a newlywed."

"She must have been devastated," I said. "Did he say why he didn't wait for her—or even write to her?"

"Later, when she came here to live, he did," Lissette put in. "He told her he wrote, but I think *Maman*'s family didn't give his letters to her."

Christine bumped Lissette's arm with her shoulder. "How do you know that?"

"*Maman* told me. Meanwhile, Monsieur Ducasse waited for her to reply while his family pushed him to marry Gabrielle. After several months, he did."

"Returning to the time of Lissette's birth," Christine said, "once Julia learned he was married, she didn't speak to him or try to see him. It had to be over for them. Since marriage was not a possibility, Julia and her sister-in-law needed another solution." She turned to George. "That's when they found my mother and me. And this farm."

"*Maman* Granger." Lissette smiled warmly as she pronounced the name. "She was just like a mother."

"What happened when Ducasse found out about you?" George asked Lissette.

"Nothing, at first. *Maman* was afraid he would want to take his place as my father, perhaps introduce me to society when I turned eighteen. She wanted no part of that."

"No, she didn't," George said. "She had me draw up some documents to keep that from happening. That was when I first learned you existed. I wish I had asked more questions about you then." He let out a tsk. "The papers Ducasse signed would have kept him from pursuing custody of you. It sounds as though that worked?"

Lissette had just forked a bite of ham into her mouth, so she simply nodded, then looked around at our intent expressions and took a drink of milk. "It worked for a while. Then, a few months ago, he asked to meet me properly. He came here a few times to visit me. He seemed like a nice man, but it was hard to see him as my father."

Christine buttered her bread with a great deal of energy. "I don't think he would have made a good parent. Even without the potential scandal for Julia, I think she was right to keep him from claiming Lissette. He barely visited her."

Lissette shrugged. "Maybe three times?"

"Were he and Julia on friendly terms?" I'd forgotten about my plan to let George ask the questions.

"I think so." Lissette nudged Christine. "What do you think?"

"They were friendly, I suppose," Christine said. "But Julia was protecting herself. She must have loved him a great deal long ago. Sometimes I saw something in her eyes when she looked at him, or she'd touch his hand when she spoke to him, and then she'd pull herself back. Maybe it was simply because he was married, or maybe because she didn't want to be hurt. She didn't want to love him again."

"How sad," I said. "But I can understand her not wanting to fall back in love with a married man."

"That might have been her reason, but I think she came to

realize the kind of person he was. From what I could see, Paul Ducasse could never love anyone more than himself. Anyone who fell in love with him would be doomed."

That was becoming a familiar refrain. "If you are correct, then that's another reason she might not have wanted him to have much contact with Lissette." I turned to the girl. "She might have been protecting your heart."

Lissette shook her head. "That's all I know about my mother and father, at least about them together. He once was a poor artist. Then he was a great artist. He was married. I am his only child."

"The Ducasses were a socially prominent couple," Christine offered. "Julia preferred her artist friends."

"Of which Ducasse was one, was he not?" George asked.

"Yes, but he could move between the two social circles easily. He grew up as part of the upper class."

"Does any of this help you find my mother's or father's killer?" Lissette asked.

George and I exchanged a look. "Not yet, I'm afraid," he said. "Which is why I think I must return to Paris and continue the investigation."

Lissette gave me a wary look before returning her attention to George. "By yourself?" she asked. She was afraid George would leave me here with her. Frankly, I wouldn't care much for that option, either.

"I think that depends at least somewhat on you," he replied. "I don't wish to meet you and run off, but I am investigating your mother's murder, and that requires me to be in Paris. Frances is part of the investigation, too, but I hesitate to leave you here alone."

I nearly snorted. Lissette would likely prefer to be left on an uncharted island rather than in my care.

"You needn't concern yourself with me. I am fifteen years

old—almost a legal adult. I can take care of myself perfectly well, and I have Christine for companionship. I have no need of a guardian."

"Be that as it may," George began cautiously, "your mother did ask me to take on that responsibility."

Lissette didn't bother to look up from buttering her bread. "Fine. I absolve you from that responsibility. You are free to go about your life without any thought for me. In fact, that is my preference."

"I'm afraid it won't be that easy." George had stopped eating and was now eyeing her with growing impatience. "Your mother has already decided the matter. You are stuck with us at least for the next few years. Besides, we must meet with her solicitor and find out how she has settled everything in her will."

Lissette sank against the back of her chair. "Can't he come here to us? Or send us a letter?"

"He probably could, but we would be waiting much longer," George said. "And it is best if everyone is present at the reading of the will."

"You should hear for yourself what your mother's wishes are," I added.

Lissette parted her lips to speak but was stopped with a gesture from Christine. They must have some secret between them. Perhaps at some point they'd trust us, but for now, we were clearly outsiders.

At least Lissette now seemed to be considering coming with us. If I were in her shoes, I would want to be doing something—something productive about her mother's murder. I would want justice.

"You may not realize it, Lissette," I said in an offhand way, "but you could be a great help to us in finding the person who killed your mother, just by your knowledge of her and her life and habits."

I caught some hesitation in George's expression, which said he didn't quite approve of involving Lissette, but I ignored it when I saw her expression grow curious.

"How would that help?" she asked.

"You would know who her friends are, who she did business with, anyone she might have been in an argument with lately."

Christine and Lissette exchanged another look. "Excuse us a moment," said Christine, who came to her feet and motioned for Lissette to follow her out the back door. Throwing us a suspicious glance, Lissette was right behind her, leaving George and me staring at each other in confusion.

George dropped his hands to his lap and gaped at me. "They left."

"I noticed."

"But what happened? What are they doing?"

"I believe they are conferring about whether to go with us."

"I wondered if it was a mistake to request that they go. I should have simply told them."

"They are used to being independent, George," I said, thinking that I rather admired them. "Ordering them would not have worked."

"They are too young to be independent." He tossed his napkin onto the table. "You weren't like that at Lissette's age, were you?"

I snorted. "Heavens no. I followed my mother's orders like a dutiful daughter. I can't say that was a better path."

"Whatever their decision, we can't leave them here alone. We don't know why Lissette's parents were murdered. What if she is next on the killer's list? She's an easy target out here."

"Why didn't you tell her that?"

George frowned. "I didn't want to frighten her."

"If they decide to stay here, you may have to explain that to her, whether it frightens her or not."

We stared at the door. On the other side of it, the girls deliberated, the rise and fall of their voices commanding our attention.

"I can't make out what they're saying," George said. "Can you?"

"No, and I believe that was the point. They wanted some privacy."

"They're plotting." George turned to me, and I'd swear there was fear in his eyes. "Is this what it is to be a parent?" he asked.

I shushed him as the kitchen door banged shut and Christine and Lissette returned to the table.

"Well?" he asked. "What is the verdict?"

Lissette cast a glance at Christine. "I suppose we must all go to Paris."

"I think that would be best," I said.

It was a simple matter for Christine and Lissette to pack for a week's stay in Paris. In truth, we had no idea how long we'd be there, but it was easy enough to return to Chartres if necessary. Since George and I had barely unpacked, we were able to catch the last morning train and arrived back at the Kendricks' apartment early in the afternoon.

The détente Lissette and I had begun building that morning had not held up. She had returned to being distant with me, so I had Bridget help settle her and Christine in two of the guest rooms, while I checked with Madame Fontaine to see if there had been a response to any of my telegrams. She handed me the pages, and I returned with them to the salon, where George met me a few minutes later.

He gestured to the messages in my hands. "From my siblings?" He trailed his fingers across my shoulders as he walked past me and to the window.

"They are," I said. "Fiona apologizes that her husband cannot come with her, but she'll arrive in Paris tomorrow. She intends to stay at the Ritz so as not to disturb us."

"Pricey," he said with a grimace.

"And not particularly convenient." I twisted in my seat to see him gazing out the window, his hands resting behind his back. "I took the precaution of sending a wire to Patricia Kendrick yesterday, telling her of the death of your aunt and your new guardianship. She replied as I had hoped, saying we should consider the apartment our own and use the guest rooms as necessary if relatives travel from England."

George glanced at me, a frown between his brows. "Are you saying you want Fiona to join us here?"

"I am. You and I are trying to solve a crime—no, two crimes. We have two young women to look after. We also have to deal with your aunt's will, and we ought to have some sort of memorial so her friends can pay their respects. Fiona could be very helpful in that regard."

"She is quite organized," he said. "What of my brothers?"

I pulled a message from the stack and held it out to George. "Nothing yet from Colin, and Brandon is unable to come to Paris at this time, but he has sent instructions for you."

George huffed as he took the page from my hand. "The devil, you say!" He scanned the few terse paragraphs. "Can't bother himself to come here but thinks he can tell us what to do, does he?"

Brandon was the eldest of George's siblings, and as such, upon their father's death, he had inherited the earldom, the estate, and a certain responsibility for the family. It really wasn't out of keeping for him to act as decision-maker regarding family matters. Regardless, I had wondered if George would find his note a bit imperious.

"I think he's trying to be helpful," I offered. "Unless Lady Julia has expressed an alternative in her will, his suggestions make sense, don't you agree?"

"That's hardly the point," he said. "This is just an excuse for Brandon to be high-handed. You know, lord of the manor and all that rot. The fact that his instructions are reasonable is completely irrelevant."

"You Hazeltons," I said. " 'Don't tell me what to do' should be your family motto." It was difficult to manage the words while choking back my laughter.

"How can you say that? Fiona, perhaps. Aunt Julia, definitely. But me?"

A bubble of laughter erupted. I held up a hand. "Please don't get me started, George, or I shan't be able to stop."

His own lips began twitching as I watched him. "Perhaps Aunt Julia has her own instructions, as you suggested." He pulled his watch from his pocket and noted the time. "I telephoned Monsieur Hubert as soon as we arrived. He will be here in about thirty minutes to go over Julia's will with us."

That thirty minutes gave me time to scratch out a message for Fiona to come to the apartment tomorrow, rather than to the Ritz, and hand it off to the housekeeper to send. I also alerted the girls to Hubert's impending arrival and pulled Bridget into service in changing out of my dusty traveling clothes and into an afternoon gown.

We were just taking our seats in the salon when Hubert arrived. He greeted us with all the solemnity the occasion called for. After a short consultation as to our language preference, he put on a pair of spectacles and got immediately to the business of reading the will in English.

"I, Julia Gertrude Hazelton, being of sound mind and body, do hereby declare this to be my final will and testament," he began.

Hubert explained that a *notaire*, a public officer, would act as the executor: he would pay Julia's debts and funeral expenses and ensure that everything was settled appropriately. Then the will moved on to Lissette and George, whom Julia had interestingly bound together, in a financial sense at least.

"I don't understand," Lissette said when Hubert had concluded the reading. "My mother has left me all her worldly goods, but I can't do anything with them?"

The arrangement took George by surprise, too. "Correct me if I'm wrong, Hubert, but Aunt Julia has left everything in a trust. Until Lissette's twenty-first birthday, any withdrawals from that trust require two signatures, hers and mine. Similarly, the business will also require both of us to make a single decision."

"That is exactly so," Hubert said.

Lissette stared at the two men in horror. "Why would she do such a thing?"

"It's actually rather clever," George said. "I suspect she wanted me obliged to explain any expenditures to you, so you will learn to manage your finances by the time you come of age."

Lissette waved away his explanation. "I will not be able to make my own financial decisions for the next several years."

"I am not some sort of ogre, Lissette." George seemed rather affronted by her objection. "You will take part in all your financial decisions. I will simply assist you."

She flopped back in her seat and crossed her arms. "You don't understand."

George turned to me in such confusion I had to take pity on him.

"She's a Hazelton," I murmured. When his brows rose, I continued. "Remember your reaction to Brandon's telegram?"

His eyes rounded in what might be fear. "Egad, you are right. I may not survive these next few years."

I was certain they'd both be fine, but there was something about the will that wasn't—Julia's complete neglect of Christine. If she'd been nothing more than a loyal servant for fifteen years, she deserved some sort of gift or remembrance in Julia's will. It appeared to me that Christine was more like a member of the family and a partner in the business, yet there was no mention of her whatsoever.

For all my concern, Christine appeared completely undisturbed. She'd brought some needlework with her into the room, and she continued even now working at it. Had she expected nothing from Julia? I knew little of their relationship, but Lissette seemed to care a great deal for Christine. If she didn't already plan to help the young woman who had helped to raise her, we would have to point out her obligation. It sounded, after all, that Lissette would have assets worth a respectable amount and possibly an income from the perfumery.

Hubert was packing away his paperwork. "I don't know if you are aware," he said, "that Mademoiselle Hazelton is also remembered in Monsieur Ducasse's will."

All conversation ceased as we regarded the solicitor.

"Do you mean to say Ducasse named Lissette in his will?" George asked.

"I doubt he went so far as that." Hubert came to his feet and closed his briefcase. "I was told only that he left a bequest to his children."

"Children?" I asked.

"Plural?" Lissette added. Her eyes narrowed as she watched the solicitor intently.

Hubert adjusted his spectacles. "That is so. Now, we have documents, signed by Monsieur Ducasse, that prove Lissette Hazelton is his child, but because of the word 'children,' the *notaire* is performing his due diligence to determine if there are any other children to consider. Perhaps I shouldn't have mentioned it until all was known, but I thought you should consider it in your planning for the mademoiselle's future."

"It is good to know," George said. "May I assume you will keep us apprised of the matter?"

Hubert agreed and left the room with George.

I remained in my seat, wondering about the possibility of another Ducasse child—or children. Ducasse had claimed to love Julia, but what about the mother of his other child? If he had dismissed her and her child, might she not have harbored some resentment? Might that be enough for her to murder him and the woman he couldn't bring himself to dismiss?

Chapter Fifteen

"I feel awful that Christine was left out of Julia's will," I said. It was the following morning, and George and I were getting dressed for the day.

"Hubert ought to have warned us that she wasn't named," he said, holding out an arm so Blakely could install his cuff link. "It was unnecessarily hurtful to have her join us."

"The distressing part was that after all their years together, Julia chose to leave her nothing. No matter how Christine learned that fact, it would have hurt. I feel badly for her." Bridget had finished with my hair, so I came to my feet and observed my reflection in the mirror. My dress was a very pale pink linen with an overlay of lace. It would act much less like an oven than what I'd worn the past two days.

"Perhaps we can do something for her," I said. "Or you and Lissette can put her in charge of the perfumery or something of that nature."

I turned when a knock sounded at the door. Before Blakely could get to it, Lissette pushed it open and peeked around the edge.

"Good morning, Cousin George," she said.

He responded and gestured to me. "Frances is standing right here, too, Lissette," he said.

I glanced at our young ward, who clearly wished I were somewhere else. Good manners prevent me from naming the place.

Lissette dragged out a sigh and planted a fist on her hip. "Bonjour to you, as well, Frances." Before I could reply, she turned back to George. "I'd like to see the place where my mother died," she said. "Will you take me?"

"Now you're getting ahead of me," George replied. "I don't like the idea of you wandering around the city until we find your mother's killer."

Her jaw tightened. Her eyes narrowed. I feared for George's safety.

When he glanced at me, I shrugged, as if to say, "Why not?"

He gaped, as if to say I'd lost my senses.

I gave him a pleading look.

"You are in agreement with her?" he asked.

Since he had spoken the words aloud, I took that as a win, though I might come to regret it. "We asked Lissette to come here to assist in the investigation," I reminded him.

"Do you realize she may not be safe?"

"Then we will have to keep her by our sides and watch out for her." I shifted my gaze to Lissette. "Otherwise I fear she is likely to venture out on her own."

Lissette confirmed my suspicion by folding her arms over her chest.

George sighed. "I suppose there is some sense to that. I see the Hazelton stubbornness in the set of her chin. All right, we will take you, but there are some rules I expect you to follow."

"Rules?" She made a face, as if the very word was offensive.

"Rules," he repeated. "They're like laws but with lesser penalties. First of all, until we know better, we shall all assume you are in danger."

She tutted. Not a good idea.

"Lissette." George's voice was more of a growl. "Your father and mother were killed within a week of each other. We would be fools not to be concerned about your welfare. Frances and I are offering you protection. Take it."

"What sort of protection can she offer me?" She gestured wildly to me, then quickly tucked her arm back in place to maintain her implacable stance.

"You would be surprised," I said. And, indeed, so would I.

"The first rule is when we are outside this house, you never leave our sight. Can you manage that?"

"Yes, I suppose I can. Is that it?"

"That's the most important one, but I reserve the right to add new rules as we go along."

"That's not fair. How will I know if I've broken one?"

"Oh, I will be sure to inform you. Now, make yourself ready, and we'll leave right after breakfast. Christine is welcome to join us, too."

When she left us, George turned to me. "I begin to wonder if we'll survive this guardianship."

It might be a close thing at that.

It took less than an hour for the three of us to eat, get ready for the excursion, meet the cab at the gate, and be on our way to the exposition grounds. Christine chose to stay at home and write to her Paris relations.

"I hope to call on them while we are in the city," she said when we assembled in the foyer.

"If you do go out, be sure to take Bridget or Blakely with you," I told her as George shepherded Lissette and me out the door. "With all the visitors to the city, it's not safe for a young lady to walk the streets alone."

I noticed George had brought the tube containing Julia's so-called painting. He saw the direction of my gaze and replied to my unvoiced question. We were becoming quite adept at silent communication. "If we have time," he said, "I'd like to take this to the studio and ask the artists for their opinions."

George had hired the cab for the day. When the driver dropped us off near the Champ de Mars, George told him we'd return in about an hour. Lissette's reaction to her first sight of the exposition grounds was much like mine had been—astonished, overwhelmed, and amazed. She stared, wide-eyed, as she turned in a circle to take in every part of the grand pavilions. With her long hair tied back underneath the beribboned boater hat, she didn't look much older than Rose. It took a moment before she became aware of the hundreds of people around her and moved closer to us.

"Are you certain you wish to see that spot?" George asked.

She indicated that she was, and he led us to the collapsed footbridge across the avenue de Suffren, which now was concealed behind a barrier. It would remain in place until the bridge was repaired. With the road blocked off, few people came this way. It was possibly the quietest spot at the exposition. Lissette settled herself on a bench and seemed lost in her thoughts. George wandered around the perimeter of the area, then paused near the barrier.

I had found a bench of my own and watched them both. The Champ de Mars, with its crowds, was only a block away. Towering over the surrounding buildings was the top of the Eiffel Tower in its newly painted gold glory.

A vendor with his pushcart rumbled around the corner, pulled a sandwich from the cart and, with a questioning glance at me, took a seat on the other end of my bench.

He noticed George examining the barrier and shook his head. "You found the one place for peace and quiet," he said. "There was a terrible accident in this place the other day, but now I come here to get off my feet for a moment, away from the crowd."

"My husband and I were here when the bridge collapsed." I gestured to Lissette. "Along with that young lady's mother."

His expression softened. "Her mother, was she injured?"

"She did not survive."

He let out a series of tsks while shaking his head. "A terrible thing. There was a man here that day with one of those cameras that take moving pictures. I don't know why anyone would want to watch such a tragedy, but I suppose there is a market for everything."

I couldn't quite believe what I was hearing. "Are you saying one of those people who make cinematographs was in this spot filming that day?"

He nodded but looked at me with different eyes, clearly disconcerted that I'd be interested in something so morbid.

I waved frantically to George to come over. Heavens! Perhaps there was some evidence for Julia's murder, after all!

George joined us, and I relayed what the man had told me about the cinematographer. When George asked for a description, the man gave us a look of confusion. "He looked British, tall, skinny, blond hair, and blue eyes."

"Then he must be known to the British contingent," I said. "We can go to their exhibit and inquire."

"You should stop by le rue de l'Avenir on your way," the vendor said. "That's where I saw him last."

Apparently, we had grown excited enough to draw Lissette's attention and engage her curiosity enough to join us. "The avenue of the future?" she echoed while George and I stared at the man in confusion.

The vendor sighed over our ignorance. "It is an exhibit. Surely, you've heard of the *trottoir roulant*. The moving sidewalk."

Lissette huffed. "How can sidewalks move?"

"It is magic, mademoiselle," the vendor said.

"The magic of engineering," George said. "But I understand

the sidewalk surrounds this section of the exposition. Where do we find him?"

"The whole route is no more than two miles in a circle. Start at the quai d'Orsay. If he is not there, he will soon be back." The vendor directed George, while I explained to Lissette why we wanted to find the cinematographer.

George thanked the man and turned back to us. "Shall we go?"

We all fell into step, heading toward the Seine and the crowds. "I'll walk with you as far as the quai d'Orsay," I said. "If the man isn't filming at the exhibit, I'll go on to the British pavilion and request information about him while you and Lissette try to find him at the moving sidewalk. I'll join you there when I'm done."

George agreed to my plan. "The vendor says he saw him not an hour ago, but who knows how much time he spends filming each location? I'd rather have a name and a way to contact him than to chase him around the exposition grounds."

We arrived at the appointed site but found no cinematographer. George frowned. "You will be all right on your own?"

I waved away his concern. "Of course. Go on, you two. I'll meet up with you soon." I watched as George and Lissette took the ramp that wound up to the *trottoir roulant*, which looked like a sliding platform, elevated to the height of a single-story building. Hundreds of people were already on the platform, yet traffic on the stairs was relatively smooth. I speculated that this must be one of many entrances and exits. I shook off my curiosity and headed toward the river and the Street of Nations.

I'd noticed the British pavilion when we passed by in the steamboat on our previous excursion to the exposition. It was situated across the river from the Old Paris exhibit, between the pavilions of Hungary and Belgium, the latter a Gothic building I had just passed. My destination was straight ahead. Britain had entries in most, if not all, of the large exhibits, but this building was where I was most likely to find the administrative type of personnel.

The pavilion was a reproduction of an English country manor. It felt a bit disconcerting to be entering what looked like Kingston House from Bradford-on-Avon here in the middle of Paris. I'd barely had a chance to step out of the flow of visitors, get my bearings, and decide where I might find assistance when I heard my name. I looked about me to see none other than Alicia Stoke-Whitney approaching from a staircase.

"Frances," she said again, weaving through a cluster of tourists. "How lovely to see you. Most of the people coming to view the pavilion are foreigners."

It's odd how our relationships with people change over time. A year ago, I'd be grinding my teeth at the mere thought of Alicia. A few months ago, I'd felt sorry for her. At this moment, I was quite delighted to see her. As part of the British commission for the exposition, and as someone who had little respect for rules, she was precisely the person I needed.

"How lucky to find you here," I said. "I had assumed your involvement was limited to planning and promoting."

She pulled me aside and out of the hearing of a couple admiring the furniture in the replica drawing room. "Arthur had volunteered for everything," she said.

Arthur was her late husband.

"Since I've stepped into his shoes, I find that I'm a part of almost every committee. Initially, I found it quite dull, but I am ever so happy I agreed to take it on. There's really nothing to it, and it has done wonders for my daughter's social status. I am rather enjoying myself."

Alicia was not one to say things she didn't mean, a trait that made her less than popular among British society matrons. But if I had any doubt of her sincerity, the sparkle in her eyes corroborated her words.

"I'm very happy to hear that," I said. Alicia's daughter, Harriet, was a kindhearted and lovely young woman. How she managed to be so with parents like hers was a wonder I'd never understand. "And I'm pleased to see you here. Perhaps you can help me?"

"But of course. I've become quite knowledgeable about the pavilion."

"My question is actually about a British cinematographer. I am assuming he is part of your commission. He's been traveling the exposition grounds and filming the various activities and displays."

"Yes, that would be Henry Standish. He sends the film back to London every week, and they have been showing it at various clubs."

"Yes, I attended one of the viewings myself a few weeks ago. You are correct. He is the man I need to contact."

"You won't find him here. I believe he's out on the grounds, but you can leave a message. Come with me."

With a pivot, she led me up the stairs and beyond the exhibits depicting country homes in Britain that were completely out of the reach of the average British citizen. Up here, the smells of construction, which had somehow been eradicated in the exhibit area, lingered in the air—predominately paint and plaster dust.

We passed through a final door into an office where a handful of people worked. Alicia led me to a desk where a young man clacked away at a typewriter. "Timmy, we are in need of your assistance," she said.

Timmy appeared to be about twenty. He looked up from his work with eyes magnified by the round spectacles perched on a narrow nose. Those eyes, in fact his whole expression, softened when he saw Alicia. I suspected that Timmy would do anything for her. "Yes, Mrs. Stoke-Whitney. How can I be of service?"

"Do you not share a flat with Henry Standish?" she asked.

He pushed his spectacles up his nose. "There are several of us in that flat, but yes, Henry Standish is one."

"Would you be so kind as to deliver a message to him for me?" I asked. Then, thinking of how Alicia's associations with young men had affected her reputation, I corrected myself. "For me and my husband, that is."

"Of course, madame," he replied, handing me a tablet of paper and a pencil.

"My lady," Alicia corrected. "This is my friend Frances, Countess of Harleigh."

Before I could correct her, the young man apologized. "Forgive me, my lady. I wasn't aware."

I waved away his apology and began writing my note to the cinematographer, which earned me Alicia's curiosity.

"What is it you need from him, Frances?"

I considered putting her off, but Timmy's presence reminded me of my manners. "He may be in possession of some film we'd like to see. Actually, we'd like the police to take a look at it."

Timmy became instantly alert. "Do you mean from the ruckus when the bridge collapsed? I saw that. It was quite horrifying."

I finished my note, letting Mr. Standish know where he could contact us.

"But why would you want the police to view it?" Timmy continued.

"It may provide evidence of a crime."

His interest deepened. "What crime?"

"You aren't with the newspapers, are you?" I asked, folding my note.

"No, ma'am!" he said.

"What is it, Frances?" Alicia asked. "You can be sure it will go no further."

Why not? If the information that Julia was murdered wasn't

yet public, it was inevitable that it would be soon. "George's aunt, Lady Julia Hazelton, was murdered, stabbed, during the surge of the crowd when the bridge collapsed."

Alicia gasped and brought her hands to her mouth.

Timmy stared.

Alicia recovered first. "I'm so sorry, Frances. How tragic. I had heard there were some deaths as a result of the bridge collapse, but I had not yet heard anyone was murdered. Why, it makes me feel almost patriotic that one of our own may have film that sheds some light on who might have perpetrated such a dastardly act."

Timmy offered his sympathies, scratched his head, then leafed through some files stacked on his desk. "You say she was stabbed?" he asked. "Might it have been with something like this?"

Nothing could have prepared me for what he found in the stacks of clutter on his desk. Opening a stiff paper file, he held it carefully so as not to touch the object inside.

I stepped closer to take a look. Lying on the paper was a dagger of sorts, but with a thin pointed blade.

And was that blood?

Chapter Sixteen

It was blood.

It was also disturbing. Alicia, for one, did not appreciate seeing it.

She backed jerkily away, waving her hand, seemingly on the brink of screaming. We were already drawing the attention of the other people in the room, who cast surreptitious glances our way. I pulled Alicia to my side and whispered what I hoped were calming words while gesturing to Timmy to cover the thing up.

I settled Alicia at an empty desk a few feet away and leaned her forward over her knees. When I returned to the young man, I was bursting with questions. He pulled up a chair for me next to his desk. I settled into it gratefully.

"First of all," I said to him, "do you have a surname?"

"Yes, ma'am. It's Ryder."

"Thank you. Now, Mr. Ryder, how do you come to have that weapon in your possession?"

"Like Mrs. Stoke-Whitney said, Henry Standish and I share a flat here in Paris. He found this on the ground the day the bridge collapsed, after he was done filming, and after the police sent everyone away."

I was stunned. "He just found it on the ground and picked it up?"

"He tried to give it to one of the officers, but the bloke just waved him off without even looking at it. Probably didn't help that Henry doesn't speak French. Anyway, he left with it, and later on he showed it to me. I thought it looked like some kind of relic, and reckoned it belonged in the Old Paris exhibit. Have you seen it? They have players there in costume from the Middle Ages. Very authentic. Why, this thing"—he pointed to the weapon—"would fit right in. I never thought that blood was real. I assumed it was just for effect. Henry handed it over to me, and I was planning to take it to the exhibit after I finished work today."

Unbelievable! I wondered how many bits of evidence were lost to people who simply didn't know what they were looking at. I was torn. Dare I trust this young man, who was currently making cow eyes at Alicia, to take this weapon to the police and provide the requisite explanations?

No. It was too great a risk. "How much longer is your workday, Mr. Ryder?"

He retrieved a worn, silver watch from his waistcoat and snapped it open. "I ought to be gone now. This correspondence took longer than I anticipated."

"Have you finished it, then? Are you ready to leave?"

"Yes, ma'am." He gave me a resigned look. "I suppose you want me to take this to the police?"

"Actually, I'd like to accompany you, but I've one stop to make first where we may come across your friend Mr. Standish."

"All right, then. If you're coming with me, it won't seem like such a daunting task." He pulled a length of fabric from his desk drawer and used it to cover his typewriter, closed the paper file over the frightful stabbing instrument and picked it up. As he came to his feet, he cast his gaze once more at Alicia. "Do you suppose Mrs. Stoke-Whitney will be all right?"

I was eager to be off, but Alicia did look rather shaken. I stepped over to the desk to assure myself that she was well and able to go about her business. She waved us off, with a promise to call on me in the coming days to hear the details.

Once Mr. Ryder and I left the British pavilion, we retraced my steps along the river toward the Champ de Mars. From there, it was a short walk to the platform, where the concessionaire collected his fees for a ride on the *trottoir roulant*, which was where we found George, Lissette, and another young man, who raised his hand in greeting to my companion.

George appeared concerned when we approached their little group. "We've been waiting quite some time," he said. "Mr. Standish is willing to go to the police with me, but I hesitated to leave before I knew what had become of you."

"Forgive me for the delay, but I think you'll find it was worth it." I introduced Mr. Ryder as a friend of Mr. Standish. "I was leaving a message for Mr. Standish when Mr. Ryder showed me what may well be the murder weapon."

George, just about to speak, let his jaw go slack. He recovered himself almost immediately. "I cannot conceive how you manage such things. We are spending our time seeking and then interviewing a witness, and in that same amount of time, you, while ostensibly leaving a message for the witness, come back with the murder weapon." He wagged his head. "How do you do it?"

"I'm sure I don't know, George. Sometimes it just happens that way. But I'm glad you've waited to go to the police, because Mr. Ryder has agreed to go, as well."

"Excellent." He turned to Mr. Ryder. "Might I see it?"

Mr. Ryder was gazing at Lissette with a distracted smile on

his lips. Alicia would not like that. Neither did I, once I thought about it. Lissette was only fifteen.

"Mr. Ryder," I said sharply.

"Yes, yes, of course," he said. He opened the file, using his body to shield the grizzly weapon from Lissette's view. She shifted around behind him in an attempt to see it.

"It's some sort of dagger, don't you think?" I asked.

"It's a poignard," Lissette said after catching a glimpse of it by peeking between Mr. Ryder and George. "I've seen pictures of them."

"Perhaps you can enlighten us as to what exactly that is," George said.

"Obviously, it's a type of dagger, but they were carried by noblemen of France in the last century and earlier. That one looks quite old. Maybe the late eighteenth century."

I hadn't yet examined the weapon thoroughly, but even from a foot away, I could see the handle was intricately detailed, and was that the glimmer of a jewel? It looked expensive.

"How do you know about such things?" George asked Lissette.

"I am a good student," she replied. "Just ask Christine."

"You can see why we thought it belonged to the Old Paris exhibit," Mr. Ryder added, closing the file and handing it over to George. "But I'm happy to get it off my hands so you can turn it over to the police."

"But you must come with us," Mr. Standish said.

Mr. Ryder demurred, stating that he was not the one to find the weapon, and the two young men proceeded to argue the matter.

George lifted his eyes heavenward and cleared his throat. "I would appreciate both of you coming with me. It should not take long, but the sooner we are off, the sooner you may return to your regular plans."

That seemed to settle the matter, except for one small issue that came to my mind. "I noticed you didn't include Lissette or me in your plans."

George turned slowly to Lissette, who placed her hands on her hips and glared back at him. "Ah, yes. Lissette."

His gentle tone sounded forced and made me wonder what had happened between George and his ward.

"It might be best if Lissette returns to the apartment," George said, turning back to me. "Would you mind taking her?" Poor George. He had been a stepfather for only a matter of months before becoming guardian to a fifteen-year-old, very independent girl. The fact that she resented me should not stop me from taking part in that guardianship. I'd been letting him handle everything. It was time I took charge.

"You wanted to take that painting to Julia's studio today," I said, indicating the tube under his arm. "I can take it, and unless you insist Lissette go back to the apartment, she may wish to come with me." I shrugged, as if it made no difference.

She cast a hopeful glance at George, who released a sigh. "You may go with Frances, but no more misbehavior."

Misbehavior? I wondered what she'd done—and what I'd gotten myself into. As we organized ourselves to go our separate ways, George touched my arm. "Good luck," he said.

I don't think he was talking about the painting.

Before the men left us to return to our cab and head to the Sûreté, Mr. Standish explained that Lissette and I could take the moving sidewalk toward the esplanade des Invalides. A block or two from there, we would be more likely to find a cab to take us to Montmartre and Julia's studio. I admit the idea of a moving sidewalk had me eager to see it for myself. I paid the concessionaire one hundred centimes for the two of us. Oddly enough, he gave Lissette a glare as she joined me on the first platform.

"How did you manage to earn his ire?" I asked as I took

hold of one of the vertical poles and stepped up to the second platform. It moved just a bit faster than the lower one. The morning had grown warm already, and the slight breeze created by the movement was delightful. Glancing around, I marveled at how many of us were traveling by simply standing on this platform. So, this was the street of the future, was it?

Lissette hopped up to my level. "I snuck past the concessionaire and jumped on without paying."

"I can see how that might annoy him," I said. "And your cousin. You did agree not to wander off."

She gave me a look that young people reserve only for adults when we say something they find absurd. "The platforms go in a circle and only around this section of the grounds. It would have brought me right back here."

I tipped my head to the side. "Shall we try the fastest one?"

She grinned, and we both stepped up to the next level. I didn't use the pole this time and had to take a step to steady myself. The thrill made me laugh, and Lissette joined me.

"This sidewalk is fun," she said.

"Indeed. What did you mean when you said it *would* have brought you back? Did you get off?"

"Cousin George made me."

"He did?"

She sighed. "He must have noticed I'd left, and the man was yelling because I hadn't paid, so Cousin George jumped on and ran along the platform to catch me. He runs rather fast. When he caught up to me, I thought it best to go back with him."

I turned my head, struggling not to laugh. That would have been priceless to see, but George must have been furious, not to mention terrified that he'd lose her or that something horrible would befall her. When I had myself back under control, I found Lissette grinning at me, which made me start laughing all over again.

"He was very angry with me," Lissette said.

"I think it was more fear than anger. Remember, he's trying to keep you safe."

"That's what he said." She sighed dramatically. "I just wanted a moment to myself."

Something tweaked my imagination. "How did he miss seeing you board the sidewalk?"

"He was talking to that man about the film and what he'd seen."

And what he'd seen had killed Julia. We'd have to be careful involving her in this investigation. It was her mother who had been killed, after all. I noticed several people disembarking ahead of us. "I think this is where we must get off."

We quickly worked our way to the slowest platform and stepped off just in time to exit to the rue de Constantine. We walked for a block or so until we noticed a cab dropping off passengers at the corner ahead of us. A few quick steps and a wave of my hand caught the driver's attention. My mother would cringe at the thought of me chasing after a cab, but I was rather proud that we'd managed to snag it before anyone else.

The drive to Montmartre was quick and quiet, each of us contemplating our own concerns. It seemed to me that Lissette might want to look around the studio and take something of her mother's for herself—perhaps everything. On the other hand, this might be too emotional a visit for her. But we had arrived, and there was only one way to find out.

I paid the driver and stepped up beside Lissette, who waited for me outside the door of the studio. "I'd forgotten that you've been here before," I said.

"Yes, many times." Her expression was eager and a bit wistful.

I pushed open the heavy door. "The place is unlocked. I wonder if the artists are here."

The wooden floors creaked as we stepped into the room, announcing our entrance. Martine, wearing a canvas smock covered in dust from her morning's work, lounged in a chair near where Edouard leaned against his table. Hmm, it seemed they did get along now and then.

Martine's expression softened when she saw Lissette. "*Enfant*," she cooed. Lissette ambled over to the table, where Martine hugged her and Edouard squeezed her shoulder. I wondered if I should give the three of them a few minutes, but Martine gestured for me to join them as she carefully removed her smock and draped it over the chair.

"The police were here yesterday," she said as I approached. "They went through Julia's things up in her little garret and pawed through everything down here."

"I think that was to be expected," I said. "They are hoping to find something that will lead them to the culprit. Did they stop and talk with you?"

She huffed. "The only talking they did was to announce their arrival and to ask us to touch nothing."

"Why would they want to speak with us?" Edouard asked. "That inspector interviewed us just the day before."

"That was about Julia's death. Now they are also investigating Ducasse's." I surveyed the room. "Did they take anything away when they left?"

"Yes," Martine said, waving her arm. "They took my tools. Do they think I killed her?"

I glanced at Martine's dust-covered smock.

She flushed. "I had some extra chisels at home."

"If they thought you did it, they would have arrested you," Edouard said. I think he meant to reassure her, but Martine continued to mope.

"I'm sure you will have them back soon," I said. Particularly if the poignard turned out to be the murder weapon.

Lissette had wandered over to her mother's work area to browse through her canvases. She seemed to be paying us little attention, so I thought it safe to make a few inquiries of my own. "Do either of you recall the last time you saw Ducasse?"

They glanced at each other and turned back to me. Martine stretched out her arms, taking in the room. "It would have been here on the tenth."

"That was the day he died, wasn't it?" I asked.

"Yes," she said. "But we had no idea what was to happen, and as usual, we were all here working."

"Are you sure there was nothing different about that day?"

Martine bit her lip. "Julia had taken the train in from the country that morning, and she was too tired to work. She was upstairs sleeping. Or at least trying to sleep." She angled a glare at Edouard. "Paul and this one were having a row."

"We were arguing. There was nothing unusual about that." He scowled at Martine. "Why do you want to make something out of nothing?"

"It was a very heated argument," she replied. "He told you several times to stay out of his business, but you persisted."

"Were you hanging on our every word?" He pointed to the kitchen area, which was closed off on three sides. "We were in the kitchen. Did you have your ear to the wall?"

"I could hear perfectly from where I worked, but anyone who had heard you before would know that you were fighting over the fair Julia—again." She said the last word as if she was heartily sick of hearing those arguments.

"You are jealous," Edouard shot back. "There is no other reason for you to make something of our disagreements." He turned to me. "Julia had made it clear to Paul that she could not see him in a romantic way, because he was married. Yet he persisted in romancing her. He was making her life very hard."

"Speaking of jealous," Martine said in a singsong voice. "You wanted Paul to leave her alone so you would have a chance with her. But you could not understand that she was simply not interested in you."

My head was spinning. They had started the conversation with such congeniality. Then their voices had grown positively venomous as this argument wore on. I didn't quite know how to stop it. Nor was I sure I wanted to do so. Did one of them kill Paul Ducasse? Did one of them kill Julia?

Edouard's expression had grown rather frightening. His heavy eyebrows were drawn downward, narrowing his dark eyes and sharpening the angles of his chin and cheeks. If I were in Martine's shoes, particularly if I were her size, I would have backed down, but she continued to attack.

She pointed a finger at his chest. "You had your chance with her, but it just didn't work out. She may not have wanted to involve herself with Paul, but she was still in love with him. There was nothing you could do about that."

"You wish I had been able to turn her head. Then you could have had Paul to yourself."

Had they both forgotten about Gabrielle? "Paul was married, after all," I ventured.

"As if that mattered," Edouard sneered at the same time Martine snorted.

"Their marriage was for form's sake only," she said. "Their families wanted them to marry, so they did, but it's not as if Paul would have given up his art or his friends, and Gabrielle would have no part of them. They had nothing in common. She was immersed in the world of society and committees and parties, while Paul was immersed in art."

"You women give him far too much credit." Edouard picked up a rag, plucked a paintbrush from a jar of cloudy water, and used the rag to dry it. "His family threatened to cut him off unless he married her, so he did. He did not marry her in good faith, as he had no intention of giving up his bachelor ways. He was back on the prowl the day after the wedding, much to his family's disappointment."

"I'm confused," I said. "His family was disappointed with his marriage? I thought they had wanted it."

"They expected Gabrielle to have more influence over him

and hoped she would convince him to give up art as a profession and take up something more respectable, like banking, the family business."

"The Ducasse family are bankers?"

"One of the biggest," Martine said.

"When Paul didn't comply, the family cut him off financially." Edouard raised a hand, palm upward. "But what did that matter when he had Gabrielle and her family money? Ultimately, when Paul's work began to command attention, they welcomed him back to the fold and reinstated his allowance. Paul had become an important artist, and they were happy to bask in his fame."

"You are proving my point," Martine said. "Even while his wife and family pushed him to take his place in high society, he devoted himself to his art."

Edouard made a rude noise. "The problems in that marriage had less to do with his devotion to art than his devotion to himself. He treated all of you who were close to him terribly, yet you all still adored him. At least Julia realized she would never have his love, and she moved on."

"Until Paul learned Lissette was his child," Martine added somberly.

"Even then, Julia knew he would never be a responsible parent and that she was better off without him," Edouard said.

I wasn't sure Lissette would have felt the same. It was with that thought that I recalled that she was in the room, which meant she had heard every word the artists had said about her father. I turned my attention to Julia's work area, where I'd last seen Lissette, but she wasn't there. A look around told me she wasn't in the room at all.

Bother! I'd lost her.

Chapter Seventeen

"What is wrong?" Edouard caught on to my distress quickly.

"Lissette." I waved my hand to Julia's work area. "She was right there, and now she's gone. I'm afraid our conversation upset her. Ducasse was her father, after all."

"She is probably upstairs," Martine said.

The stairs had been in my view the whole time I'd been here. I was quite sure I'd have noticed Lissette climbing them, but it was worth a try. "I'll check, but would one of you look out front and one out back? She slipped away from us earlier, and I'm afraid she might have done it again."

To their credit, they both moved with alacrity to the opposite doors. I headed up the stairs, calling for Lissette. There was no answer. Nor did I find her in Julia's small room. Bother! I should not have let my curiosity get the better of my judgment and should have remembered that Lissette was listening in to that conversation. No wonder she had run off.

After stuffing the tube with Julia's painting in it under the mattress, I headed back downstairs. Martine was entering through the back door, shaking her head. "Not out there," she said.

I pulled open the front door to see Edouard walking toward me from the corner. "I didn't see her on the street," he said once he reached me. "She could be anywhere."

"Then I suppose I shall have to look everywhere."

He spread his hands. "Why not wait until she returns of her own accord?"

"Both of her parents have been murdered. We don't know why. I don't want to risk anyone hurting her. For all we know, someone has been lying in wait for just such an opportunity."

"You can't believe that," he said. "What possible benefit could come from hurting her?"

"If I knew the answer to that question, I might have a better idea of where to look for her. Would you stay at the studio in case she comes back?"

He agreed, and I set off on my quest, then stopped after a few steps.

Where to go first? I was unfamiliar with Montmartre, but I assumed Lissette would be, too. I looked around me. Higher up the hill were three- and four-story buildings. It seemed to be a working-class neighborhood, with lodgings, shops, and cafés. Around the hill and toward the bottom was a veritable entertainment mecca with music halls, cabarets, café concerts, even circuses. I had noted that area when George and I drove here the first time we met with Julia. I thought the studio was located just a street or two away from there, but it was midafternoon, and those places were not open yet, or at least there were no performances.

The door opened behind me, and Martine joined me on the sidewalk.

"I don't know which way she'd go," I said to explain my lack of progress.

"Why don't I look with you?" Martine said.

"That would be very helpful," I said, pointing uphill. "She could lose herself better among those twisting streets, but so could I." I turned in the opposite direction and sniffed the air. "This way. I smell lunch."

She nodded. "There are several cafés downhill. I can search the streets from here up if you'd like to search them from here down."

"That is kind of you. Yes, let's split up."

I took the curved street that followed along the side of the hill and slowly wound downward. The area became more commercial as I proceeded. And more crowded, though I saw no sign of Lissette's blue dress among the people I passed. I walked by shops, bakeries, and cafés and found myself opening doors and checking inside where I could. If the establishment was not open, the best I could do was peer through the windows. In this manner, I made my way through a few blocks.

As I rounded a corner, I was hit with the unmistakable scent of crepes. A café was directly ahead of me. Several diners were seated at the outside tables. None of them were Lissette, but the door was open, so I checked inside. No sign of her. To keep track of my whereabouts, I noted that I was now on rue des Saules.

The sign was affixed to a building across the street. Beneath it, Inspector Cadieux leaned against a streetlamp, arms crossed over his chest, watching me. He lifted a hand in greeting and zigzagged his way through the traffic to cross over to my side.

"Have you lost her already?" he asked as he stepped up next to me.

How could he know? "Whoever do you mean?" I asked instead.

He lifted his brows in reply. "I am referring to Mademoiselle Lissette, of course. Is there someone else under your care who has managed to slip away from you?"

Had I really thought him charming when we first met? I glared at him. "Have you been following me?"

"Just for a short time. You caught my attention when you

ran after a cab, waving your hands in the air." He gave me a look of amusement. "I was under the impression that a lady wouldn't behave in such an uncultured manner."

The man was positively cheeky. No hint of charm whatsoever. "Spare me your criticism, Inspector. I have a mother, who does it far better than you. I assume the person you are really following is Lissette."

"Both her parents were recently murdered, so when I saw the two of you climb into the cab, I thought it prudent to see where you were taking her."

"I assure you I mean her no harm. We were at her mother's studio. I asked the other artists about Ducasse, and the conversation might have been too upsetting for Lissette, so she slipped out."

"So I saw."

I waited for him to elaborate and barely repressed a growl when he did not. "Did you happen to notice where she went?" I asked through clenched teeth.

"You are right next to her, madame."

He gestured to a building on the corner with a long table and a couple of benches under a tree outside the door. It had a most unusual sign—the image of a rabbit, wearing a soft hat, red cummerbund, and tie, jumping out of a saucepan and balancing a bottle of wine, I believe, on the back of one hand. The other hand waved a jaunty hello.

A sign in the window announced it was Le Lapin Agile. The Agile Rabbit? I supposed I'd heard stranger names for drinking establishments. The same sign announced it was a cabaret. I turned back to Cadieux. "Would they allow a fifteen-year-old girl in there?"

He lifted his shoulders in a shrug. "It would appear so. I saw her go in. She has not come out."

"Very well. I'll fetch her." The man annoyed me so that I would love to have simply walked away, but I did owe him my gratitude. "To thank you for your help, you should know that my husband is at the Sûreté, delivering a piece of evidence we found."

Cadieux maintained his air of insouciance, but a flicker of interest lit his eyes. "Indeed? What is this evidence?"

"The murder weapon. At least we think so."

It might have been my imagination, but I thought I saw a smile cross his lips before I turned and headed to Le Lapin Agile. Lettering on the window claimed it would not be open until five; however, the lights inside and the fact that the door was standing open told another story. I had second thoughts when I poked my head inside. The air was stale, and the floors were dirty. This was definitely not where the delicious aroma had come from. Instead, I detected the smell of grease enveloped with cigar and cigarette smoke.

I walked into the large room—a little brighter, sorely neglected. Benches lined the walls, with narrow wooden tables in front of them and stools on the other side. A guitar stood in the corner on one side of the room, but there was no sign of a stage for performers. A bar ran along the wall on the opposite side. A man with his back to me stood behind it, wiping glasses with a towel. And right in the middle of the room, seated with a gentleman, was Lissette.

I was euphoric for having found her, yet angry that she could just run off with no care for the fear she put me through. Honestly! To top off all the emotions, I now had to extricate her from the strange man, who very likely thought her company was for sale.

Then I recognized the man—Lucien Allard—and breathed a sigh of relief. At least I could strike that concern from my list.

They both glanced up as I wound my way through the tables. Allard at first looked startled, almost as if he would run. Perhaps he thought I was coming to defend Lissette's honor. But then he seemed to recognize me and relaxed. Lissette had the opposite reaction. Crossing her arms, she put on her stubborn front but refused to meet my eye.

Allard came to his feet when I arrived at the table, and pulled out the third stool for me. "Won't you join us?"

I had to think about that. It might be an appropriate form of torture for Lissette if I joined their little tête-à-tête. She probably expected me to react with anger, but why should I become ruffled or agitated? Let her just wonder what my reaction would ultimately be. Since he had spoken in French, I thanked him in the same language and took the seat.

"May I offer you some wine?" he asked, raising the bottle. That was when I noticed Lissette had a glass of wine. As if she'd seen my gaze, she took a healthy swig. It was not as if wine was new to her, I reminded myself.

I turned back to Allard. "In truth, I would dearly love a cup of coffee, if that is possible."

"Of course." He returned the bottle of wine to the table and excused himself. "It will be the work of a moment," he said.

As soon as he was far enough away from the table, Lissette leaned across the rough, pitted surface toward me, nearly knocking her glass over in the process. "Must you follow me around?" she snapped.

I steadied her glass as it tipped. "You make me sound as if I'm your jailer, Lissette, when I'm only trying to keep you safe."

She sneered. "You would wrap me up in wire wool, as my mother's family did to her."

I closed my eyes for a moment, trying not to laugh at the image. "The idea does sound tempting, but I believe you mean *cotton* wool. In any event, both options go far beyond my intentions. I simply want to keep you from following in your mother's footsteps. Or your father's, for that matter." I reached for her hand, which she snatched back to her lap. "Can you not see that you may be in danger until we learn who killed them?"

Lissette raised her glass to her lips and drained it. She probably hadn't even tasted the wine, which, in an establishment like this, might not be such a bad thing. Upon returning the glass to the table, she refilled it. At this rate, she would sail right past tipsy and become drunk and unmanageable. Not that she ever was manageable. I had to get her back home, but first, I had to convince her to come with me.

Allard returned with my coffee and placed it on the table in front of me, sloshing just a bit of the liquid over the rim and onto the table. I wondered how long he'd been here drinking before Lissette found him. He seemed far more jovial today than he had at the Ducasse exhibit. I suspected his mood was a product of the wine, since I couldn't believe Lissette had been charming company up to my arrival. She was still scowling, which reminded me of why she had run off from the studio.

"What brought you to this place, Lissette? I understand why you left the studio, but why come here?" I asked her.

Allard gave me a superior look. "Is there something wrong with this place?"

"I'm not certain anything is wrong with it, but I wonder if it is appropriate for a fifteen-year-old girl." I turned back to Lissette. "How did you decide to come here? I didn't know you were familiar with the area."

She stared at me for a moment, perhaps wondering if she should bother to answer, then sighed. "I don't know the area. I just picked a direction and walked. When I saw this place, I remembered my mother talking about it. She said many artists came here. It is a friendly name, isn't it? A nimble rabbit? So I came inside and found Monsieur Allard, who I know was a friend of both my mother and father. I could hardly be in safer company, don't you think?"

Her disdain made me want to shake her. Friend of her parents or not, he was still a stranger to her. "A friend indeed," I said, turning my gaze to Allard. "Christine Granger told me you were thoughtful enough to arrange an appointment for her to meet the great designer Worth to discuss their perfume."

He blinked a few times as he gazed at me, then shook his head. "The idea—and it was just an idea, mind you—was that I would introduce Julia to Gaston Worth. She would take it from there. There was no appointed time, and Christine was not involved at all. Why would Worth speak with anyone but the owner?"

"Perhaps she misunderstood," I said, wondering how I could ask what had happened between them at the Ducasse tribute.

Allard's expression held a hint of mischief. "Maybe she sought to make a deal between the designer and herself for the perfume."

"She wouldn't do that." Lissette's tone implied she was highly offended by the suggestion.

Allard turned to Lissette with a shrug. "You would know better than me what she would do." He snapped his fingers. "Did your mother tell you how this place got its name?"

Now that he had changed the subject, I was left to wonder if Christine would have tried to sell the perfume on her own.

"There's a story about this nimble rabbit?" Lissette asked. "Are you saying there actually was a namesake rabbit?"

"There was no rabbit," he said, pouring himself another glass of wine. "No real rabbit, at least. Only the one on the sign. Some twenty-five years ago, an artist by the name of Andre Gill painted that sign." He tipped his head and lifted a brow. "Do you begin to understand?"

Lissette laughed. "It was Gill's Rabbit," she said. "Le Lapin à Gill."

"That sign does not look twenty-five years old," I said.

Allard laughed, sending winey fumes my way. "It is not," he said. "The original was stolen."

I raised a brow. "So, perhaps not such a friendly place."

"Do you wish to hear what this place was called before Gill's painting?" Allard gave us a mischievous grin. "Cabaret des Assassins."

That hit a little too close to home for Lissette. Her grin quickly flattened to the scowl I was so familiar with. Yet this time it looked false. Put on perhaps in an attempt to hide her pain, though that was clear in her eyes. Allard was taken aback, glancing at me as if asking, "What happened?"

"You may not be aware that the police believe Lissette's mother was murdered," I said. "And they now suspect her father was, as well."

His eyes softened as he turned to Lissette. "Forgive me, *enfant*." He pulled her hand away from her glass. She allowed him to take it in his. "I should have known better than to speak of such things in jest. Of course, I heard of the misfortune that befell your poor mother. What a tragic thing to happen right on the heels of your dear father's death." He released her hand and turned back to me. "But do you say the police suspect Ducasse was murdered, too? What do they base this on?"

"I'm not entirely certain," I said. "But once the medical examiner looked at the notes from the coroner and then spoke to the funeral director, he convinced the prosecutor to investigate. I would say that means they suspect foul play."

"But that is incomprehensible," he said. "I will not believe such a vile thing happened to him. Ducasse was so amiable. Everyone was his friend. I cannot imagine one of them murdering him."

"It may well have been a stranger," I said. "But whether you can conceive of it or not, the inspector is likely to interview you."

"Me? What could I possibly know? I last saw Paul several days before his death."

"But you were close to him. You would be surprised what information could be useful to an investigation."

"Where did you last see my father?" Lissette asked.

Allard ran a knuckle along his mustache. "It must have been when he delivered his paintings to the exhibition, so we would have been at the Grand Palais."

"Are his paintings still on exhibit?" she asked.

"Oh, yes. Your father's star was on the rise. He had to be included." He sighed and swiped at his eyes with the back of his hand. "Sometimes I forget he is gone. And I cannot believe he was murdered." He gave me a dark look. "You must have that wrong."

"Well, I don't believe—" was all I managed to say.

"Why are you involved in this at all?" He truly looked angry now. "A woman in a murder investigation. It's ridiculous."

Lissette backed her chair away from the table.

"It is certainly possible that I am mistaken, Monsieur Allard. In any event, I am very sorry for the loss of your friend and partner. I think it's time Lissette and I were on our way." I came to my feet. Lissette hesitated a moment longer.

Allard's hand covered hers. "Are you sure you want to go?" he asked. "Or would you like to finish our chat? You are so like your father. You have that rebellious spirit. He would want you to live your life as he did, not allowing someone else to make your decisions." He tipped his head toward me while I waited by my chair. "I'm sure Madame Hazelton cares for you, Lissette, but you can decide when to leave. She has no control over you."

I was seconds from strangling the man, who clearly disliked me as much as Lissette did. What was it about me that was so off-putting lately?

While I didn't care about his good opinion, I truly resented him urging Lissette to defy me. She hardly needed the encouragement. Before I could speak out, she shook off his hand and stood.

"Neither do you have control over me," she said. "I make my own decisions, and right now, I prefer to go with Frances."

With that, she linked her arm with mine, and in my stupefied state, I allowed her to lead me to the door. Will wonders never cease?

At the door, she turned back to me. "Don't think this means I like you."

A very short-lived wonder. "I wouldn't dream of it." But I was making headway.

Chapter Eighteen

I saw no sign of Cadieux as we walked back to the studio. Lissette was surprisingly congenial. Not that either of us said much. Our single exchange was me asking if she still felt up to looking through her mother's things and her giving an affirmative response. After that, we plodded along the streets, picking our way over the cobblestones. Even walking side by side, we were both too caught up in our own thoughts for conversation.

Lucien Allard seemed to be drinking away his sorrows, taking solace in a glass of wine—or a bottle, as it were—over the loss of his good friend. Edouard had said Ducasse abused the friendship of those closest to him. It was clear what that entailed when it came to his wife and Julia. He would never be faithful. But what form did that abuse take regarding his male friends? Or did he have any? Though Allard cared about Ducasse, they were business partners, after all. Even so, that was a relationship based on trust, and since it involved his work, one would think Ducasse would have taken care not to abuse Allard's trust.

But that left me with suspects like Gabrielle, the woman he

cheated on; Martine, the woman he might have cheated with; and Julia, who seemed to be the woman he truly wanted. A point that might have made the other two jealous of her. Speaking of which, Edouard Legrand could not be let off the hook as a suspect once one considered his jealousy that Ducasse had a strong link to Julia in the form of Lissette.

This was going to take more digging before we could reasonably eliminate any of our suspects. And, of course, there might be others we didn't even know about yet.

Martine was outside smoking when the studio came into view. Her expression brightened and she tossed the cigarette into the street when she saw Lissette. "*Enfant!* I am so happy to see you well." She drew Lissette into a hug. "I was worried."

Martine glanced at me over Lissette's shoulder. "I searched all the way up to Sacré-Coeur and just returned myself. I'm so glad you found her." She released Lissette and shook a finger at her. "You should not go off alone like that. This place is not safe for one as pretty and young as you. Where were you?"

Lissette squirmed self-consciously. Martine had a quiet voice, but there were many people on the street, and we were drawing their attention.

"Why don't we go inside," I suggested. "It must be past one by now, and we still have to go through your mother's things before we can find a cab and go home." We slipped into the studio, where Legrand dropped his paintbrush and engulfed Lissette in a hug.

Martine hung back and tapped my shoulder. "Where was she?" she asked when I turned around.

"The Lapin Agile."

Her expression turned to one of dismay. "This is why Julia kept her in the country, I suppose," she said. "What is to become of her?"

"She is to be pitied," I agreed. "It is tragic to lose one's parents so young, but she does have family who will love and care for her. She is not completely alone."

When I saw Martine's blank look, it dawned on me that she didn't know about Julia's wishes. "Julia had made arrangements for my husband to be Lissette's guardian should something happen to her. Hazelton is her cousin, after all, and she has more cousins in England, along with assorted other relations. We will take care of her."

"You cannot mean to take her away from France?" Rather than being happy for Lissette, Martine sounded outraged.

"At some point, yes, we will take her to England," I said. "But you may rest assured that we will always consult Lissette's wishes in making such decisions. Why wouldn't she want to see new things and meet new people? She will have the option of coming back." It dawned on me that Lissette was likely listening to me make these random promises. George and I had not had a chance to discuss any of this in detail.

I gave Martine a reassuring smile. "No decisions have been made about Lissette's future, nor will they be made without her, and it's not as if we'll be going anywhere before we learn who killed her mother."

I turned to Lissette. "Shall we go up to the flat?"

She agreed, and we made our way upstairs. Neither of us spoke until I unlocked and opened the door to Julia's room. I directed Lissette to the stack of paintings leaning against the wall and let her go through them while I looked around to see if the police had taken anything. The room looked as though nothing had been touched since George and I left it.

"Are you and Martine close?" I asked after a few moments of silence.

"We used to be," she said, taking a seat on the bed. "For at least a year now, I haven't seen her as much as I had in the past. My mother didn't want me coming here, and I had my lessons with Christine and work at home to keep me busy." She shrugged. "I think *Maman* kept me from Paris because she didn't want my father to see me, but because I also saw her friends less, they came to feel more like strangers to me. Maybe I'm just not good with people, like Edouard said about my father."

"Many people loved your father, so don't give too much credence to what Edouard says."

"Is he jealous?"

"I think he may be." If Ducasse had some hold on Julia's affections, it wouldn't be strange for Edouard to be jealous. "Were he and your mother close friends?"

"Not the way you are thinking," she said.

I let the comment rest, wondering if she had more to say on the subject. In a few moments, my patience was rewarded.

"I think he was in love with her. Maybe he still is."

"What makes you think that? Did he ever visit her in the country?"

"No, but when I came here, I saw how he acted. He always tried to be close to her. He would stand behind her and watch while she painted. He would touch her arm or her shoulder." Still facing away from me, she stroked her own arm to demonstrate. "I told her it bothered me, and she must have said something to him, because it stopped."

Her shoulders rolled forward as she lowered her head. "Now I feel badly about it. If I had left it alone, maybe he would have been around to protect her."

The sob in her voice tore at my heart. I reached across the bed and touched her shoulder. She jerked away, so instead, I stepped around the bed and sat down beside her. "If your mother thought of Edouard romantically, she would have tried to make the two of you friends. The fact that she rejected his advances instead could mean that she felt the same way you did."

She took a swipe at her eyes before looking at me. "But what if he is the one who killed her . . . because she rejected him?"

That was certainly possible. I held back a shiver. "Then it still wasn't your fault. Your mother had every right to make

that decision without any repercussions." That thought reminded me that Julia had made the decision to keep Lissette
away from her father.

"How did your mother manage to avoid Monsieur Ducasse
when she brought you here?"

"He didn't work here then, remember? *Maman* was shocked
the first time she saw him in the studio."

I could imagine. What had she thought upon seeing Ducasse
for the first time—at least I assumed it was the first time—in so
many years? Had she still clung to her love for him even as she refused to be his lover? Or had she excised him from her heart and
wanted nothing more than to protect her daughter from him?

Why had she felt Lissette needed protection from her father?
Could Julia simply have feared Ducasse's selfishness would ultimately hurt Lissette? Or was there another reason?

Lissette seemed slightly less prickly at the moment, so I ventured a question. "Do you know why your mother wanted to
keep you from your father?"

She turned around and faced me. "She was afraid of losing me."

"Christine explained that society would have rejected your
mother, but are you telling me that if your father had recognized you as his child, you would have had to leave your
mother?" Were things in France that different from England?

"He said not, but my mother worried. He was charming.
He offered me a glamorous life. She feared I might choose that
over her."

Julia might have been correct to worry. I was beginning to
think Ducasse would have promised anything to get what he
wanted. "You should never be forced to make such a decision.
Tell me about your father. Did you get on with him?"

"I suppose so. We didn't really know each other enough to
have a disagreement."

"I thought he visited you in Chartres?"

She shifted around on the bed so that she sat with her back against the wall and her legs stretched in front of her. She hugged a pillow to her chest. "He came a few times to spend the day. He was fun. He brought me chocolates. We went for walks, just the two of us. Sometimes he'd sketch. He didn't push. It was just nice to be together. The third time he came, he talked to me about Gabrielle. He said she wanted to meet me, and if she and I got along, I could live with them."

Her eyes were damp when she faced me. "I didn't want to leave my mother, our house, or Christine, so I told him I didn't want to live with him. After that, he never visited again." She looked down and picked at a loose thread on the coverlet. "Now he's gone."

Poor child. "You did nothing wrong, Lissette. You have every right to want what you want, and to express that to your own father." I longed to hug her and tell her that things would get better. She was far too young to feel such regret. Since she wasn't ready for any show of affection from me, I'd have to make do with words.

"Your mother seems to have been terrified of losing you, and it sounds like your father gave her good reason." In fact, it sounded to me as if he wanted to use Lissette to pull Julia back into his orbit—not something Lissette needed to hear right now. "None of this was your fault," I said instead.

She showed just the slightest bit of interest. Enough to make me think she might believe it someday.

"Christine spoke of Ducasse as if she knew him, too," I said. If I remembered correctly, she spoke of his selfishness. It made sense that Julia, having had another woman nearby, might have wanted to confide in her. "Christine might know more about what went on between your mother and father and why his visits stopped. Have you ever asked her?"

Lissette frowned and shook her head.

"Perhaps you should." She didn't answer, so I thought our time for sharing confidences was likely over and got to my feet.

AN ART LOVER'S GUIDE TO PARIS AND MURDER   201

"In any event, we should gather whatever you want to take to the apartment and head back. I don't know about you, but I am getting rather hungry. Are there some paintings you wish to take?"

She slipped off the bed and bent to go through the canvases. "There was a particular one I was looking for, but I don't see it here."

That reminded me to pull the tube out from under the mattress. It caught Lissette's attention, so I opened it and removed the canvas, then unrolled it on the bed. "I hope this isn't the one," I said.

"What happened to it?" Her tone held a note of disgust.

I wasn't sure what to tell her. "I assume Julia didn't like it."

Lissette examined the painting. "There's not exactly anything to like, is there?"

"What I meant was that she may have disliked whatever is beneath the black paint. Thus, she painted over it."

"She would not have done that. Canvases are not cheap. If she didn't like a painting, she'd have scraped it, perhaps turned the canvas around, and begun anew. I've seen her do it many times." She made a face at the painting. "I've never seen her do this."

I considered the idea of telling Lissette how we came to have this canvas. "What if she wanted to leave a clue?"

"A clue to what?"

If I were Lissette, I'd want to assist in this investigation, and frankly, I thought she could help. I blew out a breath. "Before your mother died, she painted this canvas, put it in that tube, and gave it to Monsieur Hubert with instructions to deliver it to George if anything should happen to her."

Lissette sank back down on the bed, her eyes wide and glistening. I shouldn't have told her. Regardless of her independent nature, she was still Julia's daughter. This was too much for her.

She actually allowed me to squeeze her shoulder and slowly

lifted her gaze to meet mine. "If there's a clue, it must be under the paint."

"Under the paint?" In my lifetime, I'd painted a few watercolors. They were awful. My sister, Lily, had the artistic talent in our family. I knew nothing about oil paint. Because of that, and because Lissette was showing her first spark of interest in our investigation, I didn't want to dismiss her suggestion. "Is it possible to remove only the black layer of paint and see what is underneath?"

"I don't know, but shouldn't we try?" She rubbed a finger over the surface. "It may not be completely dry."

"It should be done by a professional," I said.

She gave me a wry look. "There's one downstairs, but I don't know if we should trust Edouard."

For once, Lissette and I were in complete agreement. "I brought this here, hoping to ask his opinion, but now I don't think that would be wise."

Lissette chewed on a fingernail while we both studied the black square of paint. "I know someone," I said. "Monsieur Beaufoy. I think we can trust him. At least he has no reason to lie to us."

"That will have to be good enough."

Lissette rolled up the canvas, and I slid it back into the tube. We were ready to leave when I heard someone coming up the stairs. While Lissette tucked the tube under the pillow, I opened the door to the hallway and leaned out. After a few more steps on the stairs, the person came into view.

Gabrielle Ducasse.

She stopped in her tracks when she saw me. "Madame Hazelton." Her tone was less than enthusiastic. "I'm surprised to see you here."

I stepped into the hall and gestured to the open door of Julia's loft. "I brought Lissette. She is going through her mother's things."

"Is this where Julia stayed while in Paris?" She tsked. "Not exactly proper lodgings."

"What brings you here?" I asked.

She lifted her chin a notch. "Well, I've just learned that my husband kept a few odds and ends in one of these rooms up here."

"Did he?" I had a feeling there was more to it than just storing a few possessions here. I couldn't argue with Gabrielle. These were sorry accommodations, but that was exactly what they were—a place to sleep, even if just for a night or two. Thus Ducasse, who owned a home in Paris but chose instead to live on a houseboat on the Seine, also kept a garret above his studio. One his wife hadn't known about.

Or so she said.

"Did Monsieur Legrand inform you?" I asked.

"Yes. I received a note from him yesterday." Gabrielle gave a smile to Lissette, who had come to stand in the doorway. "Like Lissette, I thought I ought to come here and see if there is anything I'd like to keep or if there are any paintings that should go to Lucien, before I have someone clean the place out."

"Of course." I nodded amiably, assuming she wished to be about her business, yet she remained frozen to that spot in the hallway. "How are you faring, Lissette?" she asked.

"I am well, madame," Lissette replied in a meek voice, which she'd certainly never used when speaking to me. "And you?"

Gabrielle bobbed her head. "Fine, fine," she said, then lowered her gaze.

It occurred to me that she would rather do anything than enter her late husband's loft. I could imagine how she felt. "Would you like me to accompany you, madame? It must be very difficult to do this alone."

I half expected her to tell me to mind my own business or something of that nature. Instead, she looked at me and nodded. "If you would be so kind. I would appreciate the company."

"Of course." I gestured for Lissette to stay, but she stepped into the hall and proceeded to stick to my side. The two of us accompanied Gabrielle to her husband's door, which was right next to Julia's, something none of us chose to mention. There was no lock on the door. She pushed it open, and I followed her just inside the threshold, where she stopped and took in the room.

Giving her some time, I glanced around myself, repressing a tsk. Paul could have used a housekeeper. The room was just as small as Julia's and held even fewer furnishings—an unmade bed pushed against the wall, with a small table beside it, and two chairs near a large stove. Though it also had a sink attached to the wall, Paul had clearly not used it to do any sort of cleaning in here.

Gabrielle stepped tentatively into the room, and I noticed the floor had an uneven coating of dust. "It looks like there used to be a rug here."

"Maybe it's out for cleaning." Lissette eyed the room with disgust. "Everything in here needs cleaning. And this"—she stooped to pick up a small yellow rug from in front of the stove—"belongs next to the bed. If the marks in the dust are anything to go by."

She lifted the rug and turned in one motion, leaving a large stain on the floor exposed. I let my gaze follow Lissette, about to tell her to put it back, when I saw the underside of the rug had the same stain.

Heavens! It looked like blood—a lot of blood!

Chapter Nineteen

After instructing Lissette to put the rug back where she'd found it, I wasted no time in ushering her and Gabrielle out of the room.

"What is wrong?" Gabrielle asked when I closed the door behind us.

Lissette's wide-eyed expression told me she might have worked out the problem for herself. "That was blood on the rug, wasn't it?" She shuddered. "Ugh! I touched it."

"You can wash up in your mother's room," I said. When she scooted down the hall, I turned to Gabrielle. "Lissette was right. There was blood on the rug and the floor. I want the police to look at the room before we spend any more time in there."

Her hand rose to her chest. "I don't understand. Do you think my husband was killed in that flat?"

I took her arm and led her to the stairs. Lissette joined us at the landing, grimacing and still shaking water from her hands. "It's possible," I said. "If that room is a crime scene, we don't want to disturb anything until after the police have examined it."

"A crime scene," Gabrielle echoed, as if she couldn't quite grasp the idea. She stilled for a moment; then her legs seemed to crumple beneath her. One step above, I caught her under her arms and called out for help.

Both Martine and Edouard arrived at the foot of the stairs. The latter ran up and took Gabrielle's weight from me.

"What happened?" Martine asked, taking us in. "Did she faint?"

Edouard carried a half-conscious Gabrielle down the stairs and around the wall that partitioned off the kitchen. Lissette found a chair for her, and he maneuvered her onto it. She rested her elbows on her knees and dropped her head into her open hands.

"What is wrong with her?" Martine asked.

"She's had a shock." I faced the curious expressions of the two very confused artists. Lissette seemed to have pulled the threads together, figuring out what a crime scene in the flat of the late Paul Ducasse meant. "I believe Madame Ducasse found the site of her husband's murder."

"I thought it was at his houseboat," Edouard said.

"Something dire happened up there." I didn't want to go into too much detail. Gabrielle was already upset.

Edouard was unwilling to let it go. "Are you saying he was murdered right here, and none of us knew?"

Martine slumped against the wall. Lissette ran to fetch a second chair for her, while Edouard helped me pull the woman to her feet.

"Will you alert the police?" I asked him. "Perhaps there is a telephone at one of the businesses down the street."

"I know where to find one." He settled Martine gently into her chair, then headed for the door.

"Please ask for Inspector Cadieux," I called after him. Although, the way Cadieux had been following me, he might be waiting just outside the door.

"Now what?" Once Edouard was gone, Lissette watched me with a look of expectation. If she thought I had any answers, she was about to be disappointed. Both Martine and Gabrielle were settled. Neither in danger of fainting or falling. In fact, Martine seemed recovered at this point. Gabrielle, on the other hand, appeared almost lifeless.

I took a step toward her and touched her shoulder. "Is there anyone we can send for, Madame Ducasse? The police will be here soon and will want to question you. Would you like to have someone here with you?"

Her gaze drifted up to meet mine, her eyes conveying abject misery. "Why did he have such a place? Why was he there? Why did he insist on coming here and associating with these people?"

"We were his friends and comrades." I could almost hear Martine gnashing her teeth.

Gabrielle found the strength to rise to her feet, her hands fisted, and turned to Martine. "You people took him from me," she choked, "and now you've killed him."

"Now, now," I muttered ineffectually. Why could I never think of something of more consequence to say under these circumstances?

Gabrielle took hold of my hands. "You were a widow," she said, her eyes brimming with tears. "You understand my difficulty."

Little did she know how well I understood her situation. My late husband had shut me out of his life, too. And while he'd been discreet in his affairs, that hadn't made his cheating hurt any less. Regardless of my sympathy, I could find no comforting words. Her husband had been a louse.

"No one took Paul from you," Martine said. "He left of his own accord."

"What is happening here?"

We all jumped at the sound of Inspector Cadieux's voice. Perhaps he really had been waiting outside.

Cadieux stepped into the kitchen and gave Gabrielle a slight bow. "Has Madame Hazelton upset you?"

"Me?" How dare he make such an insinuation? "I am doing my best to comfort her."

He took us all in with a glance. "But why are you all back here? What has happened?"

"Didn't Monsieur Legrand tell you?" I asked.

"I have come to speak with Monsieur Legrand." His gaze took in Martine. "And you, as well, mademoiselle. But I have not seen the man yet. Is there some reason I should have?"

"He just left to contact you," I said, "because we believe we have found the location where Paul Ducasse was killed."

Upon hearing my words, Gabrielle broke down again. Tears streamed down her cheeks as she found her way back to her chair. I had feared that if we spoke about this in front of her, this would happen. I gave Cadieux a pleading look and tipped my head toward the stairs, hoping he would interpret the gesture to mean that we should discuss this out of her hearing.

Surprisingly, he did.

"Madame Hazelton, will you take me to this location?" Gabrielle made as if to stand, but he held up a hand to stop her. "It is not necessary to put you through this pain again, madame. Wait here, where you have friends to comfort you. I will return shortly."

I wasn't certain that Martine and Lissette would consider themselves Gabrielle's friends or that they wanted to comfort her, but I agreed that she ought not come with us. I motioned him to the stairs before he could change his mind and followed him up. He stopped when he reached the landing at the top. I stepped around him and would have moved forward, but he put out an arm to stop me.

"As much as we appreciate all your contributions to this case, Madame Hazelton, you should not assume we cannot perform our jobs without you."

Well!

"I have the highest respect for the Sûreté and am very much aware that you have been solving case after case long before I came along. I have no intention of meddling in police matters, Inspector, but sometimes things like this"—I waved my hand toward the hallway—"simply happen around me. And it was not I who found the crime scene, but Gabrielle Ducasse."

He narrowed his eyes. "And did you accuse her of the crime?"

I pushed his arm aside with far more force than was necessary. "I did not. A grieving wife had a difference of opinion with a grieving friend. They each had their own image of Monsieur Ducasse."

He frowned. "That is all?"

I stood firm. "That is all."

He studied my face, as if he wasn't quite sure I was telling the truth. The nerve! Finally, he nodded. "I am pleased to hear that. You see, Madame Ducasse has already been questioned about her husband's death. Right after his body was found and before we even considered foul play."

"Now that you have considered foul play, perhaps she ought to be questioned again," I said.

Cadieux wagged his index finger at me. "There you go again, suspecting we don't know what we are doing. Why would we question her again, eh? To see if she has an alibi? We already know she does. She was in charge of a gala affair for the exposition. She spent most of the day surrounded by her staff, organizing the event. Then spent the evening and well into the night at the celebration itself." He took a step closer. "With the prefect of police himself. Who could ask for a better witness, eh?"

He extended a hand, indicating I should precede him down

the hallway, which I did. "So, you see," he continued, "Madame Ducasse is not a suspect in her husband's murder."

I stopped at the doorway to Paul Ducasse's room. "I also see that she has very influential friends," I said.

"She is influential enough in her own right."

"Family connections?"

He nodded. "Bankers, financiers. They have interests both in and outside of the country. They are very wealthy and make significant contributions to this city. We tread very carefully around her, but that doesn't mean she could get away with murder."

He pushed open the door, then wrinkled his nose in distaste at the sight of the room.

I directed him to the rug. "It's covering what I believe is a bloodstain. Quite a bit has seeped into the rug."

He raised a brow. "She saw this?"

I assumed he meant Gabrielle. "Poor dear. Not a very pleasant scene, is it?"

"Now you have sympathy for her?"

I reminded myself that pummeling a police inspector was a bad idea and threaded my fingers together to quell the instinct. "I have always had sympathy for her. Any indications to the contrary exist only in your suspicious mind."

He shook his head. "Fine. We'll leave it at that. Thank you for bringing me here. You may go now."

"Indeed?" I leaned against the doorframe and crossed my arms. "That's rather insulting."

He looked at me as if I were barmy. "How so? I thanked you."

"Then dismissed me, like some sort of underling."

"Huh." He reached into his coat pocket, removed a notebook, and handed it to me. "If you are to stay, you must be useful, and you will follow my rules. You are not to cross this threshold, and you will record everything I tell you." He made an exaggeratedly confused face. "To me, that sounds like an underling, but if you agree to those terms, you may stay."

"I'm certain I can manage your terms."

"You are a very strange woman, Madame Hazelton. I've never seen anyone so eager to be around blood and gore."

I wrinkled my nose. "Hardly eager, but I might feel a bit proprietorial. You may recall that Julia Hazelton asked my husband to investigate Paul Ducasse's murder while the Sûreté still thought his death was an unfortunate accident."

He lifted a brow and placed his hands on his hips.

The move didn't intimidate me. "I'm not claiming any rights because we were here first . . ."

"How very fair-minded of you."

"Somehow I don't think you really mean that."

"You don't want me to say what I really mean." He gestured to the book. "Now, are you staying or not?"

"Of course I am." I opened the notebook, pulled out the expected pencil stub, and prepared to record his every word. "Carry on."

He surveyed the small room.

"You'll notice," I said, "there was a larger rug in this room at one point. That smaller one was used to cover the bloodstain."

He gave me a look of utter disbelief. "No!" He dragged out the word as he gestured to the floor. "Do you mean this big rug-sized clean spot in the dust? Thank heaven you told me, madame. I might have missed it."

"Sarcasm does not become you, Inspector."

"If you do not wish to hear it, you may go. I'll wait until an officer arrives."

"Are you expecting an officer?"

"You say Monsieur Legrand has called for one." He threw me a mischievous grin. "Perhaps you can take down our notes with both hands."

"Not if you want to read what I've written."

"Noted. Since you are here, shall we continue and finish before he arrives?"

"I am at your service."

He moved to the stove and pushed at the pipe with a long, thin object. I squinted. It was a pencil—a full-size pencil, the miserable wretch. Using the little nub, I scrawled the word *stove* on the page.

"Perhaps the other officer will bring a camera," I said. "Do you photograph crime scenes? Did you photograph Ducasse's houseboat?"

"So curious, madame," he said. He craned his neck to examine the ceiling. "The pipe is disconnected. No blackening up there." He got down on all fours next to the stove. "Scrapes in the floor here. It's been moved." He sat back on his heels, still gazing at the stove. "Looks heavy, don't you think, madame?"

"Are you asking my opinion?"

He peered over his shoulder at me, his lips twitching. "We did send a photographer to the houseboat. We also scraped and tested the substance smudged on the deck. It was blood."

"So someone attempted to clean that blood off the deck while leaving it on the edge of the boat, to make it look as if Ducasse merely fell and struck his head before entering the water."

"*Exactement.* Now, your opinion?" He gestured to the stove.

"Far too heavy for me to move," I said.

"For me, as well." He leaned forward until his face was almost touching the stove. "Aha!"

"Shall I write that down?"

He glanced at me over his shoulder. "We have blood."

I directed my gaze to the yellow rug. "I believe there's a great deal of it."

"On the stove." He gestured to the notebook while I stood staring like a fool. "You should write that down."

"Oh, yes." I shook myself from my stupor. "Of course."

"It looks like Ducasse had a scuffle with his assailant and some attempt was made to set things to rights. This chair was knocked over and turned back upright, and the missing rug you so kindly told me about went missing very recently."

"How can you tell that?"

"Monsieur Ducasse was not the best of housekeepers," he said, pointing to the floor. "This beautiful layer of dust records everything that happened on this floor. You can see a sweeping motion here. As if the rug was dragged to the door."

I took one tiny step into the room and looked at the floor. He was right. In addition to several shoe prints, marks in the dust indicated where the chair had been sitting at one time; then a swirl in the dust showed where the chair had been swiveled and set upright. I turned next to the marks near the door and had to move my foot aside. "The rug was dragged out of the room," I said.

"Indeed." Cadieux waved a hand over the room, as if setting a scene. "If he was struggling with someone over here, by the stove, he might have fallen against it."

"Which is how it was moved," I suggested.

"It would have taken some force to move it, so that's very possible. It's also possible the wound that was found on his head came from here." He pointed to the area on the edge of the stove where he'd found the blood.

"Head wounds bleed quite excessively," I said.

"How do you know that?"

"I have a daughter who likes to ride horses and has frightened the wits out of me on more than one occasion."

"Yet you are far from witless, madame."

"It's just an expression, but thank you for that."

"Ah, you are correct about the bleeding, too." He turned his back to the stove and lowered himself to the floor beside the yellow rug. "It pooled quickly here."

With the pencil, Cadieux lifted the edge of the rug to examine the wood floor beneath.

"Blood?" I asked.

"Indeed." He came to his feet, and I recorded the information in the notebook.

"So, I imagine the assailant rolled or pulled the body of Ducasse onto the missing rug. Perhaps wrapping it around him so he could remove the body and, ultimately, throw it in the Seine."

"Leading everyone to believe he drowned," I said. "I suppose the rug is at the bottom of the river."

The inspector smiled.

I gaped. "You already have it!"

"Courtesy of Madame See-nothing. It obviously didn't come from the boat. Nor was it from his house." He huffed. "We didn't know about this place."

The sound of boots on the stairs caught my attention. I leaned back into the hall to see Edouard leading a young, uniformed officer up to the landing. Cadieux came to the door and slipped the notebook out of my hands before greeting the reinforcement. Edouard headed back down the stairs.

While Cadieux brought the new officer up to speed, I moved out to the hallway. I was sure the inspector meant for me to leave, but I hoped to linger—and listen—as long as possible. I let my gaze wander to the window. It looked like the clouds were finally lifting. A bit of air would be refreshing after the stuffiness of Ducasse's room. My hand was on the door to the balcony before I realized what I was doing.

"This door leads to the balcony," I said. I turned around to see Cadieux staring at me as if I had just divulged the secret of life.

I pushed the door open, and both men followed me out to the timber balcony, which ran parallel to the hallway along the back of the building and ended in stairs down to the alley below. "Is that blood?" I asked, pointing to a smear on the top step.

The junior officer worked his way slowly down the stairs, examining them for signs that the body of Paul Ducasse had been dragged down them. Cadieux and I remained on the balcony so as not to mar any evidence he found.

"There's a stable across the alley," I told him. "The killer could have hired a cart or wagon to haul the body away."

"A convenient way to remove the body," Cadieux said. "Once he was wrapped in the rug, it would be easy enough to drag him down the stairs and perhaps onto a wagon waiting below, as you suggest. Very neat. No need to worry about the people in the studio."

I opened my empty hands. "I hope you weren't expecting me to write all that down. And what if the killer was one of the people in the studio? Or both? Have you interviewed them yet?"

"Always asking questions, Madame Hazelton," he said. "Do you have reason to suspect one of them?"

"I'm told that one was in love with Julia, and the other with Ducasse. It might be worth your while to have a conversation with them."

He took my elbow and escorted me back inside. "You have been very helpful, madame, but it's time to allow the police to do our work."

"And here I thought you were enjoying my company," I said. "Before I go, can you at least tell me what is happening with the evidence my husband brought you today?"

Cadieux took a step back and gazed at me. "Ah, yes, the evidence you mentioned earlier."

"He took the items to the Sûreté a few hours ago, if not longer, hoping to deliver them to you."

"I was not there, but tell me, what did he have to break into to obtain his evidence this time?"

"Really, Inspector, one instance of trespass and you brand him as some sort of miscreant. These items were freely given.

One is film taken at the time the footbridge collapsed. The dagger was found at the scene."

Cadieux's expression told me he was impressed. "I look forward to examining them, which I will do once we are finished here. But I begin to wonder if I will ever be finished here."

"That sounds as though you are telling me to leave." It also sounded as if he was entirely out of patience with me.

He gave me a sharp nod. "I am telling everyone to leave. This is a crime scene, and we can't allow anyone to contaminate it."

Cadieux told the other officer he was clearing the building, then led me downstairs, where the two artists waited with Gabrielle and Lissette. "I'm afraid you must all vacate the premises for now," he announced to the group at large.

"I must leave my own building?" Edouard said in a voice of outrage.

Cadieux escorted both the artists to the door. "It is temporary, I assure you. I'll take your statements tomorrow and let you know when you can return."

I turned to Gabrielle. "May we drop you somewhere, Madame Ducasse?"

"That won't be necessary," Cadieux said as he closed the front door. "Officer Andrade." He gestured to the young policeman coming down the stairs. "You will take madame home. Then stop at the Sûreté for a camera."

Cadieux nodded to me, so I turned to Lissette. "Are you ready? I suppose we shall have to find a cab."

Lissette moved to Julia's work area and picked up the tube containing her canvas. She must have slipped upstairs when I was in the next room with Cadieux.

"What is that?" Cadieux gestured to the tube. "I'm afraid you may not remove anything from the premises until the police are through with it."

"Oh, no, monsieur. This is my work that I brought to show Monsieur Legrand." Lissette gave Cadieux such a solemn gaze,

I almost believed her myself. "I wanted his opinion as an artist."

"Very well, then, you may take it with you," he said.

I had no intention of correcting her and instead held the door for her to exit in front of me. Once on the street, we walked around the corner, where we might find a cab, and I looked at her with new eyes. "Cheeky little thing, aren't you?"

She grinned. "I don't know what that means, madame, but I think I like it."

Frankly, so did I, and at least her actions had produced the result we wanted. "Let's get that painting to Monsieur Beaufoy, shall we?"

Chapter Twenty

❧

We took a cab to Monsieur Beaufoy's home in the sixth district. He answered the door himself and greeted us warmly when he recognized me.

"Come in, Madame Hazelton." He gave me a courtly bow and spread his arm to the side, ushering us through the door. "Unless, of course, you are here to arrest me," he added, reminding me that George and I had been rather suspicious of him at first.

"I am not the police, Monsieur Beaufoy, so have no fear." I introduced Lissette as Lady Julia's daughter. "We are here about a matter of art. A rather technical matter. I'd hoped you might lend your expertise."

"Excellent. Then you must come to my office." He led us through a sitting room to his wood-paneled office. Ignoring the desk, he seated us around a low tea table and gestured to the tube Lissette carried. "It looks as though you have something to show me?"

"It's something Julia Hazelton very specifically wanted my husband to have," I said. "It's a painting of hers."

His attentive expression faltered a bit. "I hope you are not here to ask about its value."

"No, it's in need of some repair. Someone has painted over it, and I hoped you knew if, and how, that paint could be removed without damaging the work beneath."

His gaze sharpened once again. "May I see it?"

Lissette removed the canvas from the tube and spread it on the table. Beaufoy didn't attempt to hide the shock in his expression. "Does this have something to do with Lady Julia's murder?"

"I suspect it might," I said. "Obviously, in its present state, it's difficult to know what it might represent, but I hope once we reveal whatever is hiding under the black oil paint, we'll have a better understanding." I sighed. "What is your opinion? Can it be done?"

He frowned. "Perhaps. But I wonder, madame, why have you not taken this to the police?"

Lissette parted her lips to reply, but I spoke first. "I feared they would leave it too long. Since the paint is not completely dry, I thought this must be done quickly and by an expert. This is a delicate process, is it not?"

He muttered some words that I took for agreement, so I continued. "We all want justice served, particularly Julia's daughter." I gestured to Lissette. On cue, she dropped her head and folded her hands in an attempt to look demure.

"To that end, we are taking the extra step to ensure this is handled properly," I continued.

A look of satisfaction crossed his face. The flattery was working.

"And if the painting does shed some light on the case," he said, "I assume you will then hand it over to the inspector in charge of the investigation?"

"Of course," I said. "We are all on the same side, after all."

He held up a hand to stop me. "I am happy to help you. It is

tricky, and I may damage the original painting, you understand, but I can see the black paint is fresh. I should be able to
remove it."

"Thank you, monsieur!" Lissette's voice held relief.

Beaufoy would work on the painting immediately and hoped
to deliver it to us in a day or two at most. I gave him our Paris
address and offered to compensate him for his time, but he waved
me off.

"It is my pleasure, madame, to help you to solve this most
heinous crime."

"You are very kind, Monsieur Beaufoy," I said.

He walked us to the door, and we said our farewells. As Lissette and I crossed the courtyard to the outside door, her steps
slowed.

"Monsieur Beaufoy has no reason to purposely damage
the painting, does he?" she asked. "If it is a clue, he could destroy it."

Her question gave me a chill and made me want to turn
around and wrench the canvas from his wicked hands. Except
he really had no motive to damage the painting. He was not a
suspect in the murders—was he? "The art world here is small,"
I said. "I think we can trust him."

Lissette nodded. "We have to trust someone."

Once we left Monsieur Beaufoy's building, I looked up and
down the street, hoping to find a cab. My eye was caught by a
figure emerging from the building on the opposite corner. She
shook the hand of a gentleman, who then disappeared inside
the building.

"What is wrong?" Lissette asked, coming to a stop at my
side.

"Is that Christine?" I directed her gaze to the young woman.
With the traffic moving in both directions across the broad avenue, it was difficult to see her clearly before she climbed into a
cab and drove away.

Lissette frowned. "It might be her. I think she has family in Paris."

I took a second look at the building I'd seen her emerge from. It looked . . . expensive. "Would she have family in this neighborhood? You saw what Monsieur Beaufoy's home looked like. I didn't get the impression Christine came from wealth."

"No, I don't believe she does. But there are also businesses on this street. Maybe she was shopping."

Lissette was right. I saw a few shop fronts along the street, but Christine had come through a courtyard door, as we had. There were private residences inside. It was possible that she had been conducting business with the gentleman who had escorted her out, but what kind of business?

"I'm sure that's all it is." Lissette took my hand, as if to hurry me along the street. "Christine was probably visiting a friend or maybe family who work there. We should find a cab."

If Christine was innocently visiting family, she would have had Bridget with her, but somehow, she had managed to leave the apartment by herself. And who was this family? She'd told me her mother's people had turned her away. Her own father had abandoned them. Considering this bad blood, it seemed hard to believe either side of her family would have opened their arms to her in response to a note she had penned only this morning.

Christine was up to something, and I had a feeling Lissette knew what it was. I fell into step beside her and wondered why she was lying to me.

My attempts at conversation on the carriage ride back to the apartment were fruitless. Either Lissette didn't want to talk or she didn't want to talk with me or she didn't want to talk about Christine. All three could be true, but I suspected the last. She'd already proven that she was willing to lie for her friend.

I did ask a few questions aimed at learning Lissette's opinion about Christine's future: Was she surprised Lady Julia had left nothing to Christine in her will? Had Christine made any plans? Did she hope to continue making perfume?

Her answers were all various forms of "I don't know," followed by a series of shrugs and blank expressions.

Finally, we arrived at our building. Lissette rang the bell while I paid the driver. By the time I'd turned around, *madame la concierge* had opened the gate. I'd become used to seeing both husband and wife wearing stern expressions of disapproval whether we were coming or going and regardless of the time of day. I'd come to the conclusion that they simply didn't like to be disturbed. Perhaps they ought to have some other occupation.

The expression she wore as she let us into the courtyard was different than usual. This one was far more concerning and eerily familiar. It fell somewhere between the look my late husband used to give me when he was about to deliver some criticism and the one my mother used when I was a child that meant I was in deep trouble. My sense of dread was compounded by the fact that the Kendricks' housekeeper stood behind her, wearing a similar expression. Whatever the problem was, there would be no putting it off.

"You go on in, Lissette," I told her. "There's something I want to discuss with these ladies."

Lissette gave the women a friendly smile and headed for the stairs. She turned back when she reached them and frowned when she realized we all watched her. Gathering her skirts, she trotted up the stairs to the apartment. As soon as the door closed behind her, the two women spoke at once.

"Madame, you must exert some control over the members of your household—"

"I'm sure it is not your fault, madame. You could not possibly know—"

"Expect some propriety—"

"You must take her in hand—"

"Out the window—"

"Would not want to tell Madame Kendrick—"

"Stop! *Mesdames, arêtez!*" I held up my hands in protest. "I cannot keep up. I am only catching a few words at a time from each of you."

They stopped talking, and the housekeeper folded her hands in front of her, leading me to believe she was the more patient of the two. I turned to the concierge. "Madame, are you telling me that someone in my household threw something out the window?"

Her face was pinched with impatience. "No. I am telling you one of your household took *herself* out the window and climbed down the trellis to the street."

I gasped, which brought some relief to the housekeeper's expression as she realized that I did not condone such behavior. Even *madame la concierge* bobbed her head in approval of my reaction, though it did not stem the flow of her grievance.

"In broad daylight," she continued, "where anyone could see her and wonder about the people who live in this building. I will not have it, madame!"

"Nor should you." I turned to the housekeeper. "I assume we are speaking of Christine Granger? Has she returned?" At least now I knew how she had managed to leave the house without Bridget at her side.

The housekeeper nodded, and I returned my attention to the concierge. "This behavior will not happen again," I told her. "Thank you for making me aware of it. I will address the matter with Mademoiselle Granger immediately."

The concierge bobbed her head and took a step back, rather as if she had run out of steam. The housekeeper, too, seemed calmer. Perhaps they had expected some sort of argument or denial.

"Is that all, then?"

They both agreed that it was, so with nothing further to detain me, I headed for the apartment and my confrontation with Christine. The housekeeper followed behind me, then passed me on the stairs and opened the door.

"Pardon, madame," she said. "I forgot to tell you Monsieur Hazelton's sister has arrived."

While that information lifted my spirits, I could see it was just one more chore for the housekeeper. "We have made a hectic day for you, haven't we?"

She lifted her shoulders in that French manner, which could mean just about anything. "It is my job," she said.

"Has Monsieur Hazelton returned yet?"

"No, madame."

That decided me. I'd check on Fiona first. If no one had been here to greet her when she arrived, she deserved my attention now. After all, she was probably desolate.

And that decision had absolutely nothing to do with putting off my conversation with Christine. Nothing at all.

I found out which bedroom she'd been given and headed upstairs, where I tapped on her door, one room down from ours, and let myself in. I found my sister-in-law seated at the table on the narrow balcony, enjoying a cup of tea. The sun cast a bronze sheen on her chestnut hair as she turned to greet me. Seeing her there, with her patrician features and her eyes the same green as George's, I found the scene so familiar, so calm, so British, that it rather choked me up. And once it did, the sobs simply escaped me uncontrollably.

After a moment of surprise, Fiona moved to my side and led me to a chair at the table. Then she seated herself and poured me a cup of tea.

I was horrified. What was the matter with me?

"Drink," she ordered. "You'll soon feel better."

I drank, and she was right. The sobs relented, and as soon as I could speak once more, I apologized. "Forgive me, Fiona. I ought to be consoling you on your loss, and instead . . ."

"I suspect you've been under a bit of pressure over the past few days. When you saw a friendly face, that pressure exploded," she said.

"Yes! I had no idea all that was just lurking inside me, waiting for an excuse to come out."

"It's understandable," she said. "You, too, are dealing with the death of a relative. I'm certain you've had to console George and then Julia's daughter, and you've been doing everything in another language. That's a great deal to have on one's plate. Your own emotions and the pressure of coping were bound to come out at some point."

"I'm glad that they waited until I was with a sympathetic friend. And speaking of which, I'm so sorry for your loss, Fiona."

She reached across the table for my hand and squeezed it. "Thank you, Frances. I'll admit anger is my primary emotion regarding her death. My aunt finally had the life she wanted, and some horrible person took it away from her. I understand her daughter is here. How is she managing?"

I parted my lips to speak, then paused as I realized what she'd said. In fact, this was the second reference she'd made to Lissette. "How long have you known that Julia had a daughter? Did you know she lived in Paris?"

Fiona gave me a look of incredulity. "Don't be ridiculous. Of course I knew. Do you honestly think there could be such a secret in my family and I would be ignorant of it? Come now, Frances, you know me better than that."

"No one compares to you when it comes to ferreting out the details of a secret, but I'm convinced that Julia wasn't aware you knew about her life here. How did you find out?"

"I'll confess. It was no great feat of espionage. My mother told me." She shrugged upon seeing my expression of surprise. "I knew something must be going on with all the trips Aunt Julia made to Paris. Then she'd return with a single gown or sometimes completely empty handed." She let out a huff and raised her eyes to heaven. "I don't know why my father never became suspicious."

"He probably wasn't paying as close attention as you were. Julia was his sister. If she wasn't announcing an impending wedding, her actions had little to do with him." I sipped my tea and settled in for the rest of the story.

"You could be right. Regardless, Mother required only the tiniest bit of prodding to reveal the whole story. Aunt Julia was very independent and insisted she could manage everything herself. Mother thought that would be her downfall, and she considered it best that Julia had an accomplice, whether she knew about it or not. Lissette was around four years old when Mother entrusted me with their secret. She made me promise to keep it and to keep my knowledge a secret from Aunt Julia."

That gave me pause. "What a shame. It might have been comforting to Julia to know she had an ally in the family even after your mother passed."

Fiona pursed her lips. "It looks like she chose George as her ally."

"Don't be envious, Fiona. She chose George only for his legal expertise." I thought about that for a moment. "And perhaps because he didn't ask a lot of questions."

"Yes, I did ask a great many questions, some of which my mother even answered. After she died, I had to be content to keep an eye on Julia and Lissette from a distance."

"What do you mean? How did you keep an eye on them? Did you have spies?"

She grinned.

"Not Christine Granger?"

"The foster mother's daughter? No. The neighbor. The tenant farmer. I've been paying him for a number of years." She frowned. "Is there something I should know about Mademoiselle Granger?"

I glanced out at the street below the balcony. It wasn't such a very long drop, but I wondered how Christine had the courage and audacity to climb down. I looked back at Fiona. "Christine is something of a mystery and"—I sighed—"possibly a suspect."

I explained how we'd seen Christine first at the Ducasse tribute. That she'd told us she returned the following morning to the farm, but I'd learned from the neighbor, Fiona's spy, that Christine wasn't at the chateau when he stopped by at midday. And even though she tutored Lissette for a number of years, acted as housekeeper, and helped Julia with the perfumery, Julia had not mentioned Christine in her will.

"Julia leaving her with no security might be a motive," Fiona said. "And you say she was in Paris when Julia was murdered?"

"She might have been in Paris. What we know is that she was not at Julia's house, where she claimed to be."

Fiona frowned. "That is rather suspicious."

"It gets worse," I said. "Today she said she'd be writing to relatives in Paris. I told her to make sure Bridget accompanied her if she left the apartment. Instead, she climbed out the window. I assume to avoid Bridget. Lissette and I saw her leaving a man's house when we paid a call across the street."

Fiona glanced down at the street and back at me with a look of horror. "She climbed out from this floor?"

"The concierge saw her and complained to the housekeeper, Madame Fontaine. Both of them pounced on me when I returned. I am supposed to be speaking to Christine about the incident now." I chuckled. "But thankfully, you had arrived, which allowed me to put it off."

"I can't blame you for that. What do you think she was up to that she had to avoid your maid's company?"

"I've no idea." I ran my finger around the rim of my saucer while I thought and Fiona patiently waited.

"The problem," I said, "is that she is an adult, or very nearly one, and she is entitled to some privacy. For all I know, she was seeking employment. She has experience in managing a household, and in managing a business, now that I think of it. Perhaps she was applying for a position in the perfume industry."

Fiona looked doubtful, but I forged ahead. "The point is, she is not my daughter, my ward, or my employee. I don't have a right to know her business. I simply wanted to keep her safe."

"Climbing out of windows is hardly safe, and if she is living in this house, you have a right to expect that she will not make a spectacle of herself by doing such a thing."

"Yes, but I think that's as far as I dare go. Lissette has just lost both her father and mother. I don't want to be the reason she loses her longtime friend, too."

"If Julia left Christine with no security, no financial reason to stay, Lissette had better give her one, or Christine may leave her, anyway."

That would be unfortunate, but with nothing left to lose, I feared Christine could be planning something far worse than simply leaving.

Chapter Twenty-one

I felt much better after my conversation with Fiona. In part because she had agreed to take on the arrangements for a memorial service for Julia here in Paris—after consulting with Lissette, of course.

As expected, my conversation with Christine did not go half so well. She was horribly embarrassed to learn she'd been seen climbing out the window and down the trellis. That was something, I suppose, and it gave me reason to believe it might not happen again.

As to why it had happened in the first place, she claimed she was simply uncomfortable having a maid follow her around. She insisted she'd always gone about on her own at home and pooh-poohed my observation that Chartres was not Paris. Still, she agreed to take some member of the household with her the next time she needed to venture out.

I took that as a victory. It was my only one. When I asked where she'd gone, she made some vague mention of a long-lost relative. Since that was what Lissette had suggested, I assumed she and Christine had discussed their cover story. I wondered what they were up to.

The five of us had dinner at home. George arrived just in time to greet his sister and introduce her to Lissette and Christine before we were called to the dining room. Lissette warmed up to Fiona quickly. Quite a contrast to her coolness toward me, though I do believe her attitude at that point was more a matter of form than an active dislike of me. At least that was what I told myself.

We kept to polite conversation throughout the meal. Fiona asked for Lissette's opinion regarding the memorial service—where it should be held and who should be invited. She offered to take Christine and Lissette shopping for something suitable to wear. Both of them agreed eagerly. Once dinner was over, the girls returned to their rooms, and George, Fiona, and I retired to the salon to have coffee and to open the topic that was at the top of everyone's minds—the murders.

"It's one thing to discuss Aunt Julia's will with Lissette," George said, forgoing a seat to pace behind the sofa, "but I simply can't bring myself to mention the details of the investigation while she's in the room."

Fiona and I took the two chairs facing the sofa so George wouldn't be walking back and forth behind us. "I obviously misjudged the situation when I suggested she help us. I neglected to take her age into consideration, and of course, the victims are her parents. Investigating with us today was difficult for her." I told them how Lissette had run off this afternoon while I was discussing her father with the artists at the studio. "I suspect that is why she ran away from you at the exposition, George. It became too much for her to bear, so she simply removed herself."

"Now that I'm here, you needn't take her with you," Fiona said. "But shouldn't the police be investigating?"

"They are," George said. "We are just providing assistance."

"You were at the Sûreté quite late," I said to him. "Were you waiting for Cadieux to return?"

"I was. I had no intention of leaving our evidence in the hands of anyone else. It was Cadieux or no one." He stopped his pacing and joined Fiona and me, though he still didn't take a seat.

"The police must be very grateful to you if your investigation turns up such significant items," Fiona observed, causing both of us to laugh.

"I'd say he was intrigued with the items," George said, "but annoyed that I was the one who brought them."

"He wasn't particularly happy with me today, either," I said. "Did he tell you he was at Julia's studio this afternoon?"

"Yes, he mentioned that." George finally settled on the sofa and poured himself a cup of coffee. "It sounds like Ducasse was not murdered on his houseboat, after all."

I shook my head. "That was just a good place to dispose of him."

Fiona made a sound of distaste. "If the two of you were discussing matters like this in front of Lissette, I completely understand why she was distressed."

George and I denied doing any such thing, then gave each other guilty looks. "She was there when I realized Ducasse might have been murdered in his garret," I said. "In fact, it was she who uncovered the blood."

"It's possible I mentioned a few details in her presence that might have been better left unsaid," George added. "Now I feel badly for having upset her."

"Since we're talking about guilty feelings," I said, "there's something I must confess." I peeked over my shoulder to make sure the door leading to the foyer and the stairs was closed. When I turned back, they were both staring at me as if I were about to confess that I was the murderer. "For goodness' sake, I didn't do anything. I'm just suspicious of Christine."

"What do you think she's done?" George asked.

"She thinks Christine murdered Aunt Julia," Fiona said.

"No," I said. "Well, perhaps. I've caught her in a few lies, and that leads me to be suspicious of her." I reminded George that Christine had said she'd returned home the morning after the Ducasse tribute. "But the neighbor told me she hadn't returned by lunchtime that day. I'm not saying she is our murderer, just that she lied about where she was at the time."

"Then there was her deception today," Fiona said.

I recounted to George the story of Christine sneaking out the window. "And finally, there was the reason she gave us for her appearance at the Ducasse tribute."

George stared up at the ceiling for a moment, then suddenly snapped his fingers. "She told us that Lucien Allard had arranged for her to have an interview with Gaston Worth, the designer," he said, "to convince him to sell Julia's latest scent."

"That's what she said," I agreed. "But Lucien Allard had a different story. He said he had promised to introduce *Julia* to the designer, but that introduction had never taken place. He denied ever making an appointment for Christine or telling her he would do so. He scoffed at the very idea of the great Worth speaking to anyone but the owner of the perfumery."

"A misunderstanding?" George drummed his fingers on the arm of the sofa.

"Perhaps, but he made a suggestion that has me troubled." I threw another glance at the closed door and leaned over the table toward George. Fiona followed suit. "What if," I continued, "she was offering to sell the formula for the perfume, so Worth could have it made himself under the Worth label?"

Fiona gasped. "It isn't hers to sell, is it? Why would she do such a thing?"

I held up my hands. "I don't know that she would. Monsieur Allard planted that seed in my head, and it has taken root. She had a hand in creating the scents. Julia has left her no part of the business, or anything else, for that matter. And she's been acting mysteriously. If she's not stealing perfume formulas, she may be up to something even worse."

"That sounds as though you do think she may have murdered Aunt Julia." Fiona looked more concerned than shocked. "But she had motive to do so only if she knew that Julia was leaving her nothing."

"Not necessarily," George said. "If Christine knew she'd inherit nothing, she'd be better off with Aunt Julia alive."

"I disagree," I said. "If Christine wanted the perfumery for herself, she'd find it much easier to steal it from Lissette than from Julia."

"Good point," George said. "I doubt she would have to steal it. Christine knows very well how to get Lissette to do as she wants."

He was certainly right about that. "Lissette may not have been lying for Christine today, but she was ready with excuses for her."

Fiona shook her head. "What about the two artists you spoke of? Both of them were crossed in love. One loved Julia, and the other Ducasse."

"If unrequited love is a motive, they qualify," I said. "As far as Julia's murder, they were in the area when she was killed. And they both lied about it."

"As did Christine," George said.

"We need to get to the bottom of this quickly," I said. "I don't know if Christine Granger deserves our sympathy and assistance or if she's a murderer."

"Or just a thief," Fiona added. George and I looked to her for an explanation. "If she is trying to sell the formula for one of the perfumes, then she is effectively stealing from Lissette."

"And I think she's quite fond of Lissette," I said. "She wouldn't want to harm her."

Fiona gave me a hard look. "I'd say killing Lissette's mother would fall into that category."

I dropped my head into my hands and massaged my temples. "This investigation has me so confused. It's the two murders. Evidence and suspects keep crossing from one case to the other."

"That's because the two murders are connected," George said. "Aunt Julia knew something about Ducasse's murder, and that's why she was killed."

"If the same person murdered them both," I said, "then who had access to them both?"

"And a motive," Fiona added. "For Ducasse, I'd say his wife. And if the man was in love with Aunt Julia, why wouldn't she want to kill her, too?" She tossed her head. "In for a penny, in for a pound, I say."

"The police questioned her as soon as Ducasse was found to be dead," George said. "They say she has an alibi."

"She was at an event with the *préfet de police*," I said to clarify. "In fact, I believe Cadieux said she was hosting the event."

Fiona studied her fingernails. "*They* say. *He* said. Did either of you verify this alibi yourself?"

No. George and I stared at each other until he spoke. "We have no reason to think the police got it wrong, but I'll check on it tomorrow."

Pleased, Fiona pushed on. "What about the two artists?"

I shook my head. "They had motives and opportunity, and with all Martine's sharp tools, they certainly had the means."

"But?" George lifted a brow.

"They were both at the studio the night Ducasse was murdered," I continued. "And I saw them together in the Tuileries—so, near the exposition grounds—not long before Julia was murdered."

"I see," George said. "The problem is that they were together."

Fiona stared at us, waiting for an explanation.

"If Martine wanted to murder Julia to have Ducasse to herself, and if Edouard wanted to get rid of Ducasse so he could have Julia, neither of them would stand quietly by while the other murdered the person they loved," I said. "Besides, Ducasse was murdered days before Julia. Even if Edouard killed him, thinking he was a rival for Julia's affections, there would be no point for Martine to kill Julia, because her love was already dead. Murdering Julia would not have brought back Ducasse."

George nodded his agreement, but Fiona wasn't convinced. "After all the months or years of unrequited love, don't you think they might simply have decided that if they can't have the people they love, then no one will have them? So, they each murdered their own loved one, then took solace in one another."

I stared at her in horror. "That is . . . possible." I turned to George, who also looked rather ill at the picture his sister had painted. "Isn't it?"

"Yes," he said. "It's very possible."

Fiona flapped a hand. "Of course it is." She reached for the coffeepot. "Now I know why you two find this occupation so endlessly engrossing. Have you any other suspects?"

George and I were alone at the breakfast table the following morning. It was early, and there was no sign of Fiona or the girls. I had to think of another way to refer to them. Christine was hardly a girl, and Lissette probably wouldn't appreciate the sobriquet.

After our discussion last night, we'd made our schedule for today. George and I had an early appointment with Monsieur Hubert at his request. We assumed he must have something new to tell us about Julia's will. After that, we'd head to the Sûreté and check in with Cadieux regarding the film and the dagger. Once we finished there, we'd return home, and I'd go shopping with Fiona and the girls, while George would find a way to verify Gabrielle Ducasse's alibi. All in all, a full day.

George consulted his pocket watch. "Our appointment is in thirty minutes. Are you ready?"

I blotted my lips with my napkin, then dropped it on the table as I came to my feet. "I'll just fetch my hat."

Blakely had gone down the street to hire a cab for the day. *Madame la concierge* opened the outer door to reveal the cab waiting on the street just as George and I crossed the courtyard. "I hope everything will be quiet today, madame," she said as I passed her.

Quiet was far too much to hope for, but at least I didn't think anyone would be dangling from the trellis. I gave her my assurances and let George hand me into the cab after Blakely climbed out. As we pulled away from the curb, I glanced out to see that Blakely had said something to make the concierge laugh, which put a smile on my face.

Fifteen minutes later, a secretary led us to Monsieur Hubert's office, where the solicitor gave us a cheerful greeting. Ah, presumably, we weren't summoned for bad news.

"I have heard from the *notaire* for the Ducasse estate," he said once we were all seated. "He feels confident all of the late Monsieur Ducasse's offspring are accounted for, and will proceed to apportion the estate. It could still take several weeks, of course, but I thought you would like to know things are moving ahead."

"That was rather fast," George observed.

"Nine days since Ducasse passed," Hubert mused. "That isn't much time, but I suspect the Ducasse lawyers already had the details of his other child, and the *notaire* needed only to verify that the person was alive and interested in collecting an inheritance."

"Does that mean Madame Ducasse, Lissette, and this other child will split Ducasse's fortune?" George asked. "I wonder if Ducasse had much of a fortune to disburse."

Hubert looked flustered by George's words. "I'm afraid I know nothing about his assets, or how they are to be divided, but the man was an artist of some renown, with many paintings still unsold. I would imagine they are quite valuable."

He didn't say the words *now that Ducasse is dead*. He didn't have to. Since there would be no future Ducasse paintings, those remaining would become far more valuable.

"Yes," I said. "I would imagine valuations could take some time."

"I will certainly keep you abreast of the progress."

"Do you know the identity of the other child?" I asked.

" I do not, madame." Hubert frowned in disapproval. "Even if I did, it wouldn't be proper to share that information with you."

"The other beneficiary is Lissette's half-sibling," I continued. "After losing her mother and father, she may wish to form an acquaintance with this person."

Now I had George frowning at me. "She may not wish to do so. We ought to check with Lissette first."

"Do that and let me know," Hubert said. "I can make her wishes known to the Ducasse lawyers. If both parties agree to a meeting, it could be arranged."

He and George came to their feet. Hubert reached over the desk to shake George's hand, then noticed I had remained seated. "Is there something else you wish to discuss, madame?"

"Yes, regarding Lady Julia. Did she ever discuss Mademoiselle Granger's role in the perfume business with you?"

He lowered himself to his chair while George eyed me with curiosity. "She had no official role in the company. It was a sole proprietorship. Everything was in Madame Hazelton's name, though both her daughter and Mademoiselle Granger did some sort of work for her."

"I see. Then did Madame Hazelton ever talk to you about copyright or patent protection of her products?"

Hubert adjusted his spectacles and peered at me. "For her perfumes? No, indeed she cannot copyright the recipes, or formulas, if you prefer. The courts do not allow it. Even if they did, it would require the perfumer to release to some agency what is usually a closely guarded formula. Most feel they can better keep the secret themselves."

George and I exchanged uneasy glances before I continued. "But what if someone within the company makes off with the formula and attempts to sell it?"

"Most perfumers are small family businesses. Even so, these formulas are known by only a few people." He paused to gauge our insistence, then sighed. "Should such a betrayal happen, the rightful owner could sue in court. They would have to prove the scoundrel has no right of ownership."

"Have you seen anything in Lady Julia's documents that gives the right of ownership of her scents to Christine Granger?" George asked.

Hubert's brows lowered. "I most definitely have not, or I would have conveyed that information to you at once. Are you telling me that Mademoiselle Granger is producing one of Lady Julia's products and calling it her own?"

"At the moment, we have only suspicions," I said. "We wished to know how to act if we find that is the case."

"That would be terrible." Hubert tut-tutted. "After all Julia has done for that girl, it would seem most ungrateful."

"We will alert you if any lawsuit becomes necessary," George said. "Thank you for your time, monsieur. I assume we are done here?"

"Actually, I have one more question," I said. Hubert, who had half risen, sat back in his chair and raised his brows. "Did Julia Hazelton know Paul Ducasse planned to leave a settlement for Lissette?"

"She never mentioned it to me," Hubert replied. "I learned of it only when the Ducasse attorney notified me."

I turned to George, who shook his head. "She never said anything to me about the state of Ducasse's affairs. I'm not sure she would have approved," he added. "To avoid argument, Ducasse may have simply kept this to himself."

Since Monsieur Hubert could enlighten us no further, George and I took our leave.

"What was that about?" George asked once we were settled back in the cab, on our way to pay a call on Inspector Cadieux.

"I have an idea taking form in my head," I said. "But if I try to grasp it now, I fear it will vanish." I gave him a helpless look. "It needs some time to become solid."

"I understand," he said. "Ignore it for the moment and let me ask you this. Do you suppose Madame Ducasse knew her husband was leaving a large legacy to his daughter?"

"She knew he had a daughter, but it's difficult to know if Ducasse kept the bequest from her or if he reveled in the drama of telling Gabrielle his plans."

"She can't have been happy to hear she'd be sharing his fortune with his illegitimate children," George said. "If he had told her about it, this might give her a motive for his murder."

"But murdering her husband would only hasten the undesirable outcome," I said. "Besides, she has an alibi, remember? I know you'll be looking into that, but now that I've seen the murder scene, I don't think Gabrielle could have put up the sort of fight that apparently happened there."

George was not convinced. "You said he hit his head against a stove. All she had to do was put him off-balance. The force of a fall against such an object could cause a fatal blow."

"If the body had been found in the loft, I might agree with you. Moving it to the Seine is well beyond her strength. Besides, she's been kind to Lissette, and I'm certain she was not feigning her shock and distress at the studio."

"Yes, I suppose it is not always the spouse, is it?"

"I'm not entirely prepared to rule her out. Since we are calling on Cadieux, anyway, we ought to convey this new bit of information, don't you think?"

"Indeed. I also wonder if the film has brought any revelations."

"With everything that happened afterward, I'd completely

forgotten about the film. Have you not seen it, even after waiting for Cadieux?"

"I have not," he said, sounding quite disgruntled. "As I mentioned yesterday, Cadieux was not particularly pleased to find I had brought in the evidence, and was in no mood to share. He had me give a statement to one of his officers while he went off to find his dinner. At least that's what I suspect. It was late, and now that I know he'd been working all day, I suppose that was all I ought to have expected."

We'd come to a stop at the aged limestone walls of the Sûreté building. George climbed out and reached back to assist me.

"Hopefully, the inspector is here today," I said as we made our way inside.

There were quite a few people scattered around the lobby, sitting, standing, leaning against walls. None of them looked particularly nefarious. We spotted Cadieux among them and approached him as he gestured impatiently to two women. Upon seeing us, he handed them off to a uniformed officer and motioned for us to follow him down a long hallway to a small room, where he closed the door behind us.

There was an old wooden table in the center of the room and a scattering of chairs around it. Cadieux waved us to the chairs and leaned his hip on the corner of the table. "The newspapers printed a story about the bridge collapse and included a statement that we are eager to interview anyone who was in the area at the time." He tipped his head in the direction of the lobby. "They've been filing in nonstop all morning."

"That sounds like a positive step," I said.

"It is an act of desperation," he said. "One I don't think was necessary. At least not yet."

"It hasn't proved helpful?" George asked.

"Everyone is eager to tell their story, but no one saw anyone stab Madame Hazelton." With a wince, he amended his statement. "The other Madame Hazelton."

"I assumed as much," I said. "What about the film George turned over yesterday? Did that produce any leads?"

Cadieux moved around the table and slumped into a chair. He pointed to his eye. "Do you see these eyes? I'm surprised they even work anymore."

George let out a tsk. "They do look rather red, now that you mention it."

"I watched that film over and over throughout the night. The camera never had a view of Julia Hazelton. It showed how the crowd surged, but identifying the people in it would be impossible." Cadieux waved his hand to emphasize the last word.

"The only time individuals became clear is when they managed to separate from the crowd and moved toward the camera." He gave us a wry smile. "I appreciate your effort, but I'm afraid it wasn't particularly helpful."

"Then the film brought nothing to light, and the newspaper asking for witnesses hasn't been helpful." I mentally crossed those items off my list.

"That has been the opposite of helpful. If it had mentioned what the people were meant to have witnessed, we might have had one or two good leads show up at our doors. As it is, we must interview everyone, because they might have witnessed the murder, even though ninety-nine percent of them surely did not."

"Any luck with the murder weapon?" George asked.

Cadieux sighed. "We have experts helping us with the poignard, and we have confirmed it is blood on the blade."

"Does someone keep track of who sells and buys such antiquities?" I asked.

"We may get to that, but right now, they are simply trying to identify the coat of arms on the grip." At my look of surprise, Cadieux explained. "Such an item would have been custom made for some aristocrat, possibly even a gift from the king for an accomplishment in battle."

"Yes, something like that would have been personalized. I hate to ask, since you are so busy with Julia's case, but have you learned anything more about Ducasse's murder from the crime scene?" I had told George about how we believed Ducasse's body had been dragged out the back stairs.

Cadieux nodded. "I sent a team out there last evening to collect the various bits of evidence. They also managed to interview the owner of the stables across the alley from the studio. It seems something very strange happened there, and he was quite sure it was on the night in question."

"When Ducasse was murdered?" I asked.

"Indeed. Someone unknown to him borrowed a horse and cart."

George leaned forward. "Borrowed?"

"The animal and the cart were waiting in the courtyard when the owner arrived the following morning. Assuming the horse didn't simply decide to hitch himself to a cart and take a walk in the middle of the night, someone must have borrowed them."

"Ducasse's murderer," I said.

"More than likely," Cadieux said. "But the owner found no harm done and didn't report it to the police. He simply returned his horse to the stable. The straw that was in the cart was soon soiled and disposed of, leaving us with no physical evidence. Though I do believe we now know how and where Ducasse was murdered and how his body was disposed of, we are no closer to finding a who."

"We do have some information for you that might go to motive," George said. "We've just come from Monsieur Hubert's offices. He was my aunt's solicitor. Are you aware that Ducasse left a significant settlement to his two children?"

"I was aware he left something for Mademoiselle Hazelton. But there are two children, eh? Why does this seem important to you?"

"Only that it is money that would normally have been directed elsewhere. One must wonder how that person feels about sharing."

The lines in Cadieux's face eased. "You are, of course, referring to Madame Ducasse. Cherche la femme, eh? In this case, *la femme* is wealthy in her own right, while Paul Ducasse was relatively poor. My understanding is that the amount that will remain to be divided between his wife and his children will be negligible."

"How is that possible? The man was a renowned artist whose work was in demand." As I spoke, I recalled that Allard had referred to Ducasse as "on the rise." Perhaps he wasn't doing as well as I had assumed. "He also has many paintings yet to be sold," I added.

"Ah, yes, he does have those assets." Cadieux shrugged. "I spoke to the family lawyers. Ducasse had no fortune. I also spoke to Gabrielle Ducasse. She has an alibi, a sizeable fortune, and I don't see her as someone who would mind if her husband chose to take care of his offspring."

He came to his feet with his hands on his hips. "Anything else?"

I considered telling him my suspicions about Christine, but at this point, it was just a matter of what she might be up to. I thought it best if we gathered a little more information first. "I suppose not."

"Excellent, because as you saw, I have several interviews to conduct." He opened the door and sighed. "Should anything else arise, I will be here."

Chapter Twenty-two

George and I showed ourselves to the lobby. "That poor man—" I said, then cut myself off when I saw Martine waiting in a chair, with her shoulders rounded and her arms and legs crossed. She looked up when I called out to her, her expression one of great relief. She met us near the hallway.

"Have you been called in for an interview, as well?" she asked.

"We've both had a few interviews," I said, "but this time we were here making an inquiry."

"The inspector sent a message to my apartment last night, asking me to come in and answer some questions. I suppose I understand if Paul was murdered at the studio." She blinked away a tear. "I still can't believe that."

"I'm sure they just want to inquire about everyone's routine," I said. "And your observations on that day."

She shook her head. "I think they will accuse me. Especially if they have already spoken with Edouard or Gabrielle."

Just as she said his name, I spied Edouard pushing through the door. Easily a head taller than anyone else in the room, he scanned the assembled so-called witnesses in a rather desperate manner. He saw my raised hand and came barreling our way, passing by me in favor of Martine.

"Thank goodness you are safe," he said, taking hold of both her hands.

She frowned. "What are you doing here?"

"When you weren't at the studio, I thought you might be here." He looked her up and down. "They have not questioned you yet. Good."

Martine jerked her hands free of his. "What do you care?"

"Of course I care." His raised voice and the way he growled the words at her made him less than convincing. He was also drawing the attention of the people around us.

"You think I killed her!"

Every head turned in our direction. All conversation ceased.

"No! I know you are innocent of any wrongdoing. That is why I'm here—to protect you."

She eyed him suspiciously while everyone in the room seemed to be holding their breath, including George and me.

"And?"

He took her hands in his again. This time she allowed it. "And," he said, "to confess my love for you."

The crowd heaved a collective sigh.

"Kiss him!" someone shouted.

Martine eagerly obliged, throwing her arms around his neck. Edouard lifted her off her feet and spun her in a circle while the onlookers applauded.

I turned to George to see him staring back at me. "What is happening?" he asked.

"I think they just acknowledged that they are in love with each other."

He frowned. "They can barely speak to one another without arguing."

"I don't think that matters."

The crowd lost interest before long. The newly declared lovers turned their glowing faces back to us, and I lost no time in satisfying my curiosity. "On the day Julia was killed, I saw you both in the Tuileries Garden, arguing, but when we asked where you were that morning, you lied and told us you were elsewhere."

Their stunned expressions brought me up short. Perhaps I ought to have offered my good wishes before interrogating them.

George laughed awkwardly and stepped forward. "Of course we wish you every happiness."

"We certainly do," I said. "But could you answer my question?"

Martine's gaze crept up to meet Edouard's. "May I tell them?" With his nod, she faced me. "When you saw us, Edouard had just found out that I entered one of his works into an exhibit. He did not appreciate my effort."

"Your effort? You went behind my back. Took one of my paintings. Not my best work, either, I'll have you know—"

"You never think your work is good enough!" She jabbed a finger into his chest. "It was perfect for this exhibit, but if I had asked, you would have refused."

He loomed over her. "I will not have you pushing me!"

"Someone must push you."

George leaned toward me and whispered, "Do you truly require an answer?"

I waved my hands between the two combatants. "I think I'm coming to understand that you both lied about your whereabouts because Edouard didn't want anyone to know his work was entered in the exhibition. Is that right?"

"Martine was trying to remake me in the image of Paul," Edouard grumbled.

"You are far better than Paul," Martine said, placing a hand on his cheek, "but I wouldn't mind if you made the kind of money he did."

"The Ducasse family have told the police that Paul wasn't making money," George said. "At least not a significant amount."

"Don't start another argument," I warned under my breath.

"That's not true," Martine said. "He was doing very well. His paintings were selling every day."

"We don't mean to imply Ducasse wasn't successful, Martine," I said.

Edouard came to her defense. "Martine is right. He was earning enough money that he had to hire Lucien to manage his sales."

That was true enough.

"You should speak with Lucien. He would know about Paul's finances," Martine suggested.

"Why are you so certain Ducasse was doing well?" George asked. "Did he discuss it with you?"

"*Mais oui!* We were friends," Martine said. "We worked together for many years and celebrated each other's success. Last summer one of his paintings sold for one thousand francs! I could live for a year off that. Do you think he would have kept such news to himself? He also had lesser sales, but plenty of them."

"That is contrary to what the police have been told," I said. "When you speak to Cadieux, I hope you'll tell him about this."

"We shall," she said. "Perhaps he should interview Lucien again. If the family insists Paul had no money, Lucien should explain where it went."

Martine worded that statement so succinctly and put her finger on exactly what had been bothering me. Had Allard been stealing from Paul, his close friend and business associate? I could see from George's expression that his thoughts were moving in the same direction.

"Just what sort of explanation do you think Monsieur Allard would have?" George asked. "Is there a chance he might have been cheating Ducasse?"

She frowned and glanced at Edouard.

"They were very good friends," he said.

George nodded. "So Ducasse would have trusted Allard."

"They trusted each other," Martine was quick to reply. "Paul created, and Lucien took care of business. Lucien managed Paul's money because if left to himself, Paul would have squandered it. I don't think Lucien would betray him like that. I bet he has Paul's money in another account, that is all. We will mention it to Cadieux. He can ask Lucien."

"That's a splendid idea," I said. But I suspected that if Ducasse's money was in a separate account, that account had Allard's name on it.

"Do you plan to wait until Cadieux has time to interview Monsieur Allard?" I asked George as we stepped back out on the street.

"The inspector seems rather busy at present, don't you think?" he replied. "He could do with a little help."

"And you happen to be in possession of Allard's address, if I'm not mistaken. If Ducasse had been earning money, I think it's time his business manager explained what happened to it."

George fished Allard's card from his pocket. "Glad I thought to bring it."

"This is hardly fair," I said. "We have a clue to follow at last, and I can't go with you."

"That's right. You have that very important shopping trip." He grinned. "In that case, I'll let you take the cab." George gestured to the vehicle that was waiting on the street and opened the door for me to get in. "I wouldn't put too much value on this clue," he said. "Theft and murder are completely different crimes. Thieves rarely end up murdering anyone."

"I recall at least one instance of a thief committing murder to cover up his crime. And if the thief in this case is stealing from a dear friend, which is what Monsieur Allard called Ducasse, then is confronted by that friend, I could see a fight ensuing, which is exactly what happened at Ducasse's room over the studio."

George pondered the idea for a moment. "An accident, then?"

I scoffed. "One doesn't accidentally dispose of a body."

"Good point. Perhaps a fit of anger. I'm glad to be going alone. I'd hate to take you into a dangerous situation."

"If I am safely out of the way, what is to stop him from killing you?"

George huffed as if he were insulted. "My superior skills, perhaps?"

"In the words of your mother, George, be careful."

He grinned. "That's my middle name."

I let out a tsk and seated myself in the cab. George gave the driver instructions to take me back to the apartment and closed the door. "All right, then. Wish me luck so I can get this over with."

"I wish you all the luck in the world."

As the cab pulled away, he blew me a kiss. "I'll meet you back here around four o'clock," he said.

I nodded, then settled into the seat. Though I felt a bit guilty about leaving George with all the work, not to mention envious at leaving him with all the excitement, my task shouldn't take long. It also gave me a chance both to spend some normal time with Lissette and to observe Christine. I still hadn't grasped that elusive idea that kept teasing me, but I was fairly sure it involved her.

When the driver let me down at our gate, I asked him to wait in the hope that my companions would be ready to depart. Two of the three of them did not let me down. I ought to have known Fiona would still have some last-minute detail to attend to, but she didn't keep us waiting for long.

She put an arm around Lissette and guided us all to the door as if *we* had delayed *her*. Not only did Lissette allow Fiona to lead her, but she also smiled. I had a feeling Fiona would be good for her.

Outside, the two young ladies took the lead, fairly skipping down the stairs and across the courtyard, while Fiona and I walked behind them. "The cab is at the gate," I told her. "Have you any idea where you'd like to go?"

Fiona, of course, had several suggestions. I listened while she enumerated the benefits of one shop over another. *Madame la concierge* opened the gate, and Christine and Lissette walked out to the pavement a few steps ahead of us. She gave me a nod as we passed through, so all must have been calm while I was gone. Before I could say anything to her, there was a loud bang from the street, and the wooden gate swung toward us.

"What was that?" Fiona had ducked back into the courtyard and was peering around the gate.

"A gunshot," I said, taking in the scene on the street. My first thought was for Lissette. She had jumped away from the cab, which rolled forward as the driver tried to control the frightened horse. To our left was another disturbance, as startled pedestrians shouted and pushed each other to get out of the way.

"Get back inside," I snapped just as a scream tore itself from Lissette's throat.

I followed the direction of her gaze to see Christine on the ground, slumped against the wall, the blue sleeve of her dress dark with blood.

The sight of the ever-increasing bloodstain was horrifying. My head reeled. My ears rang. I stumbled the few steps to Christine and landed on my knees beside her.

"Christine!" Lissette was right behind me, clutching at my shoulders, as if to get past me to her friend.

She could not be out here.

I pushed to my feet and, gathering her up, shoved her at Fiona. "Get her off the street," I said. "Take her inside."

Fiona hustled her into the courtyard. As I turned back to Christine, I caught a glimpse of something out of the corner of my eye. A bullet, the dull gray metal standing out against the red paint, was lodged in the thick wooden gate. That the bullet wasn't still in her gave me a little hope.

I crouched beside her. The red stain on her sleeve was spreading quickly, her face was pale, and her eyes drooped. "Stay with me, Christine. We're going to get you some help." After standing up, I turned back to the cab. *Madame la concierge* had the horse's harness in her grasp while she argued with the driver. Both of them spoke so fast, I could make out only that she questioned his lineage while he threatened to take his whip to her. When she caught my eye, she waved me over.

"There is a surgery not one street over," she said, shaking a fist at the driver. "This one will take you there."

"Sir, I will pay you well for your help," I said.

The words broke through his resistance. He climbed down from his perch, and between the two of us, we got Christine onto the seat. I lodged myself in beside her and let her lie across my lap. Shouting a *merci* to the concierge, I saw a blue-coated officer jog up to her before the cab sped down the street.

When we arrived at the surgery, the driver once again climbed down and carried Christine from the cab to the door of the surgery. The doctor calmly led us to a back room, where the driver slid her onto the table like a bag of grain. Christine groaned, and the doctor shooed us away.

As promised, I handed the cabdriver a handful of francs. He tipped his hat, promised to wait, and left me pacing in the doctor's sitting room, alone with my thoughts, which raced in every direction.

Who had shot Christine? And why? Did it have something to do with Lissette? They'd been several feet apart, and it would have been difficult to mistake one for the other. I considered Ducasse's will, Christine's supposed visit with a relative yesterday, and how lost Lissette would be without her longtime friend. The niggling idea that had been teasing me all day finally took form when the doctor emerged from the back room about thirty minutes later.

"She'll be fine," he assured me.

I sank into the nearest chair. "Thank goodness!"

"I've given her chloroform to help her tolerate the procedure, and she has lost a good amount of blood," he added, "so I'd like to let her rest for now. In the meantime, I hope you will report this to the police." He made a sound of disgust and shook his head. "Les Apaches should not be allowed to run wild," he said, referring to the gangs that had taken to the streets of Paris recently.

I was quite sure this was not the work of some gang of ruffians. It was a deliberate attempt to kill Christine. While I would have liked to report the attack to Cadieux immediately, I feared one look at me and the police would think I was the victim. Maybe if I rid myself of the bloodstained jacket. I began undoing the buttons.

The doctor noticed. "You may leave that here if you like," he suggested.

And the gloves, I thought. After slipping them off, too, I turned the jacket inside out and bundled the whole thing together. Miracle of miracles, the blood had not seeped through the lining, and my blouse was unstained, though I had a few spots on my skirt. "First, I must take a message home to let them know Christine will be fine."

He rested a comforting hand on my shoulder. "Go off to the police now, eh? Leave me your address and I'll send my boy. You may return for your sister in a few hours."

I gave him my thanks without bothering to correct him. Christine might not be my sister, but I had a strong suspicion that she was Lissette's. She was the other Ducasse child.

And someone had tried to kill her.

Chapter Twenty-three

The driver was waiting for me by his cab, his head hung low. "*Désolé, madame.* You did all that you could."

That brought me up short. "No! Thank you for the condolences, monsieur, but the surgeon says she will be fine." Considering I'd had to bribe the man into service, his distress was unexpected.

"She will recover?" His eyes rounded in surprise, while his hands gestured to the cab and the street, and finally, to the stains on his coat, in reference, I assumed, to all the blood Christine had lost.

"That is nothing short of a miracle," he said, opening the cab door for me. "I was speaking to a passerby while I waited for you. I was sure the young mademoiselle had died, and I told the woman as much. I am delighted to hear I was wrong."

"As am I." I gave him a smile and asked him to take me to the Sûreté.

My intention was to report everything to Cadieux, but when the cab pulled up to the building, I had barely set foot on the pavement when I heard George call my name from down the street.

I leaned against him when he caught up with me and offered his arm. It often amazed me how I could move through adversity like a sort of automaton when necessary, but once George arrived with his support, I knew he would step in and take the weight from my shoulders.

"Shopping does not seem to have agreed with you," he said, taking in my appearance. "You look rather done in."

Hmm, no lifting of weight this time. But to be fair, I could hardly expect him to be psychic.

"We're both early," he said. "If you're looking for Cadieux, he's not expected back for another thirty minutes or so."

"Then let's find a seat somewhere. I have much to tell you."

Twenty minutes later, I'd relayed the events of the past hour or so, assured him I was fine, and told him my suspicions about Lissette and Christine being half sisters. "I can't be certain until one of them has confirmed it, but that would explain a great deal of their behavior."

"Like why Christine chose not to take Bridget when she went out yesterday," he said. "If she was meeting with the *notaire* for the Ducasse estate, she wouldn't want any witnesses."

"And the fact that he told Hubert yesterday that the other child had come forward could not just be a coincidence. Assuming we are correct, the only question now is, who tried to kill her?"

"I happen to have some information that may relate to that question. Lucien Allard has moved out from his lodgings."

I raised my brows. "I take it you paid him a call?"

"And spoke to the caretaker. Allard gave up the apartment for good yesterday." George shrugged. "He left no forwarding address, which makes me all the more eager to speak with him. However, with no idea where to find him, I returned here. That's how I learned Cadieux was out."

"I can't take Christine home until around six, so I am at loose ends, too." I gave him a sideways look. "What do you think of calling on Alicia Stoke-Whitney? I have her card, and she seemed to be on close terms with Monsieur Allard. Perhaps she knows where he's gone."

"Even if she doesn't, it's better than doing nothing," he replied.

Our trusty cab waited at the street to transport us. I pulled Alicia's card from my bag and gave the driver her address. Fortunately, she was in the sixth arrondissement, not far at all.

Alicia's accommodations were on a narrow street off the tree-lined boulevard Saint-Germain. George and I had barely emerged from the cab when I spotted her descending the steps from her building.

"What a lovely surprise to see you both," she said when we caught up to her, "but I am on my way to an engagement for tea."

"We have yet to release the cab," George put in smoothly. "If you could spare us just a few moments, we'll drive you to your engagement."

Alicia was happy to accommodate us and gave her destination as the Ritz Hotel. George provided the information to the driver, and the three of us squeezed inside.

"You aren't by any chance having tea with Lucien Allard, are you?" I asked.

"Lucien? No. Why do you ask?" She pointed to a spot on the floor. "Is that blood?"

"Public transportation," George said, with a helpless shrug.

"George just called at Allard's apartment," I said, drawing her attention once more. "But the man has left, apparently without any intention of returning."

"Indeed?" She frowned. "I might know where he could be found. Are you hoping to acquire some art?"

"Yes," I said. "Something by Ducasse."

She made a noise of derision. "How ironic. If I had to guess, that's precisely where I'd expect him to be." She paused. "Though it does seem embarrassingly soon for him to move into the Ducasse residence. Are you certain he has no plans to return to his lodgings?"

George and I both stared at her for a moment, coming to terms with what her words revealed. "The caretaker seemed to think he was gone for good. Are you saying he and Gabrielle Ducasse are involved with one another?" I wondered how to go on, but she managed to read my expression.

"Did you think he and I were together?" She chuckled. "Heavens, no. My involvement with Lucien is strictly business, but even I can see he and Gabrielle are having an affair. They are both rather clumsy about hiding it."

They weren't too clumsy to hide it from us—or the police. Cadieux couldn't know, could he? I had a feeling Alicia was simply intuitive about clandestine relationships. She was rather an expert on them.

George watched Alicia with a doubtful expression. "Allard has professed to be a close friend of Paul Ducasse," he said. "Yet he was involved with the man's wife?"

"He and Paul were good friends as far as I know, and I don't see how Paul could object to Gabrielle's affair, since he was never faithful to her. He wasn't one to concern himself with discretion, either."

"Why did they marry, then?" I asked.

She shrugged. "I understand the families insisted upon it. You know how family can be."

The cab rolled to a stop.

"Ah, here we are," Alicia said. "If there's nothing else? I do hate to be late."

I could think of no other questions Alicia could answer. I gave her my thanks and waited while George opened the door and stepped out to assist her to the street. When she took his hand, I thought of one more thing.

"Alicia, I don't suppose you know where he was on the evening of Tuesday, the tenth, do you?"

She paused, then shook her head. "All I know is he wasn't with me." With a rustle of her skirts, she stepped out.

George climbed back in, but when he closed the door, she popped up beside the cab. "Tuesday, did you say? On Tuesdays he always dined with Paul Ducasse."

Alicia skipped off to her luncheon engagement. My mouth sagged open as I turned back to face George.

"Tuesdays he dined with Paul Ducasse," he echoed.

"Things are not looking good for Allard," I said. "He was having an affair with Gabrielle Ducasse, had control of Paul Ducasse's earnings, and had a standing appointment with Ducasse on the night he was murdered."

"And now Allard is missing. We have to notify Inspector Cadieux." George instructed the driver to take us back to the Sûreté. While we traveled, we tried to think of anything that might rule out Allard as a suspect.

"Do we know if Cadieux interviewed the man already?" I asked.

"He was Ducasse's business partner. I'd certainly want to interview him," George said, "but I don't know if Cadieux has had the chance."

Nor did I. "If Allard was pocketing Ducasse's earnings for himself, that would explain the discrepancy between the sales Ducasse told Martine about and the meager amount the lawyers found in his bank."

"I agree it would, but we have heard about his sales only from his friends." George stroked his beard as he gave the matter some thought. "They may have been misinformed. He may have sold several paintings, but not for the amounts they believe."

"But the fact that Allard has disappeared is troubling, don't you think?"

"We don't know where he is," George replied. "That doesn't mean he's disappeared. It doesn't do to fixate on one suspect and assume he is the guilty party. Allard is only a suspect."

I supposed that was true, though I could envision Ducasse confronting his partner about stealing from him. If they had been fighting, Allard could have shoved Ducasse into that stove. He looked strong enough to haul the body away. But without evidence, that scene would have to remain in my imagination.

We arrived at the Sûreté to find the crowd in the lobby had barely receded since we left. The milling potential witnesses allowed us to slip up the stairs to Cadieux's office unnoticed. His door was open, and we could see him scowling from behind his desk. A quick glance showed me he was interviewing Martine and Edouard. That could be helpful.

Cadieux stopped us with a lifted hand and met us at the door. "Please tell me this is important. I have had quite enough of these lovebirds."

"It is," George said. "And those two might be able to add to our information."

He stepped aside and motioned us into the room. "I believe you all know each other?" he said as he took his seat behind the desk.

George and I entered the room and stepped around Edouard and Martine, who were completely absorbed in one another. Heavens, this version of them could take some getting used to. Cadieux drummed his fingers on the desktop, while we settled in.

"Go ahead," he said to George. "What have you learned?"

George summed everything up rather well, I thought. He started with the fact that Ducasse had hired Lucien Allard to manage his exhibitions, sales, and money. And though Ducasse was finding success in the art world, there was little money in his accounts. Cadieux appeared unmoved until George mentioned the affair between Gabrielle and Allard. At that point he leaned forward with interest.

"Have the police interviewed Monsieur Allard yet?" George asked Cadieux.

The inspector flipped through a few files on his desk, selected one, and opened it. "One of our officers interviewed Allard yesterday. He said he was dining with a friend on the night Ducasse was killed. Madame Alicia Stoke-Whitney. We have yet to verify that with the lady."

"We just spoke with her," I said. "They were not together that evening."

"In fact, she was under the impression," George continued, "that Ducasse and Allard were meant to dine together on the evening of Ducasse's death. Thus, Allard might have been at the studio that night." He turned to the two artists. "Do you recall seeing him there?"

Edouard replied immediately in the negative, but Martine frowned in thought before answering. "I didn't see him, either, but he was usually there on Tuesday evenings."

"What time did he normally arrive?" Cadieux asked.

"Any time after six o'clock. If Paul was working, Lucien would stay in the studio and chat with us. I usually left by seven. Sometimes they were still there when I left."

"Was Ducasse always working in the studio at that time?" George asked.

"No," she replied. "Sometimes he was in his flat, resting. Then Lucien would go up to collect him."

"Did Allard always come through the studio when he visited Paul?" Cadieux asked.

"Sometimes he entered through the rear, but they would leave through the front door."

Cadieux was sitting up straighter and writing in his notebook. "Let's go back to that day in particular, mademoiselle. Tuesday, the tenth. How late were you in the building?"

"I left a few minutes before seven," Martine said.

Cadieux tipped his head. "And Allard had not yet arrived?"

"Not that I saw," she said.

"Who was left in the building?"

"I was," Edouard said. "I was just cleaning up and left soon after Martine. Julia had gone upstairs to her little garret."

"Where was Ducasse?"

"He was also upstairs."

"If someone entered or left the building through the back stairs, would you have seen or heard them from the studio?"

"No," Martine said. "The floors squeak up there, but we don't notice the sound any longer."

Edouard shook his head in disbelief. "Lucien? Are you saying he murdered Paul?"

Cadieux closed the file. "I'm saying I'd like to have another talk with him."

"I'm afraid you will have to find him first," George said. "I've just been to his residence and learned he has left, with no intention of returning."

"Is that so? We are very good at finding people, monsieur. In this case, we will begin with Madame Ducasse's home."

"I don't suppose Allard was identified on the film George brought in yesterday."

"The one that plagued my eyes all night? I wouldn't have been able to identify him, anyway, but we were able to verify his alibi for the time of Madame Hazelton's murder. He was nearby, but with a group of artists inside the Grand Palais. There were multiple witnesses."

Cadieux came to his feet. "I thank you for this information. I trust we are done here?"

"At this point, that's everything we know," George replied.

Cadieux turned to Martine and Edouard. "Thank you for coming in. If we need anything further, we'll be in contact."

The four of us left his office. Edouard and Martine never took their eyes off each other all the way to the street.

Though it had not been quite three hours since I left Christine with the doctor, George and I stopped by the surgery to see if she was recovered enough to leave. We were delighted to find her up and drinking coffee with the doctor. Her arm was bandaged, and she looked frail, still wearing her blood-stained clothes.

"I could not convince her to stay in bed," the doctor said, then grimaced. "Forgive me, madame. Another emergency came in after you left, and in the excitement, I forgot to send the note to your family. My apologies."

I assured him that it was no matter, since we were on our way home. He gave us instructions for her care and some powders she could take for pain. She appeared both eager to leave yet wary of going with us. I suppose we were the lesser of two evils.

"Is Lissette all right?" she asked once we were all in the cab and heading back to the apartment.

"Your sister is fine, though I'm sure she's worried sick about you by now."

She jerked around to face me. "How did you know?"

"I didn't really. Things just added up, and I strongly suspected the relationship. Now I know, and I have a lot of questions, but I suppose they can wait for later."

"Well, here's one that can't wait." George's gaze searched her face. "Why did you hide your relationship from us? I assume you made this decision together, and Lissette does know, doesn't she?"

Christine dipped her head. "She—"

"While we spoke of her being in danger," he continued without waiting for her answer, "didn't it occur to you that you might be in just as much danger? How are we to help if you don't trust us?"

Her eyes flashed with anger. "We didn't know you," she said. "Julia told us someone murdered our father. She wouldn't say who it was, but we had a feeling she knew. She became secretive and determined not to let the killer get away with it, even when the police said his death was an accident. She never mentioned having sent for you, but after you arrived, Julia was murdered. Were we supposed to trust that you had nothing to do with that? That you were only concerned with Lissette's best interests?"

George wore a sheepish expression. "When you put it like that—" he began.

"Is there some other way to put it? We decided it was best to take a page from Julia's book and keep our secret to ourselves."

I placed a hand on George's arm to stop any further argument. "Considering their situation, it makes perfect sense for them to have been cautious about us."

George muttered something under his breath, but since we had reached the Kendricks' apartment, there was no time for him to belabor the point. The driver dropped us off at the gate. As we climbed out of the carriage, someone called out to us from across the street. Monsieur Beaufoy.

"Why don't you help Christine inside," I said. "I'll speak with him."

Surprisingly, no one argued with my suggestion, so I stood alone at the gate and watched Monsieur Beaufoy lumber through the traffic, carefully guarding the tube, which I assumed held Julia's painting.

He heaved a sigh when he reached the sidewalk and handed his burden off to me. I held it against my chest.

"Thank you for attending to this so quickly," I said. "Won't you come inside?"

"I'm afraid I haven't time to stop. The cab is waiting for me as I am late for another engagement."

"I appreciate your stopping at all. You've finished sooner than I'd anticipated."

"It was more straightforward than I'd expected. The black paint did not cover another painting, after all, so it didn't require much delicacy. I just scraped it all off." He gave the tube a little pat. "You will see what I mean. I hope it helps you."

With that, he tipped his hat and scurried back across the

street to his waiting cab. That was when I recalled *madame la concierge* and what we owed to her. Her husband waited to close the gate behind me.

"Is madame nearby?" I asked.

The man jerked his thumb toward their small flat. "She is taking a rest."

"Much deserved," I said. "I will come by later to thank her for helping us this morning, but in the meantime, please let her know how grateful we are."

Maintaining his status as a man of few words, he closed the gate, bobbed his head, and walked off.

All right, then. Holding the tube under one arm, I crossed the courtyard and headed up the stairs. The door was open, so I walked right in. Voices drew me into the salon, where I found George, Fiona, and Christine. As I deposited the painting on the nearest table, a sense of dread tickled the back of my neck.

"What's wrong?" I ventured.

"Frances!" Fiona separated from the group and moved toward me. "I was just telling George how relieved I am to have you back. I didn't know what to do."

"Do about what? What happened?"

"It's Lissette," George said. "She is missing."

Chapter Twenty-four

❧

Fiona stood before me, wringing her hands, while Christine stormed about the salon in an agony of frustration.

I glanced at George. "We should go to the police."

He stepped up to us and caught Fiona's arm. "First, we need to find out what happened." I followed as he guided Fiona to the sofa. "Calm yourself, Fi," he said. "When did you realize Lissette was gone?"

Instead of sitting, she clutched at his arms. "It's been at least two hours. After Christine was shot, I had to drag Lissette into the house. She was in a terrible state. I told her Frances would take care of her friend and tried to get her to sit down with me and have some tea."

Fiona took a seat, and I handed her a handkerchief to dry the tears streaming down her cheeks. She drew a deep breath and continued. "Lissette took to her room. I thought that would be fine, and I gave her some time to compose herself. I had tea in my room, so it was about thirty minutes later that I knocked on her door. It wasn't locked, so I pushed it open and peeked inside. She wasn't there."

Fiona was looking up at George and me, lacing and unlacing her fingers, as she spoke. "I looked for her down here, then checked with the housekeeper, who said she hadn't seen her. Finally, I went outside and asked *madame la concierge* if she'd seen her. She hadn't, but she told me a boy had delivered a message to this address. The housekeeper knew nothing about it, so I assume Lissette had answered the door herself. That was about two hours ago. I haven't found the message. Lissette was gone. You were all gone, and I didn't know what to do."

Christine let out a wail and collapsed on to the sofa. "We must find her," she said, sending Fiona into another outburst of tears.

"Yes, we must, but we can't just run off and search the streets. We need a plan. I'm going to ring for some tea." I took a step toward the bellpull.

"That will take too long," George said. He opened a cabinet along the wall and pulled out a bottle of brandy, then reached back inside and retrieved some glasses. "This should do," he said, pouring a good three fingers into one of them. As he brought the glass over to Fiona, he caught my stare. "We need to calm her, don't you think?"

Before I could answer, Fiona wrenched the glass from his hand and downed the contents in one go. We stared as her expression changed from that of a fraught woman to that of something resembling a gargoyle.

"Probably shouldn't have done that," George muttered.

"Dearest, are you well?" I asked.

Fiona lifted a shaking hand to her face. "Blech! What was that vile drink?"

George examined the empty glass with a frown. "A rather good brandy," he said.

"I was expecting something like a cordial, not that disgusting fluid."

"Can we get back to Lissette, please?" he asked.

"Yes," Christine said. "We must find her. Someone had to see her leave, don't you think?"

Fiona gave Christine a scowl. "Don't rush me. I'm collecting my thoughts. No, nobody saw Lissette leave the apartment. However, when I returned to her room, I saw that her window was open."

I sat down by Christine, who was openly weeping now, and drew her into my arms. "She could have climbed down from the balcony without anyone seeing her," she said between sobs.

"Who would have sent her a message, Christine?" George asked. "She received a message, then went up to her room and climbed out the window so no one would see her leave. Those had to be instructions from the message, don't you think? Who would have sent it?"

Christine shook her head. "The only people she knows in Paris are Julia's artist friends."

"Then it must be one of them," Fiona said.

"They have no idea where we are staying." I glanced at George. "They wouldn't know Lissette was here."

George blew out a breath. "It might have been someone who knew that Christine had been shot. The message might have been an offer to take Lissette to Christine."

Christine stiffened, her fingers digging into my arm.

"Several people on the street saw the shooting," Fiona said.

"Yes," I said, "but only one of them would want to get his hands on Lissette." I turned to George, who nodded. "The shooter."

Fiona gasped. "Then this is far worse than I thought."

Considering the circumstances, I was very much afraid she was right. I shifted around to face George, who was pacing behind the sofa. "What should we do? Contact Cadieux?"

"I wish we had more information for him. I'm assuming someone waited on the street for her, but we don't know who or where they might have taken her."

"We suspect Monsieur Allard," I reminded him. "If he was stealing from Ducasse, the last thing he would want is for Ducasse's daughters to collect their inheritance and start asking where the money went."

"That's just speculation," George said, running a hand through his hair.

"But Allard is missing, which makes me even more suspicious. That reminds me, we have yet to look at Julia's painting. Beaufoy managed to scrape off the black paint."

"You trusted him with it?" George strode over to the painting, which I'd left waiting on the table.

"He seemed a better choice than Edouard."

George removed the canvas from the tube and unfurled it on the coffee table, revealing a sketch rather than a painting.

"Does this look like Julia's work?" I asked.

Both Christine and George agreed that it was.

The strokes were sharp and bold, as if the sketch was done too quickly for any type of finesse. Yet the image was clear. Two men were in Paul Ducasse's room over the art studio. The chair was knocked over; the rug stained with what we knew was blood. One man was dragging the body of the other to the rug. The dead man was Paul Ducasse. The other man was Lucien Allard. Seeing the dark image sent a chill through me.

"The question remains," George said, "was she drawing what she saw or what she suspected?"

"She was there that night, George. She didn't have to suspect anything. Allard probably had no idea that she was in the next room at the time, but he often visited the studio. Either of the artists might have told him later. She must have been terrified he'd come back for her. Why didn't she go to the police?"

"I don't think she saw anything," George said. "As you said, she was in the next room. If she had come out and seen Allard, then he would have seen her. That place is old, and the floors creak in anticipation of one's steps. I think she heard a fight that night. Maybe she heard voices. She knew who was there, but she didn't know exactly what happened. The next day, she went back to the farm. She didn't know Paul was dead until his body was found. That's when she put it all together. I'd wager that's when she drew this sketch."

"And when she contacted you," I added. "If you are correct, she might not have thought she had enough evidence to take to the police. Especially since they declared his death an accident. But Julia told Martine she thought Ducasse was murdered. Maybe she told someone else, and it got back to Allard."

Beside me, Christine let out a gasp and clapped her hands to her face. "I told him," she said through a sob. She lowered her hands and clutched my arm, something completely unnecessary since she already had our rapt attention.

"Julia told us—Lissette and me—that Ducasse was murdered. When Lucien made me leave the tribute, he tried to shame me for coming to him about business when he was celebrating the life of the beloved Paul Ducasse. I told him I'd heard Ducasse was murdered, so there must be someone who didn't love him." She swiped at the tears on her cheeks. "He had to know it was Julia who told me."

"So he broke into her flat to scare her off," George suggested.

"Or to see if she had any damning evidence," I said. "Still, Allard couldn't have killed her. There are witnesses saying he was nowhere near Julia when she was stabbed."

"Then they are mistaken, or he hired someone to do it," George said.

As time was speeding past, I was becoming more anxious. We had to do something now. "Cadieux is looking for Allard already. It may be helpful for him to know Allard may have been here two hours ago."

George looked doubtful. "Would Lissette trust him enough to go with him?"

"She met him. He was kind to her." I shrugged. "It's possible."

At the sound of a knock, we all turned to see Madame Fontaine at the door, holding out a note. "This was just delivered for you, monsieur."

"By whom?" George asked. He took the note from the housekeeper and opened it.

"I do not know," she said, shaking her head slowly. "There was a knock at the kitchen door. When I opened it, the only thing to find was the note."

George thanked her, and she left us. The rest of us gathered around George, Fiona looking over his shoulder and Christine wringing her hands, eager to hear the contents of the note. He did not make us wait.

"We have Mademoiselle Lissette," he read. "If you wish to see her again, Monsieur and Madame Hazelton should go to Julia Hazelton's home in Chartres at nine o'clock tonight and wait for further instructions. If you arrive with the police, the girl will die."

"Short and to the point," Fiona said.

"Do you have a plan?" I asked.

"Not yet, but we have until nine o'clock to devise one." George handed the note to Fiona. "Once we're gone, take this and the sketch to Cadieux at the Sûreté. The cabman at the gate will take you."

Fiona stared at him in horror. "But the note said if you bring the police, they'll kill her."

"We won't bring the police. They will follow us." George turned to me. "You may want to change before we leave."

I'd forgotten about the bloodstains. "Yes, my wardrobe is not holding up well on this trip. If we have time, I'll go up now."

Christine looked down at her stained dress and grimaced. "I had better do the same."

George put out a hand to stop her. "I'm sorry, but you were not invited to this meeting."

Her expression hardened with her resolve. "You can't expect me to stay here when my sister is in danger."

George glanced at me, then Fiona; both of us were in sympathy with Christine. "I understand," he said. "Truly. Were I in your position, I would feel the same, but putting you in harm's way will not help Lissette. It may hamper our efforts to help her."

I held out a hand to her. "Nevertheless, you ought to change your gown."

Christine appeared resigned when I dropped her at her room, but I wasn't convinced. I stepped across the hall to mine and rang for Bridget. By the time she responded, I had removed my skirt and blouse and was washing my face in the basin. She handed me a face towel while holding the skirt away from her with two fingers of her other hand, clucking like a mother hen.

"My lady, this has to stop, or you'll need a new wardrobe."

"I'd love for it to stop," I said. "But a new wardrobe wouldn't go amiss, either." I folded the towel and left it next to the basin. "Do I have anything undamaged left to wear?"

Bridget, of course, found something. I was clean, coiffed, and dressed in a fresh gown in twenty minutes. That had to be enough time for Christine to make a decision and take whatever action she deemed necessary.

There was no response to my knock on her door. I opened it and poked my head inside the room. Her soiled dress lay in a heap on the floor. She couldn't possibly have climbed down the trellis with the wound to her arm, but she could have snuck out of the house through the kitchen door.

I stepped out to the balcony and looked over the railing just in time to see her slip around the gate and head down the street. George would not be pleased.

It didn't matter that she was ahead of us; we were all bound for the train station. I stopped at my room long enough to stuff more francs into my bag and change into some sturdier shoes, in the event we had to walk to the station.

Fiona and George met me at the foot of the stairs. "Fiona is off for the Sûreté now," he said. "And we should be on our way."

"Christine has left ahead of us."

Both their mouths popped open. They truly were brother and sister. Heavens, Fiona was speechless. If I had a calendar, I'd make note of it.

I placed a hand on her shoulder. "I fear for the state of our sanity when our daughters become young women. If Rose is like those two, I don't think I'll survive it."

"Or Rose won't," Fiona offered.

"That is also possible." I held out a hand to George. "Are you ready?"

"You let her go." His eyes narrowed suspiciously.

"Let her? You seriously overestimate my authority if you think I could stop her." I gave him a helpless shrug. "I suppose she must accompany us."

Changing my shoes might have been the first good decision I'd made all day. We had to walk at least halfway to Saint Lazare station before we spotted a cab dropping off a fare. By that point, I would have elbowed grandmothers out of the way to claim it. Fortunately, George's long stride saved the day, and we caught the cab before anyone else managed to get close.

Once inside, George eyed me suspiciously. "You knew Christine would sneak out of the house, didn't you? Yet you didn't warn me."

"I thought there was a good chance she would, yes, but there was also the chance she'd obey your orders."

He made a derogatory noise.

"We can turn her over to the custody of Suzanne Dupont, the neighbor. In the meantime, she could be useful in helping us come up with a plan. We'll be an hour on the train. She knows the house, the area, and the people."

His expression relaxed. "I hated making her stay behind. I hope Madame Dupont will have more authority than I."

"Waiting in Paris for hours with no word is very different than being five minutes away from the farm. I think Christine will be reasonable."

I didn't see her upon entering the station, but I did see that the next train was leaving at seven o'clock—in fifteen minutes. Having traveled to Chartres so recently, we purchased our tickets, found the platform, and boarded the train well within that time. That was when we found Christine.

I took the seat next to her, leaving George to sit facing us. "Nothing like a relaxing trip to the country, is there?" he said.

She watched George cautiously. "I'm sorry to cause you any trouble, but I had to go to Lissette."

George gave her a nod. "I understand. If my sister was in danger, nothing could keep me at home."

Christine gazed out the window as the train began to move.

"We have an hour's ride ahead of us," I said. "Why don't we try to work out what we'll be facing when we get there? Lucien Allard is not a professional kidnapper. Why would he have taken Lissette?"

Christine turned away from the window. "You are certain it was Lucien, then?"

"He killed Paul Ducasse," I said. "Though I have no actual proof, there is no doubt in my mind. It's very likely he was stealing from the man. He was also having an affair with Paul's wife."

"What?" Christine's eyes were wide with surprise. "Do you mean Gabrielle Ducasse?"

George grinned, delighted to have provoked a reaction. "It's rumored that they are together," he said, "but this rumor comes from a very reliable source, so I'm inclined to believe it. How well do you know Madame Ducasse?"

"The day you saw her at Julia's house was the first time I met her."

Christine's words felt if not false, at least not quite true. "But?" I urged.

"My mother had spoken of her." She glanced out the window and back at me.

"And?"

She huffed. "My mother hated Gabrielle Ducasse, which is strange when you consider it was Paul who wronged her." She blew out a breath. "Paul was playing at being the starving artist when my mother met him and fell in love. She thought he loved her and would marry her when she told him she was expecting his child. He had no such intentions. Instead, he gave her some money he had begged from his family. That helped for a few years. It paid for the flat we lived in until I was five."

"Your mother stayed in Paris?" George's voice was gentle.

Christine nodded. "That way she could keep an eye on him. She tried to get him to acknowledge me, but he wasn't interested. By that time, he had met Julia. My mother warned her not to trust him. She said he would never marry her. When Julia returned to England, Paul married Gabrielle. That broke my mother's heart. He married an aristo. He was an aristo. The poor painter she knew had never really existed.

"I'm not sure why my mother directed all her ill will toward Gabrielle," she continued. "Paul was never faithful to his wife. When Julia returned and found Paul married, she sought out my mother, and the two of them formed a kind of partnership. Julia was the best thing that could have happened for my mother. Me too."

She heaved a sigh. "I don't know why I told you all that. It has nothing to do with Lissette, and I truly am worried sick about her."

"Of course you are," George said, "but there's nothing we can do until we get to Chartres. And it's good to know more about Gabrielle. She may have a role in this mess."

"I thought you said she had an alibi for the night of Paul's murder."

I waved a hand. "It doesn't matter. Lucien killed him. The

question is, does Gabrielle have an alibi for the time of Julia's murder?"

Christine frowned. "Why would she kill Julia?"

"Why would your mother hate Gabrielle?"

"I don't think it's the same," she said. "Her husband was in love with Julia, but he'd been involved with one woman or another their whole marriage. Why would she feel the need to kill Julia after all this time?"

That was when it hit me. Gabrielle had an alibi for the time of Paul's murder. Allard had an alibi for the time of Julia's. I doubted that anyone had questioned Gabrielle about Julia's murder. If she hadn't murdered Paul, why would she have troubled herself to murder the woman he loved after he was already dead? Maybe because she loved Lucien Allard. Julia had to be murdered because of what she had seen or heard. If Allard wasn't the culprit, it might very well have been Gabrielle.

The poignard. Noblemen carried them, or they had. Gabrielle came from a noble family. If it was her family's coat of arms on the handle of the weapon, it would certainly implicate her. Was she aware it had been recovered?

"What?" Christine and George were both staring at me. "I can see you've thought of something," he said. "What is it?"

I gave them the gist of my epiphany. "Christine and Lissette are to inherit half his fortune, but there is little fortune, because Lucien had stolen it. If Gabrielle had been his sole heir, no one would have been the wiser. I think we can assume Lucien would have shared his plunder with her."

A spark lit Christine's eyes. "But now they must be worried that someone will start asking questions—wondering where the money from Ducasse's recent sales has gone."

"The *notaire* will certainly ask questions," George added. "An investigation of Ducasse's accounts might uncover Allard's theft. It might also uncover Ducasse's murder, so Allard is in danger of discovery. If the poignard turns out to be

Gabrielle's, the police will soon know, and then she, too, will be under suspicion."

"If that's true, it would be more logical for them to run." Christine spread her hands open on her lap. "Get out of Paris. Get out of France. That's what I would do."

"Yes, but put yourself in their places. They don't know as much as you. In fact, they didn't know George was Lissette's guardian until we told Gabrielle. My guess is that once Julia was killed, Gabrielle planned to take Lissette in to live with her, and no one would ever know about Lucien's theft or the murders."

"That explains why Madame Ducasse came to the farm," Christine said. "She wanted to weasel her way into Lissette's life."

"She probably thought Lissette would be easy to manipulate," I said. "At the time, Gabrielle didn't know about you or George. The two of you complicated their plot. I'm at a loss to see how they think Lissette could help them now. And if they do intend to run, and to take her with them, why notify us of the fact?"

"If they expect a payment for her safe return," George said, "one would think they'd have named a sum of money in the letter."

Christine's expression changed from thoughtful to troubled. "But you think Lucien shot me. He thinks I'm dead. Why wouldn't he go ahead and kill Lissette, too?"

"As far as Ducasse's bequest goes, they have nothing to gain from your deaths," George said. "Your shares would go to your heirs. And we have no way of knowing if he thinks you are dead."

I gasped, recalling the cabdriver. "I believe he does think she's dead. The cabdriver waited for me outside the surgery today. He said he spoke to a woman passerby. He told her he was certain Christine would die."

I gave Christine an apologetic smile, which she waved off.

"Rather an odd conversation for two strangers on the street," George observed.

"My thoughts exactly," I said. "Do you suppose it was Gabrielle?"

He nodded. "But that still doesn't tell me what they are up to." He turned to Christine. "Since they don't know you are alive, we should keep you hidden. If we get into trouble, you can go for help."

"That makes for a good beginning to our plan, but we are pulling into Chartres." I gestured to the window. "And it's already eight o'clock."

"I think we'll have to make that plan as we go along," George said.

With no belongings to gather, we disembarked quickly and found a cab outside the station. We drove silently through the gathering dusk until I saw the Duponts' cottage.

"Let's stop here," I suggested.

George signaled the driver and glanced at Christine. "Do you know the family?"

"Nearly all my life," she said. "They are trustworthy."

He nodded. "I didn't want to take the cab right up to Julia's farm. This is as good a place as any to stop."

We climbed out, sent the cab back to town, then followed the path up to the Duponts' door. Suzanne answered on the first knock.

"Frances, Christine," she said, opening the door wide. "What can I do for you?"

Could she tell me if there was a murderer at Julia's farm? Probably not.

George introduced himself. "I'm afraid I have an odd question, madame. I wonder if you happened to notice any activity at the farmhouse today—anyone coming or going?"

She frowned in concern. "It has been quiet all day. I spent

the afternoon out here on the porch, so I would have noticed any arrivals or departures. I hope nothing is wrong?"

"Everything is probably fine," George assured her. "But we are going to have a look all the same."

"Shall I send my husband with you?"

Heavens, she was the perfect neighbor.

"Kind of you to offer," George said, "but that won't be necessary. However, if we do encounter any problems, may we send Christine to you for help?"

Her brows came together as she studied us. "Of course. You go on ahead and check on things. If I don't hear from you in thirty minutes, I will send my husband up to check on you."

The thought that someone would follow us felt reassuring. I considered Christine as she followed us down the drive. "I thought we were to leave Christine with the Duponts," I reminded George. "She is injured, after all."

"I'm going with you," she said.

George stopped and faced her. "Once we assess the situation at the house, we will need you to return to the Duponts, either to fetch help or to get yourself out of danger."

She parted her lips to speak, but George held up a hand. "You are injured, and you will slow us down when our lives may depend on moving quickly."

She nodded her agreement, and we moved on to the front entrance of the property. My watch indicated we still had twenty minutes until we were expected to show ourselves at the door. George gestured for us to follow him and made for the shrubbery that encircled the property.

Our progress was slow. We crept alongside the shrubbery and rounded the side of the yard. Just as I decided this stealth was ridiculous, I heard the sound of an engine and saw lights not far in the distance, down the road in the opposite direction from the Duponts' home. We all backed deeper into the shrubbery and waited. The motorcar wasn't moving at great speed, but it still didn't take long for it to close in on us, turning a few yards in front of our hiding place into the drive of Julia's house. Interesting.

The motorcar slowed as it pulled up the drive, and I poked my head out to watch it wind around the side of the house to stop near the kitchen door. The motor cut off, the driver's door opened, and a shoe crunched into the gravel.

Peeking around the side of a shrub, I caught a glimpse of a woman slamming the door. She glanced around the yard before crossing to the doorway.

Dusk had settled in, but I recognized the face of Gabrielle Ducasse. If she was here, then so was Lucien Allard. We had less than fifteen minutes to find out why.

Chapter Twenty-five

❧

Gabrielle disappeared into the house. Now what? She and Allard couldn't possibly believe that Lissette would help them, so abducting her would be fruitless. If they were on the run, she would only be in the way.

And where was Lissette? And what were we to do about Christine?

We really ought to have made a plan.

"Are we just going to hide here all night?" Christine had moved close enough to whisper to me. How she managed to imbue so much judgment into a whisper was remarkable.

"Give me a moment to think," George replied.

While he thought, I observed the house. From the road, the house was dark, but back here a light glowed through the kitchen curtains, and if I wasn't mistaken, there was another light from an open window farther down. That must be the salon. If they didn't want the neighbors to know the house was occupied, it made sense to make use of the back rooms.

I tapped George on the arm and pointed to the window. "Let's see what we can learn."

We had Christine stay put and made our way across the yard to the salon window. I reached it first and peered beneath the half-drawn shade, then immediately sank back to my knees.

Allard was seated in a chair against the wall, while Gabrielle paced in front of him. It was no less than I'd expected, but it was still a jolt to see them, knowing they had Lissette. Wait. Where was Lissette? I leaned back toward the window to hear their conversation. George did the same on the other side.

"Impulsive idiot! Why do I put up with you?"

That was Gabrielle.

"There was nothing impulsive about it," Allard replied. "I had a chance to get rid of her, and I took it."

I slapped a hand over my mouth to silence my gasp. Had he already murdered Lissette? Were we too late?

"But you shot her! I thought we agreed they would suffer an accident."

"So, now Lissette will have an accident. What difference does it make?"

"Honestly, Lucien, sometimes I wonder if there is a brain in that beautiful head of yours. Do you ever think before you act?"

There was silence for a moment, during which I assumed Allard showed Gabrielle what he was thinking. From their conversation thus far, it sounded like Lissette was alive. We still had hope of keeping her that way, but we had to find her first.

I heard a murmur and a couple of footsteps. Perhaps Gabrielle had walked away from him. "It could have been so nice, Lucien." The footsteps continued. Closer, then farther. Gabrielle must be pacing again. "The police would have assumed Paul was attacked by some thug," she continued.

"They would have assumed he had drowned if you hadn't led them to his garret."

"That landlord kept asking me to come and collect Paul's

things. Cadieux was asking me questions. I thought it best to make a big show of it—gain their sympathy."

I muttered a curse. She'd managed to fool me.

"Besides, by that time the police already knew Paul hadn't drowned, and I found out Lissette had a guardian. Everything was ruined." She released a heavy sigh. "All I wanted was to be with you and have Paul's money. It was all much easier when he was alive."

"It's not as if I planned this." Allard sounded highly offended. "You believe Paul's death was an accident, don't you? I didn't mean to hurt him. He just came at me, and I pushed him back."

"I know, I know. Shhh, it's all right."

I rested my head against the side of the house. How long was this going to take? I just wanted to know where to find Lissette.

"I only wish you'd called on me before you took any action."

"Julia heard us fighting. If I had left his body there, I might just as well have turned myself in to the police. If you hadn't killed Julia, everything might have been fine. She was far too afraid of me to go to the police."

"But not too afraid to call in an investigator."

These two lovebirds were clearly headed for a life of bliss together. Perhaps they'd just shoot each other.

"Julia has been a menace since the moment Paul met her." She let out a tsk. "Well, it's too late to turn back now. What time is it?"

"Almost time."

There was a pause, then more footsteps. "I bought a map and extra fuel for the motorcar while I was out," Gabrielle said. "We should be ready to leave as soon as it's over. No delays. Is Lissette in the barn?"

"She is, and we should go up front to wait for our guests."

I didn't linger to hear any more. George tipped his head to the courtyard, and we moved away from the window. It took only a few moments to worm our way through the shrubs around the courtyard to where Christine waited.

"Go for help," I told her. "We'll try to get Lissette out of here."

Christine was off before I even finished the sentence.

More concerned with speed than stealth, we ran across the yard to the barn. The main door was closed but was just resting against the latch. Would they have left her here unguarded?

Once inside, I glanced around the open space, allowing my eyes to adjust to the darkness. We didn't dare light one of the lamps. Holding my arms out in front of me, I stumbled toward what I hoped were the stairs. George caught me as I tripped over the bottom step. He pointed to the upper room. Light was coming from under the door, illuminating the top two steps. I heard a shuffle across the floor overhead and breathed a sigh of relief that it had to be Lissette reacting to the noise I'd just made.

Before I could climb more than two steps, Allard and Gabrielle walked through the barn door. Holding a lantern in front of her, Gabrielle looked angry enough to kill us, but it was Allard who held the pistol. His calm demeanor did not make me feel any better.

"My apologies for not being here to greet you," he said. His tone lowered the temperature in the barn by several degrees. "We had assumed you'd call at the house."

George leaned casually against the stair rail. "One hates to be predictable under these circumstances."

"What difference does it make?" Gabrielle asked Allard. "They are here. They are alone. Let's finish this."

"I assume by that you mean to kill us." I stood behind George and two steps up.

He tipped his head back and gave me a look. "When we are standing on this side of the pistol, we don't use that word."

"She has not planted that idea in our minds, Monsieur Hazelton. We are far ahead of you." Gabrielle placed the lantern on the floor and stepped up to the long table containing the perfumery equipment and effects and, oddly enough, a hammer. She lifted the hammer and set herself to smashing the perfume bottles. Other than adding insult to injury, I didn't know what she was about.

"Madame Ducasse," George began, "I do hope you don't believe that killing Lissette and the two of us means her portion of your husband's estate will go to you."

Allard let out a huff, took a step forward, and pushed over the contraption I thought of as a distiller. It honestly looked as if the two of them were determined to destroy everything. Then I noted the liquid draining out of the equipment—alcohol. Combined with the flame from Gabrielle's lantern, this barn could become an ember in short order.

Having run out of things to smash, Gabrielle dropped the hammer on the table and walked back to Allard. Her hair had become disheveled, and the tangled mass made her look all the more dangerous. "I don't need more money," she said. "But getting you out of the way gives me the one thing I do need."

"Time," George said.

She narrowed her eyes. "How did you know that?"

I wondered the same thing.

George lifted his open hand. "Obviously, if one has ample funds, the only thing one could be short on is time. I suspect you have some covering up to do. Perhaps transferring funds from your account to one that Monsieur Allard can say was for Paul's art sales. That would keep the *notaire* from suspecting someone had been stealing from Paul."

"You do see," Gabrielle said. "It isn't about sharing the money, but I will not lose my status or reputation."

"Understandable," George replied. "After all, I suspect that's why you married Paul in the first place."

Allard leaned forward to whisper to Gabrielle. When she turned her head toward him, I leaned down, getting closer to George. "What are you doing?" I asked. "Do you have a plan?"

He grimaced. "You are quite fixated on plans. Right now, my idea is to keep them talking until help arrives. Perhaps we'll get lucky and bore them to death."

It wasn't much, but it was better than nothing. I looked at Gabrielle and Allard, who had finished their conference and were staring at us. So was the barrel of Allard's pistol. "That's enough talking," he said.

"Oh, I think, for your sake, Gabrielle, there should be just a little more talk," I said. "This has all been easy for Lucien." I waved a hand toward him while keeping my gaze locked with Gabrielle's. "You're the one who had to marry Paul. I suspect your family has experienced some financial downturns, so over the years you managed to squirrel away a large portion of your husband's fortune. Then your lover kills your husband, by accident, of course, and look at the mess he's left you in."

Allard slipped his free arm around Gabrielle and pulled her to his side. "We are in this together."

"Of course you are," George cooed. "Up to the point where the police arrest Madame Ducasse for murder."

She stared at George in horror.

"The police recovered your poignard," I said. "They know it was used to kill Julia, and they know it belongs to you."

Gabrielle turned to Allard, who squeezed her all the tighter. "If what they say is true, then there is all the more reason for haste," he said.

"We will have to leave France," she sobbed.

Blast, they had a secondary plan.

"I have to leave France because of you!" Gabrielle pulled

away from Allard, grabbed the lantern from the floor, and threw it at the table—the table drenched in alcohol.

It flamed up with a whoosh, sending me against the stair railing behind me. George ran to the door, only to be stopped by Allard and his pistol. He kept George at bay until he and Gabrielle left the barn, then bolted the door behind them.

The flames from the table had already jumped to the floor and were spreading quickly. George swept up the hammer and banged it against the door. I ran up the remaining stairs to Lissette. She, too, was locked in, but this bolt was on my side.

If only I could see it. One would think the blaze below would create enough light, but the smoke quickly enveloped the whole loft area. Finally, I managed to wrap my fingers around the bolt and unlock the door. I pushed it open, and Lissette fell into my arms, tears streaming down her face. I hugged her to me like a promise. I would do whatever it took to keep this girl safe.

"I'm sorry, Frances. I'm sorry," she said into my ear. "I was so afraid for Christine, and Madame Ducasse said she was here."

So, it was Gabrielle who had lured Lissette here. "Christine is safe. Gabrielle and Lucien are gone. Now we must get you out of here."

"Frances!"

The smoke was thickening. Down on the main floor, I could barely see George. And worse, the fire had followed me and was moving quickly up the stairs.

"I have the door open," he said, fear and panic in his voice. "But I don't think I can get you down."

Thank heavens there was another way out. "Leave before you're caught in here, George. We'll meet you at the river." I flapped my hand when he hesitated. "Go!"

"Be careful!" he called.

"It's my middle name."

"That does not fill me with confidence."

"There's another way out. Now go!"

Lissette let out a squawk when I pushed her back into the room. "What are you doing?"

I slammed the door, hoping to keep the smoke out of this upper room long enough to find our way out. "We can't get down the stairs."

"We have to!"

I heard the panic in her voice, but there was no time to calm her. Besides, I was feeling a little shaky myself as I felt my way over to the outer wall in the dark. When my fingers found the paintings, I pulled them off the wall and tossed them aside. Then I found the latch and pushed open the wooden shutters, letting the pale moonlight stream in.

"How does this help?" She stepped over to the window and glanced out at the river below. "There are no stairs."

I had already thrown off my jacket and was working on my skirt. "I'm afraid we're going to have to swim."

She stared at me, her lip quivering and one hand against her chest. "You mean jump into the river? We will surely die!"

"Only if you keep that heavy skirt on. It will weigh you down." I pulled on her sleeve, only to have her jerk away from me. I dropped my hands to my sides, exasperated. "Lissette, there is no other way. My brother and I used to do this all the time when we were children. It's not even twenty feet to the water. I promise you it will be fine."

This time she let me take her jacket. She unbuttoned her heavy skirt with shaking hands. I was already in my shift and a single petticoat, tapping my stockinged toe. "Hurry, Lissette."

Her hands stilled. "I cannot do this. I cannot swim."

"I will not let you drown."

She waved a hand and stepped away from the window. "No, just go without me. Then you can come back in and let me out."

The idea was preposterous, but she was clearly paralyzed with fear. I put my arm around her waist and slowly guided her to the window, where I had her sit on the ledge while I removed her boots. "You can do this, Lissette. You just have to trust me."

I saw the resignation, and dread, in her eyes as I pulled her to her feet and had her face the window. "This is how we'll do it." I spoke as calmly as if we were in the salon, sipping tea. "We're going to stand on this ledge, you are going to hold tight to my hand, and together we'll take a big step forward. You may want to hold your nose." There really wasn't time to explain how to breathe.

Lissette was shaking as she climbed onto the ledge beside me. I took a peek behind her to see smoke rolling in around the doorframe. "Oh, Frances," she squeaked, taking my hand. "I don't want to do this."

"Everything will be fine. Now, squeeze your nose and step off."

And shocking me to my core, she did it.

We both stepped into the inky night, with just a second to draw a breath before we broke through the surface of the river. A few strong kicks brought us back up. Lissette was flailing and sputtering, but she was alive.

"You did it," I said. "You wonderful, brave girl. You did it!"

I ducked my head as her elbow came toward my nose. "Get me out of here!" she cried.

I tightened my hold on her and kicked us the few yards to the bank, where George helped us up to the grass. Then we all scrambled away from the barn, which by then was little more than a frame for the smoke and flames.

Christine ran toward us, with Monsieur Dupont on her heels. His eyes widened and he spun around as Lissette and I came into view in our soaking, and now transparent, underthings. "If you are both unhurt, I will fetch some blankets," he said.

"I'd prefer that you alert the fire brigade," George said, shrugging out of his coat and throwing it over my shoulders before wrapping me in a hug.

Even as Monsieur Dupont rushed to do George's bidding, several neighbors were running toward the barn, laden with buckets. Lissette and I left Christine and George to direct them and made our way back to the house.

When we reached the kitchen door, Lissette stopped and spun around. "We can't go in there. What about Lucien and Gabrielle?"

I gestured to the empty space where Gabrielle's motorcar had been parked. "They are long gone by now. They would not have wanted it known they were ever here. The three of us would simply have died in a tragic accident."

She gasped. "They can't get away with that!"

"Let's discuss it inside, shall we? We are creating a distraction out here."

She relented, but once we were in the kitchen, she stopped again. "After all they did, we can't let them get away," she said.

I pushed her toward the stairs. "They won't. We did not die in the fire. We shall tell the police what we know, and they will go after them. They have not gotten away with any of it. Now, let's get some dry clothes on so we can go back out there and salvage something of your perfume business."

We dripped all the way to the bedrooms. Lissette pointed me to Julia's room, the most likely place to find something I could wear, then moved on to her own. She returned a moment later to hand me a fluffy towel. Before returning to her room, she stopped at the doorway.

"Thank you for coming for me," she said. "And for saving me."

"You are well worth saving," I said.

She stood in the doorway with her back to me, talking over her shoulder, but not really looking at me. "You are not as bad as I thought you were," she said, then hurried off to her own room.

Well, I supposed that was something. I wondered what sort of feat I'd have to pull off before she'd actually like me.

Chapter Twenty-six

Ⓩ

There was very little to save of Julia's perfume business once the fire was out. The frame of the building was largely intact, but the perfume itself, the herbs and dried flowers, the oils, and virtually every element that had been stored in the barn were broken, damaged, or burned. Julia's paintings up in the loft were singed or smoke smudged.

Cadieux and his officers arrived, then left just as quickly to pursue the criminals.

The neighbors had stayed well into the night to ensure every ember from the fire was cold. If that wasn't enough, they brought us bread, sausages, and wine for our dinner.

The following morning brought a note from Inspector Cadieux. Even better, it was hand delivered by Fiona. We all gathered in the salon to greet her.

"You can't imagine how awful it was in that apartment all by myself, waiting to hear some word from you," she said, handing the note off to George.

He scanned it and looked up with a smile. "The police caught up with the fugitives, and they are currently back in Paris, at the Sûreté."

The news allowed us all to exhale in relief and bring out the remains from last night's feast to the kitchen table. It was a warmer, cozier place than the formal dining room. Perfect for the five of us to gather. Even Christine and Lissette seemed to have relaxed after the ordeal they had each been through. Thank goodness they had one another. How had I not realized sooner the two were sisters?

I tore off a piece of baguette and listened to Lissette tell Fiona how I'd made her jump into the river. "She practically dragged me off the window ledge," she said.

"Yes, and then you dragged me under the water," I replied.

"I am just relieved that we are all still alive and well," George said. He took my hand and brought it to his lips. "I am not letting you that far away from me ever again."

"Why were they so determined to do away with all of us?" Christine asked.

"To cover up years of theft," Fiona replied, pouring herself a cup of coffee.

George and I turned to her in astonishment. "How do you know that?" he asked.

"What do you mean, how do I know?" Fiona looked quite offended. "I spoke with Inspector Cadieux, of course. Where do you think that note came from?"

George let out a huff. "And Cadieux just told you everything?"

"People do feel compelled to confide in your sister," I said.

Fiona's gaze took in all of us. "Do you wish to know the story or not?"

"Yes," we all said at once.

"Very well, then. Gabrielle Ducasse has been draining money from her husband's account for years. When his family paid his allowance, she'd leave enough in his account for his immediate needs and take the rest. When she met Lucien Allard, they became a team, and rather than hiding the money around the house, they opened an account in Allard's name, with Gabrielle as a beneficiary, of course. They assumed this could go on forever. Then Paul Ducasse died."

Lissette sputtered like a faulty motor. "That could hardly have come as a surprise to them," she said. "Lucien killed him."

"He claims it was an accident," Fiona went on. "With Paul dead, they'd lost their golden goose. Everything they did after that was to prevent discovery and scandal. Gabrielle murdered Julia because she feared Julia knew that Lucien had killed Paul. The rest of you had to go because you had claims on Ducasse's money, and they needed time to cover up their theft."

"Why didn't they just replace the money they'd stolen?" I asked.

"Excellent question," Fiona said. "I asked it myself."

George raised his brows. "And the answer is?"

"There wasn't much money left." She raised her open hands. "They spent it—on jewelry, a seaside villa in Deauville, and furnishings, of course. They didn't have enough currency on hand to convince the Ducasse lawyers that it represented even a portion of Paul's earnings."

Fiona placed her arms on the table and leaned forward. "Can you imagine the scandal if their underhanded dealings had become public? Both families would have become pariahs."

"I assume they needed to liquidate some assets," George suggested.

"Not only that, but they had to find a banker who would backdate the deposits so they wouldn't arouse suspicions." Fiona considered the matter. "I suppose that takes a special type of banker."

"A dirty one," George said. "For all their attempts at concealment, their actions will become public, anyway."

"I wish they'd been caught sooner," Lissette said. "Before anyone was killed."

Christine reached out and squeezed Lissette's shoulder. "I miss Julia, too," she said.

"As close as the three of you were, I'm rather surprised Aunt

Julia didn't see to your security in her will, Christine," George said. "It seems rather unfair."

Both girls stared in confusion. "But Christine had the perfumery," Lissette said. "*Maman* would have expected her to keep that going."

"But she didn't leave Christine an interest in the perfumery," he said.

Lissette rested her forearms on the table and leaned forward. "The perfumery belongs to Christine. She was too young, so my mother held the ownership, but she always planned to transfer it. Christine started the perfumery from nothing but some herbs and flowers we grew in the garden. She made up the oils. She developed the scents. What little money we made from it was due to her hard work. It was not my mother's business. It was hers."

I could see George was about to argue that Julia had made no such mention of this in her will, so I gave him a nudge with my foot under the table. "That makes perfect sense, doesn't it, George?"

"Ah, yes," he said, turning to Christine. "When will you come of age?"

"I will be twenty-one in December."

"Excellent," I said. "By then, everything should be settled with Julia's and your father's estates." I grinned at George. "Then you and Lissette will make your first joint transaction by transferring the perfumery to Christine. And you thought working together would be difficult."

George gave me a sour look, so I turned to Christine. "Will you be able to salvage the business?"

"Will I have enough money to help her?" Lissette asked George.

He hesitated. "I don't know much about running a business."

"My aunt Hetty does," I said. "I think she'd be willing to advise Christine about her industry."

George raised a brow. "If you're expecting Hetty to visit, you must be planning to spend a little more time here yourself."

"We must return to England to have a service for Julia and to introduce Lissette to the family," Fiona said. "But afterward, why not return to Paris?"

"Where will we stay?" I asked. "The Kendricks will need their apartment back by then."

"It isn't Paris, but it sounds as though our father has paid for a house in Deauville," Lissette said with a smirk. "And there is plenty of room in this house."

"There, you see?" Fiona said. "A solution."

She and the girls put their heads together, and George leaned into me. "I fear you and I won't make another decision for ourselves until Lissette turns twenty-one."

I rested my forehead against his. "Then Rose will take over."

"Egad. I hadn't thought of that. Well, you did say our lives were becoming too routine."

"I may have been a bit hasty. Routine isn't all that bad." I ran my finger along the edge of his beard. "In truth, as long as we're together, and people aren't trying to kill us, *c'est la bonne vie*."

George grinned. "That is not just a good life. It's perfect."

Acknowledgments

The Paris Exposition Universelle ran from April through November of 1900 and drew approximately 54 million visitors to the city. Tragically, the footbridge near the Celestial Globe really did collapse, though I took some liberties with the story. The accident happened in April rather than July, and because the bridge had already been judged unsound, no one was allowed to walk on it. Instead, it collapsed of its own weight on to the crowd passing below, injuring forty people and killing nine.

Not long after I decided to send Frances and George to Paris, I realized that I knew almost nothing about France. Since it was too late to change my mind, I had to remedy that lack, and I owe a debt of gratitude to the many people and organizations who helped me deepen my understanding of France and the French. I want to specifically thank Lucien Morin-Cognet for bringing the exposition of 1900 to life for me. I couldn't have asked for a better guide to the past.

As always, I'm grateful to my wonderful author friends. Thank you, Mary Keliikoa and Catherine Arguelles for your insights. And thank you, Barb Goffman for your editorial eye. To Team Melissa, thank you for being there when I needed support.

It's such a pleasure to work with John Scognamiglio and the wonderful team at Kensington. Special thanks to Robin Cook and Rosemary Silva, who help me polish my words, and to

Larissa Ackerman, my fabulous publicist. *Merci Beaucoup* to my agent, Melissa Edwards for always looking out for me.

Love and gratitude to my husband, Dan, who traveled with me to the most romantic city in the world, only to find himself at such locations as the Paris Police Museum. *Je t'adore!*